PRAISE

"In this warm, bighearted novel, Jim Zervanos offers us an irresistible coming-of-age story about the bonds of family, the pull of home, and the power of art. It's humane and hopeful and just the book I needed right now—I expect many readers will feel the same way."
ELISE JUSKA, AUTHOR OF *REUNION*

"Johnny Demos, with his show-biz name and movie-star looks, thinks New York is calling with his big break and he'll never again have to see that ever-rotating cylinder of gyro meat in his family's small-town Greek restaurant outside of Philadelphia. This good-hearted young man is about to learn that the gyro sandwich comes with a side of fries, dutiful obligation, self-doubt, an uncle's mild sabotage, and a two-for-one special of frequently hilarious guilt—in this rollicking family tale by Jim Zervanos."
WILTON BARNHARDT, AUTHOR OF *LOOKAWAY, LOOKAWAY*

"Jim Zervanos's spin on the ingenue-with-a-dream story is funny and smart, full of unforgettable characters you can't help but root for. Johnny Demos, the engaging hero of *American Gyro*, is a sensitive dreamer, brimming with an unspoiled optimism for the future and a charming starstruck sense of awe about the movie world he enters. Zervanos's portrait of this young man navigating his own desire to make it big while also staying faithful to his Greek family's roots is warm and genuine, at times heartbreaking and always honest. Like the sandwich in its name, *American Gyro* is as satisfying as it gets."
JOHN FRIED, AUTHOR OF *THE MARTIN CHRONICLES*

ABOUT THE AUTHOR

Jim Zervanos is the author of two memoirs, *The English Teacher: A Year on the Brink with Generation Z*, winner of the 2024 Indies Today Best Memoir Award, and *That Time I Got Cancer: A Love Story*, and the novel *LOVE Park*. His essays and short stories have been published in numerous literary journals, magazines, and anthologies. He is a graduate of the MFA Program for Writers at Warren Wilson College and Bucknell University, where he won the William Bucknell Prize for English and was an Academic All-American baseball player. He teaches at a high school in the suburbs of Philadelphia, where he lives with his wife and two sons and has risen in the baseball pantheon as coach of two Little League teams.

jimzervanos.com

AMERICAN GYRO

JIM ZERVANOS

www.vineleavespress.com

American Gyro
Copyright © 2025 Jim Zervanos

All rights reserved.
Print Edition
ISBN: 978-3-98832-178-7
Published by Vine Leaves Press 2025

No parts of this publication may be reproduced, stored in a retrieval system, or transmitted in any form or by any means, electronic, mechanical, photocopying, recording, or otherwise, without the prior written permission of the copyright owner.

This book is sold subject to the condition that it shall not, by way of trade or otherwise, be lent, resold, hired out, or otherwise circulated without the publisher's prior consent in any form of binding or cover other than that in which it is published and without a similar condition including this condition being imposed on the subsequent purchaser. Under no circumstances may any part of this book be photocopied for resale.

This is a work of fiction. Any similarity between the characters and situations within its pages and places or persons, living or dead, is unintentional and coincidental.

Cover design by Jessica Bell
Interior design by Amie McCracken

To my Bucknell Holy Trinity,
Jack Wheatcroft, Robert Love Taylor, and Dennis Baumwoll
And to my sons, Nikitas and Victor
Dream big, boys, and swing hard at anything close

CONTENTS

1 Behind Curtains 11
2 Lucky Day 37
3 Rebel Sons 57
4 Just Business 75
5 Snapper Soup 91
6 Wrong Dreams 113
7 Just Crew 125
8 Bronx Brew 133
9 Brooklyn Bridge 143
10 Shadow King 159
11 Fallen Angel 169
12 One Shot 177
13 Call Back 199
14 Last Call 217
15 Exit Demos 229
16 Wild West 239
17 Off Broadway 247
18 Johnees American 259
Acknowledgements 267

1
BEHIND CURTAINS

When I finally entered my grandfather's house, I could hear Uncle Nick on the phone in the family room, joking with the undertaker about group rates. Papou had bought enough cemetery ground so that all of us could end up together, right next to my father's grave. I stalled in the vestibule, tugging at the brim of my ancient brown fedora, book bag heavy on my shoulders. Papou had given me that hat, and I'd been wearing it constantly, relishing my newfound pleasure of pretending to be someone else.

"Hey, Chad, are they cheaper by the dozen?" Uncle Nick laughed in the distance.

I left my hat and book bag by the door and entered the family room.

The sun glowed peach and rust-colored behind the thick drapes shielding the sliding glass doors. Between rushed bites of baklava, Uncle Nick turned to me and waved. He covered the mouthpiece and whispered the undertaker's name to me, "Chad Taylor." Chad Taylor was the son of a wealthy Greek mortician, who had changed the family name to Taylor. Uncle Nick wiped syrup from the coffee table and licked a finger. His brown wingtips pushed and pulled against the worn shag orange rug. Another laugh came to a quick stop, along with his shoes. "Okay, Chad. Yeah, thanks, Chad. We'll call you as soon as … well, we'll call you."

When Uncle Nick stood from the chair, his red tie rested flat on his chest. "Hey, Shakespeare. How's the actor? Ready to come back to work?"

"Show's this weekend," I announced, as if I played a crucial role.

"C'mere." I stepped back—he rushed at me, grinning and slumping, with a flurry of fake jabs and uppercuts that stopped just short of my chin. "You eat?" He grabbed the back of my head like a football and scooped me into his belly.

"Uncl—"

He released me. "You got me running the place by myself." He planted his hands on his knees, catching his breath, wide-eyed, anticipating some retort, though he knew about rehearsal.

I stood there, heaving right along with him.

"Sunday," I huffed. "I'll be back for good."

We'd been through this. I needed to give the play my total focus, or so I'd tried to convince him. When you were in the family and you worked at the restaurant, you didn't just wash dishes or just wait tables. You ran all over the place, splitting oysters and manning the grills. At the end of a shift, you didn't go home and recite soliloquies. You passed out.

In the past month I'd secretly determined that the restaurant would not be the death of me. Instead, I'd latched on to vivid dreams of myself as an actor, though I couldn't say with any confidence how this future I imagined might take shape. It seemed to me, at eighteen, that there was a point from which there would be no turning back in life, and I dreaded that I might be approaching that point, if I hadn't passed it already.

When Uncle Nick reached for my hand—truce—a whiff of shellfish danced with the scent of steak. A drop of sweat fell from his chin and made a spot on his shirt right next to a small, faded circle of fat. His clothes were always freshly washed, but they never lost the faint smell of the kitchen or the indelible brown of old grease splatter. He pressed a fist to his chest and drew in a long, deep breath. "I might not make it till Sunday …" He winced and winked for effect. I pretended to hold him up. We were a theatrical bunch, if not theatergoers.

He steadied himself and gazed at the ceiling: "I might beat Papou to it."

My stomach sank at the thought. I grimaced, not pretending.

We braced ourselves for the scene that awaited us upstairs, still shaking hands like two gentlemen.

"When I was in high school," he gasped, "we had to memorize a speech."

"Macbeth," I said, and shivered at the sense of danger the name conjured.

"How'd you know?" He grinned.

I was happy to stall here with my uncle, as we grew sad, his grip on me still firm.

"*Tomorrow, and tomorrow*—"

"And tomorrow and tomorrow," I joined in, as I always did—at my uncle doing his Shakespeare bit.

That had always been the joke, and our routine, Uncle Nick repeating the single word he remembered from Shakespeare, until I chimed in along with him, neither of us knowing what came next.

Only this time he whispered, "*I have almost forgot the taste of fears.*"

In an instant my uncle was no longer himself. He held my teary eyes with his.

"*I have supped full with horrors …*" He squinted—in pain?

"What is it?" I asked.

"*Out, out, brief candle!*"

My hand shrank in his tightening grip. It was as if he were waiting for me to burst with the tears I was obviously fighting back.

"*Life's but a walking shadow, a poor player that struts and frets his hour upon the stage and then is heard no more.*"

I would be speechless forever, in awe of this uncle of mine, who harbored secret worlds within. Those words hovered over us, along with ghostly images I could hardly bear.

"You like that?" Uncle Nick chuckled. "*A tale told by an idiot!*"

I now longed to unveil my shame—the embarrassing truth: these past weeks I'd been missing work to help out as a member of the stage crew. Worse than that, I'd gone on, like a fool, secretly rehearsing for the lead, behind curtains, in the shadows, and again at home, behind closed doors, as if the parts had not been cast and I were not a mere stagehand.

"That was amazing," I said.

"You know why my father lived a long life?" Uncle Nick mused.

I showed my proud, stiff upper lip, anticipating wise words.

He tapped a finger to his chest. "You're lookin' at him. He wouldn't have made it this long without me slugging it out with him in the kitchen. You can't make it in this business alone."

In a flash, my guilt doubled.

At last, Uncle Nick unclenched my hand. Blood rushed through my fingers. We'd been fused by fists this whole time.

"Okay," he said. "I think I'll live." With a wink, he changed roles again. "Let's a-go … Everybody is-a up-a-stairs"—his rendition of an old immigrant's broken English.

"Ahh, I see." I reciprocated with some kind of Greek flair, extending my arm and making a fist.

Uncle Nick kept a stiff upper lip as he exited the scene. He gestured for me to follow.

The sun was setting beyond the sliding glass doors and the golden lawn.

—

I stalled in the family room, feeling drawn back to the high school auditorium, where a half-hour earlier my moment in the spotlight ended before it began. The lead had just excused himself from rehearsal, complaining of another debilitating migraine. With his exit as my cue, I emerged from the shadows, transformed from stagehand to stand-in. Sierra McCloud beamed at me from the wings, with what I believed was sweet sorrow in her eyes, as if she understood, long before I ever would, that this was where I wanted to be for the rest of my life, in this pretend world, which she had led me to. Before I could utter a word, the principal's secretary was walking down the aisle, toward the stage, where she whispered her message to the director, whose eyes met mine. Somehow I'd known she was coming for me. I grabbed my things and left the theater. I took my time driving. I was in no hurry to return to the real world that awaited me.

Uncle Nick was waiting for me in the vestibule, apparently in no hurry himself. We twisted to fit between the banister and Papou's elevator-chair tracking. Recently, Papou's legs had gotten so swollen that he'd installed this electric system we'd been badgering him to buy. He'd been wearing himself out trying to get up the stairs, but he'd refused to spend the cash. "I like it very much," he eventually admitted. "We've come a long way." The chair was still on the top step.

Upstairs, Uncle Nick braced himself outside Papou's doorway before entering. I inched toward the bedroom, my shoulder brushing an old brass plaque presented to Papou by the Kornfield Kiwanis: *Some people make the world better just by being the kind of people they are.*

My mother emerged from the bedroom. She hugged me and said, "Papou looks a lot different from the last time you saw him. Just so you know." She left cold tears on my cheek and led me inside.

Papou was small and pale on top of dull white sheets that had come undone at the foot of the mattress. His eyes and mouth were open. He was motionless but for small heavy breaths that pushed out his bloated chest. His forehead looked like clay that hadn't made it to the kiln and was beginning to crack.

A semi-circle surrounded the bed: Uncle Nick knelt at the head; Aunt Helen wiped Papou's forehead with a wet washcloth; Yiayia was wedged in a chair; I stood between my mother and my cousin Big, at the foot, where Papou's calloused heels reached toward the coiled seam of the mattress. At first it bothered me that no one had fixed the loose elastic sheet, but the coarse mattress on Papou's calves didn't seem to bother him.

Big's face was pink. He greeted me with the release of air. "Hey." He pulled in another deep breath and held it.

"Hey," I said.

Big wore checkered chef pants and shrimp-bisque-glazed Converse All-Stars. With the last game of the football season only a week behind him, he'd already traded in one uniform for another, heading straight to the restaurant after school every day instead of out to the practice fields. He looked more exhausted than usual. He swiped a wrist across his nostrils. "He's not doing so hot." He let out another puff. "You hungry?" Before I could say no, he said, "I'll be back," and left the bedroom.

"Where you going?" I followed him into the hallway.

"We have to eat."

"I'll go with you," I said, but he raced down the stairs and pulled the front door shut behind him.

—

Back in Papou's bedroom, Aunt Helen handed the washcloth to Uncle Nick, who turned for the bathroom. Yiayia sat in a reupholstered navy-blue chair that had made its way home from the restaurant. Uncle Nick had refurbished the restaurant with blues and whites and dark-brown oak, covering up all the sunken and cracked red-leather furniture, even the silver legs of the chrome bar stools that Big and I used to sit and spin on during endless Sunday afternoons, watching the Phillies on the TV above the bar, while the adults talked tirelessly over coffee refills and rice pudding.

Yiayia's eyelids rose and fell, her chin resting on her shoulder. Her body filled the chair. My mother knelt down to pull Yiayia's short stockings up to her knees. Yiayia tugged at the hem of her lime-green polyester dress and sank back.

Uncle Nick came from the bathroom with the newly wet cloth and reached for Yiayia's arm.

"Mom, why don't you go lay down, eh? C'mon, why don't you take a nap?"

"No, Neeko, I stay here next to Papou." She smiled vaguely at him, buoyed up for the moment. She retrieved her arm from Uncle Nick's gentle hold, and it flopped onto her bellybreast. She didn't seem depressed or frantic, but strangely at ease. I imagined her momentarily untethered, ready to float away, even as she stayed put, anchored at Papou's side.

"All right, Mom, you stay," Uncle Nick said.

Lamplight blended with the sunshine filtering through the curtains above the bed. Sitting on the dresser, a clay dish held Papou's dry dentures on a bed of pennies. A framed postcard from Uncle Paul, a snapshot of glittering piers jutting from white sands into the Pacific Ocean, sat next to a faded photograph of three generations of restaurant owners: Papou wore the white jacket and black bowtie of a maître d'; Uncle Nick wore the usual kitchen attire—the white short-sleeved shirt, red tie, blue pants, and brown wingtips; Big, with crooked clip-on tie, his head at his father's hip, wore the spirited look of an heir eager to fit into his first busboy sport coat. A small, black-and-white passport-like photograph of Papou fell from behind the restaurant picture when I picked it up.

My mother had always talked about how handsome Papou was when he was young, but the passport photo captured more than good looks or the determined face of an immigrant. His lips were firm above the cleft in his broad chin. His forehead wrapped smoothly around the sides of his almond-shaped eyes, which seemed slightly closed but were not. This was the restful gaze of calm eyes. Confident. Invincible. Eyebrows peaked and stopped sharply where the nose became brow, narrowed at the temples and caressed the soft slopes of eyelids that dipped toward the cheekbones. A bow tie made a shadow over a pin on the wide lapel of what looked like a camel-hair sport coat. He looked about eighteen. He was dashing. Destined. On the back, faded ink announced his arrival: *Yiannis Demos, Manhattan 1920.*

"Nee-ko, I clean the toilet." Yiayia was standing in the bathroom doorway, holding a toilet brush at her side.

Uncle Nick had been kneeling at the bed, head bowed. He turned and stood up. He cackled, "Ma, what the hell are you cleaning the bathroom for now?" He took the brush from her and led her back to her chair.

Aunt Helen dabbed Yiayia's cheeks with Papou's washcloth. "Mom, you don't need to clean now," she said. "Pop needs you here. Just sit and try to be good, okay?"

"Okay, Helen. Yeh, I sit."

In an instant Yiayia was quiet again.

Big was back with food from the restaurant. He'd arranged chicken sandwiches neatly on a silver tray from downstairs and set it on Papou's desk next to the bathroom door. He opened a large Styrofoam box filled with French fries. We ate while we watched Papou. Yiayia bowed her head over a handful of fries. I held my sandwich with both hands, like some sacred thing, and chewed quietly. My mother brought up a tray of Cokes and Seven-Ups. Each of us took turns when it seemed appropriate, feeling the cold leathery skin of Papou's forearms and hands. His feet were frigid, and his chest was hardening. I disguised my fascination with solemnity. Gravity pushed against his chest, which fought back with the help of his tireless diaphragm, each thrust causing a sharp coughing sound. His ears had disappeared into the pillow. Uncle Nick took a bite of sandwich and wiped blue cheese dressing from the side of his mouth.

"Paully's coming, Pop. You gotta hold on for Paully. He's coming from California to be here with you, Pop."

Uncle Nick squatted and clasped Papou's hand. He brought the pale knuckles up to his own flushed cheek.

"We're all gonna be here, Pop. No one's gonna spoil the party."

Cheek full, Uncle Nick turned and laid his half sandwich on the tray. He laughed and swallowed painfully, red-faced and still squatting. He licked a shred of tomato from his lower lip. "Pop would always say, 'Don't-eh spoil the party!' Even the last few days, you couldn't leave without hearing, 'There goes Nicky, gonna go and spoil-eh the party.'" He nodded to the rhythm of his silent laughter, squinting to see through his own glazed eyes. He blinked, and tears fell over Papou. Aunt Helen still wiped the forehead periodically, though she no longer bothered to wet the washcloth.

The house was hot. Uncle Nick wiped his own beading forehead with his bare forearm, transferring the sweat.

"Hey, Ma, maybe Pop wants some more blankets, eh?" he teased.

I laughed silently. Papou would tell us that Yiayia was trying to burn down the house with him in it. *The woman's trying to make toast of me,* he would say. *All I want is a little grapefruit juice and some goddamn air condition.*

Yiayia tried to lift herself from the chair. "Yeh, Nicky, I keep Papou warm. I turn on-eh heat for Papou."

"Ma, sit down. Papou's not cold," my mother said.

Yiayia took a step toward the bed. Her knees buckled, and my mother caught her elbow before she lost balance.

"Her legs must have fallen asleep," Aunt Helen said.

As my mother guided her back into the chair, Yiayia responded with a defiant but harmless swat, slow-motion fingers that grazed my mother's cheek.

"*Mom,*" my mother gently warned.

I remembered my mother's brief accounts of locked closets and wooden spoons and wondered if Yiayia's temper would emerge from a dark past.

Yiayia sat. "Papou is-eh cold." She pulled up her stockings and reached for the Styrofoam box of cold French fries.

This was the Yiayia I'd known best, happiest when the world just let her be, despite her obvious suppressions. I felt sad for her. In a far-off way, I even sensed a connection with her, or with the disappointments I imagined she harbored—or maybe had forgotten. She'd left Greece as a girl, for a young man waiting for her in America, where she would never get her own footing.

Aunt Helen folded the dry washcloth in her lap. Papou breathed obliviously behind her. She gazed in my direction, as if just now recognizing my presence. "Hi, Johnny." At once she beamed, apparently pleased with the thought that had just occurred to her: "How's the play going? We miss you at the restaurant."

I nodded, all eyes suddenly on me. "Fine. I'll be back soon."

"The lead," Big pronounced, and slapped my shoulder.

"I *heard*," Aunt Helen sweetly sang. "What other talents have you been hiding from us?"

"None," I assured her.

In the silence that followed I could no longer endure the lie. I knew Papou couldn't hear a thing, but it seemed as if this were my last chance to come clean.

"I'm not in the play," I said.

My mother frowned. "You're not in the play?"

"Not exactly."

Uncle Nick snapped, "What the hell have you been doing for the last three months?"

I couldn't bear to admit it: I'd been doing manual labor in the high-school auditorium instead of in the restaurant, where I belonged.

"I'm a stagehand," I said.

Big's face twisted unrecognizably. "You quit football to be a stagehand?"

"What the hell is a *stagehand?*" Uncle Nick asked.

Their unanswered questions hovered in the room, and they would go on hovering. Never before had I so longed to escape. I glanced at Papou and then back at them. Their hard stares softened, finally, seeing that this wasn't the proper time and place to press me for answers.

Anyway, what could I have said? That I felt drawn to the stage, despite my failure to get a part? That I needed to be there, if only in the shadows? That I dreamed of going to New York to become an actor, even though I'd never been there before? Even though I'd never been in an actual play?

In my silent disgrace, I slipped out. No one tried to stop me.

—

Alone on the driveway, I stared at the bleak front yard, once carpeted in pink feathery fallout from giant mimosas. As children, Big and I had butchered those trees. Mimosa trunks had served as chopping blocks, testing grounds for drills and newly discovered hardware. I remembered Papou standing in his maître d's pose at the top of the driveway, hands clasped behind his back, saying, "You like-eh the trees, eh?" Big just nodded and kept on drilling, fascinated by the mimosas' bleeding thin sap that would turn sticky and ruin Papou's tools. I stripped the trunks with the claws of Papou's hammers, exposing pale, wet wood. Papou seemed thrilled every time we emptied the shelf in the garage. Still, we sneaked away like thieves with screwdrivers and sledgehammers. Later, hearing the muffled banging in the garage, Papou emerged once again, opening the door from the family room.

"You want Oreo Cookies?"

We grabbed two bottles of Coke from the cases by the snow shovels and headed toward him. When he smiled, you could see brown cookie fragments in his dentures.

We sat on the floor and poured Coke into ice-filled glasses while Papou handed us Oreos one at a time from the bag on his lap. "*Or-eh-o*," Papou said, trilling the *r* and stressing the *e*, "means *good* in Greek. Good Cookies."

Yiayia cried out from the couch, "Yianni, put on-eh the wrestling." Only Yiayia liked to watch professional wrestling. She sat by the phone in the back of the room. Papou was her remote control.

"Papou, anything but wrestling," we said.

Papou lowered himself to the carpet—not the wrestling Yiayia had in mind. Big and I played pinned, pounding our fists for mercy. We submitted, laughing and choking, as Papou fed us cookies from above. His hand came down like a crane.

"Yianni, the wrestling!"

Papou distracted us with imitations of squinty-eyed, bent-lipped gangsters from whatever old-time movie we were watching. "Why don't you go take Yiayia for a walk—on the highway," he said to us with a dramatic sneer. We laughed with him but didn't understand. Yiayia didn't either. She got her English from watching wrestling.

"Yianni!"

"Yeh, yeh, the wrestling," Papou said, and he finally changed the channel. Yiayia was happy, and, as long as she wasn't moaning about being sick or depressed, Papou was happy, too.

"*Valton kato, moreh!*"—Take him down!—Yiayia screamed from the couch.

Later, she would insist on Lawrence Welk, which must have relaxed her after a long day of body-slamming and head-butting.

Now, the sky was darkening over Papou's house. Days earlier, it seemed Papou might live another year, but I guess I should have known. *I've had my turn*, he'd said to me. *It's your turn now.*

I'd told him about acting in my first play and about my newfound dreams of going to New York, dreams I recognized without embarrassment as plagiarized, formulated from the stories he'd told me of himself as a young man. He was the only person I'd told about this revelation. He sat at his table in the barroom of the restaurant, his hands folded softly. I'd never been to New York, but he wasn't surprised by what I was telling him. His cheeks flushed and tears fell into a smile, and then there was no smile. For a while he said nothing, and I wanted to take back my words, to tell him I'd stay here forever and one day take the reins. His eyes brightened when he began to speak. He was retracing steps of the early days, serving sandwiches from the streets. He told me we were alike, reminding me that though I looked like my father, who had died when I was two, I took after my grandfather in ways only he could see. *New York is a good place for a young man*, he said, as if he could see my future. I kissed him goodbye and went home to rehearse my lines.

What I didn't tell him was that I was not the lead, as I had led my whole family to believe. I figured none of them would learn the truth because none of them would attend the show. After all, the restaurant came first.

"Here you are …" I startled at the sound of my mother's voice from the front porch. "Outside."

I nodded, confirming: Here I certainly was, outside again, as if I could delay the inevitable.

"You okay?" she asked.

"Yeah."

"I'm sorry about the play." She smiled warmly. "Coming in?"

I nodded.

She looked up at the dark sky and went back inside, leaving the door open behind her.

—

At eight o'clock, Big and I were sent to pick up Uncle Paul and his family at the Philadelphia Airport. We were assured that Papou would wait for us. Still, Big floored the old brown Buick, his eyes bearing down on the yellow ribbon sailing out before us on the smooth back roads cutting through vast farmland. For the full hour inside that enormous dark car, I didn't dare disrupt the silence, certain that Big wasn't contemplating Papou's imminent death, but punishing me for my secrecy, or my dishonesty, or my betrayal, or whatever he might have interpreted from my recent admission. *I'm sorry,* I kept thinking. And then, still trying to puzzle out my own feelings: *I'm not sorry.*

At the arrival gate, Aunt Dawn seemed more beautiful than ever, taller, and blonder. She'd been spending a lot of time in the sun and at the spa, she offered, perhaps reading my mind. Little Hayden wore red-striped Nikes, along with a double-breasted blue blazer and gray pants, just like Uncle Paul, whose distinguishing black tasseled loafers gleamed. We greeted each other quickly and rushed for the luggage terminal, Big and I leading the way.

"Are you gonna give me any baseball cards?" Hayden asked, trotting to keep up. Big's baseball card collection dwindled with every visit.

"Hayden, you don't just say, 'Gimme some baseball cards.'" Aunt Dawn laughed apologetically, walking briskly and ruffling Hayden's hair.

"Tie your sneakers, Hayden," Uncle Paul said.

We all stopped in a long corridor lined with stores.

"They *are* tied," Hayden said, kneeling.

Uncle Paul put his hand on my shoulder as I found my aunt's reflection in a gift shop window. "Your mom said you—Hayden! We're in a hurry!"

"My mom said what?" I asked.

Aunt Dawn answered, "She said you're the lead in the school play."

"I'm finished!" Hayden switched knees.

"So this is what you want to do now?" Uncle Paul asked. "Acting?"

The word stung like an accusation. I shrugged with emphatic indifference, as if my mother must have grossly misunderstood something I'd said. At the same time, I was trying to imagine her actually saying, *This is what he wants to do now*. I felt both guilty and giddy.

"I'll talk to a client of mine," Uncle Paul said, "Aunt Dawn's friend—she's a sitcom writer—Hayden! Dawn, what does Marcy do in L.A.? Sitcoms?"

"Not sitcoms. Just commercials."

Just commercials? In an instant I forsook New York for the fast track to Hollywood.

Aunt Dawn looked at me. "Your mom said you'd be interested."

"She *did?*" My mind catapulted toward an unimaginable conversation that my mother hadn't let me in on, and perhaps never would, for fear I might expect her support.

Aunt Dawn said, "You could stay with us …"

Before I could reply, Uncle Paul was moving on: "So how's Papou? Hanging in there?"

"Oh, he's …" Our eyes met in the glass, and I looked down, disguising my excitement behind my tragedy mask.

"Not doing so hot," Big said. "He probably won't make it through the night."

Uncle Paul contained himself, his jaw muscles jumping, betraying him. "How long's he been this bad? Why didn't someone call me?" He took off for the luggage terminal. We all followed.

"He was conscious this morning," Big said, catching up. "He's only been this way for a few hours. You were probably in the air already."

"He'll be okay till we get there?" Uncle Paul huffed.

"Oh, yeah," Big said. "He's waiting for you."

"He said that?" Uncle Paul slowed down for a moment.

"Not exactly, but I think he knows. My dad told him you were coming. I mean, a few hours ago he knew we were there. You could tell. He was holding Dad's hand."

Uncle Paul dashed toward the luggage terminal.

"He'll be okay," Big called, losing ground.

On the way home, Aunt Dawn sat behind Big, who whisked us out of Philly and back into farm country. She asked if we should risk getting pulled over, but Big pushed ahead into the night. Behind me, Uncle Paul was silent but for a few reprimands to Hayden, who leaned forward, pressing Big for Mike Schmidt cards, then for Babe Ruth cards.

"My friend's dad got like a million dollars for one."

Finally, Uncle Paul yanked Hayden back.

I was surprised when Aunt Dawn handed me a thick white envelope from her oversized handbag. She flicked a switch above us, and the interior glowed. I held the pile, as she narrated through photographs of their home's recent additions.

"The mosaic's finished. It's hard to see. That's the new guest room for when you visit …" I flipped to the next picture. "Marcy will love you. She's big-time."

"Great," I tried gloomily.

"He's breathing all right?" Uncle Paul broke his silence, reaching for Big's shoulder.

"Oh, yeah. He's breathing all right. I mean, he's breathing. It's just starting to get really heavy, and the spaces between breaths are getting longer."

Aunt Dawn tapped my arm; I turned to the next picture. "Oh—there's the boat. See the steering wheel? Your Uncle Paul *had* to have that."

"His eyes are open, sort of," Big continued, "but he isn't seeing anything. He's really sunken. You might want to look at him first before you let Hayden see him."

"Daddy lets me steer."

"Oh, yeah?" I said.

Aunt Dawn's hand rested on my shoulder, her fingernails French-manicured in creamy white and light brown, elegantly poised to point.

I returned to the beginning of the stack.

Big anticipated another question. "Dad already called Chad Taylor, so he's ready to come over when we call."

"That's the end," Aunt Dawn said.

"I can look at him, right, Daddy?"

"Hayden," I said, tucking the pictures back into the envelope. "Who's your favorite team?"

Big stared straight ahead, as Hayden went on about the Phillies and Mike Schmidt: "Best player in the league, right?" Hayden had learned baseball from his East-Coast cousins. When the conversation flatlined, Big stepped on it all the way.

I was grateful to Big for not announcing to the newcomers that I wasn't an actor on the fast track, or on any track, that I wasn't even in the stupid play. I handed Aunt Dawn her pictures, and she smiled nervously. Arms crossed, Uncle Paul seemed cold, his gaze lost in the passing fields, obscured by the night.

Hayden's eyes rested on me, still expecting an answer to the simple question.

"Yes," I lied. I couldn't bring myself to tell him that, as of last season, Schmitty was finished.

—

It was approaching midnight by the time we got back. My mother and Uncle Nick were stone-faced in the hallway, and I thought Papou must have died. Warm greetings to the new arrivals were coupled with warnings about his appearance, but Uncle Paul and Aunt Dawn survived the initial shock of the bluish body. Aunt Helen sat on the bed, stroking Papou's matted yellow-gray hair, the washcloth dry and folded on the windowsill. His breathing sounded faint and hollow, as if his chest were filling with fluid falling from his throat, like drips in a cave.

Without instruction, Hayden waited in the hallway, peering from the door's edge. Then he inched toward Big and me at the foot of the bed. He stared at Papou's pale green feet. He touched the strange skin with a fingertip. He looked up at us. "His toes are cold."

Aunt Helen rose from the bed to welcome Aunt Dawn. Uncle Paul approached the bed and stared down at Papou.

Uncle Nick backed away from the bed to give his brother space. "Paully's here, Pop. Everybody's here now, Pop." He cushioned his squat with a footstool brought from Yiayia's bedroom across the hall.

Uncle Paul unbuttoned his sport coat and lifted Papou's right hand, clasping it in an almost formal shake. He put his face into what should have been Papou's line of vision. "Hi, Pop!" He placed Papou's hand back down on the mattress and stood up straight. "Nothing," he whispered. He laid the back of his hand on his father's forehead, as if testing for fever. Uncle Paul's face was flushed but stubborn. His nostrils flared and jaw muscles flexed each time he turned his hand from palm to backside, feeling for vital spots on Papou's skin.

Aunt Dawn took Aunt Helen's place, sitting next to Papou. We all watched Uncle Paul trying to make sense of Papou's bloated chest and faint breathing.

"Listen to him," I said to Big.

"You think he knows we're here?"

All of a sudden Papou became absolutely quiet. We followed suit.

My mother whispered, "He's ready."

I looked at her.

"This is what he wanted," she said. "He just wanted us all here when he went."

Aunt Helen said, "We should all be so lucky to go this way."

I stared at Papou, my thighs pressed against the bed's footboard.

Uncle Paul lowered his chin to his chest. He stepped back, frustrated. Aunt Dawn shifted on the bed and began a circular rub on Papou's chest. The worn-out V-neck T-shirt buckled and pulled under her tan fingers. Uncle Paul stepped forward again.

"Pop, it's Paully!" He tried his long-distance phone voice again, but still no connection. "We're all here now, Pop. And Hayden's here."

He re-buttoned his sport coat, standing beside his wife, who rubbed and patted Papou's chest.

"Helen!" Yiayia awakened. "Find me black dress! In-eh the closet."

"What the hell, Ma?" Uncle Nick seemed amused, twisting on his stool, poised to rise and to tame her once again.

Both my mother and Aunt Helen stepped toward Yiayia, who clenched the hem of her lime-green dress.

"She wants out of that thing," my mother said, and walked to the closet.

I shoved my hands into the pockets of my jeans.

"I need black dress!"

"Not yet, Ma," Aunt Helen said.

"It's okay, Ma. Look. Two pretty dresses." My mother turned from the closet, displaying two dark dresses.

"O, no, I can't," Yiayia said.

One dress was black but with tiny white polka dots; the other was navy blue.

"Ma, they're fine for now," my mother said. "How about the navy?"

"Yeah, come on, Ma," Aunt Helen said, taking one of the dresses. "We'll help you."

Uncle Nick snickered, standing now, hands on his hips. "Mom wants to get this show on the road."

"There must be a black dress in there somewhere," Aunt Dawn offered, her small circles slowing down to a soft pat on Papou's elevated chest. Breaths were coming slowly.

"Ma, this is America." Aunt Helen admired the polka-dot dress draped on the hanger in her hand. "You don't have to wear all black anymore."

Yiayia didn't seem convinced.

"America, Ma, you know." Uncle Nick sang in a low voice, "A—merr—i—caa, the beauu—tiful."

I pulled my hands from my pockets and crossed my arms.

"Yeh, yeh, Nicky, I know America." Yiayia laughed.

Papou's chest began to rise even farther. Aunt Dawn turned to us with a rueful smile.

"Just go with the polka dots, Ma." Uncle Nick stood in the bathroom doorway, his eyes on Papou.

"Nee-hee-ko, please! I can't wear!" Yiayia bellowed.

"Mom!" Uncle Paul was facing Papou with his hands on Aunt Dawn's shoulders. He turned, composed and stern. He reached out and grabbed Yiayia's arms. "I want you to be a strong American woman. Do you understand?"

Yiayia wrestled free from Uncle Paul's hold on her. She flung her hands at him and then, strangely, curled her arms before her face, elbows up, like a boxer blocking punches.

"Honey, you're scaring her," Aunt Dawn said.

"She's not afraid of us. Believe me." Uncle Paul didn't turn to face his wife. He just stared at Yiayia, hidden behind those upraised arms.

"Ma, what are you doing?" My mother cleared Yiayia's frenzied arms from her face. "Oh, Ma ..." She homed in, realizing, "She's been trying to undo the zipper." Yiayia cooperatively drooped her head into my mother's hands. Everyone watched. "It's stuck," my mother said.

I turned anxiously to Papou. Aunt Dawn was patting his chest as it descended. She rubbed on the way back up. Her hand and his breathing were synchronized. Down pat, up rub. Down, pat. Up. Her hand waited.

Papou was stalling. He wanted us all to turn around.

Yiayia moaned, "Papou no like the dots."

Just find her a black dress, I thought.

"Goddamn it, Mom!" Uncle Paul took the dress from Aunt Helen.

I clenched my hands and eyed the door. I wanted to escape, but I didn't want to leave Papou.

Yiayia hoisted herself to her feet. "*Kaka pethia!*"—bad children!—she scolded and started for the closet.

"Paully, that's enough," Uncle Nick said.

Uncle Paul whipped around to face his brother. "You're not the boss of me."

Yiayia's pale arms stretched into a wall of dark clothes, her back to us. The flap of her sad green dress hung open, where she'd managed to unzip.

"Mom—" Uncle Paul started toward Yiayia. "This is not the Old Country!"

I hollered, "Just let her change!" And as if that weren't enough: "What's the matter with you people?!"

For a brief, astonishing moment, they all looked at my serious face.

I was no longer myself. I announced, "I'm leaving here someday."

They looked right through me, as if I'd already disappeared or never existed at all.

I felt a chill.

Just then Papou howled. His back arched. Aunt Dawn pulled her hand away as his cheeks sucked sharply toward each other inside his mouth. His back fell. With a cough, he released his last breath, which left his body with a spray of white foam that shocked Aunt Dawn, dotting her dark neck. Papou was still.

"Papa!" Uncle Nick slid down the wall outside the bathroom. His knees and forearms met the rug, and he crawled toward the bed. Aunt Dawn wiped her neck with the dried-out washcloth. Her face fought a look of disgust as she stepped away from the bed. Uncle Paul held the polka-dot dress. Yellow blood inched toward Papou's forehead. *We should all be so lucky to go this way.*

I unclenched my hands.

My mother and the aunts helped Yiayia to her bedroom. She cried something in Greek over and over.

Side by side the men stood over Papou, our arms stretched wide, resting on each other's backs and shoulders.

He was shrinking. I imagined him at eighteen, naturally dark from the Greek sun. He wore a hat like Bogart's, to shade his fear. The walls of the city made a dark tunnel to nowhere, but he strode toward the center of Manhattan as if he were going home. *New York is a good place for a young man.* I heard his voice. *Papou.* This small man, this gray man disappearing before a wall of grandsons and sons, it was as if the spotlight were fading from him now and we were thrust from behind curtains, shoulder against shoulder, this horizontal force somehow holding us up as we emerged from a shadow.

Uncle Nick stood before Papou's dresser.

"His teeth," he said.

Uncle Nick brought Papou's dentures from the bed of pennies and nodded to me. I helped stretch Papou's shrunken lips around the pink plastic. I held his face with both hands, and Uncle Nick braced his arm against mine. A click, then a painful, gummy smack. Papou was grinning at the ceiling.

2
LUCKY DAY

The morning after Papou died, he didn't seem gone exactly. We lingered at the house, waiting for Chad Taylor to arrive. My uncles stood sentry at the bay window in the dining room. My aunts washed dishes in the kitchen. In the family room, Big stared out the glass doors at the expansive back yard, which together the two of us had mowed since we were strong enough to push Papou's Toro; where Uncle Nick had rifled Big passes almost out of reach, while I played defender and learned the value of persistence in the face of futility; where Uncle Nick had taught his prodigiously athletic son to run like a torpedo and to protect the football from defenders like me, who figured their only shot at Big was to try to make him fumble, swatting at the ball in his vise-grips.

Yiayia sat on the sofa, gazing at the dull pink phone on the corner table, as if hoping for a call. When it didn't ring, I half-expected her to call some secret number herself, plunging her finger into the holes, one after another, soothed by the steady pulse of the dial rotating back. It occurred to me that she could not live here alone and that soon the house would be sold. My mother was inching off the edge of a nearby chair, holding her hands out toward Yiayia and repeating, "Ma," as if pleading with her, but saying no more. She might have been devising the lies she would have to tell or telling herself that a better daughter would go on playing housemaid and nursemaid.

In the dark corner, I pressed my palms to the surface of the giant, lifeless TV, bedecked with a dozen framed school portraits of the three grandsons, exhibiting in upright fashion the progress of our brief lives. I couldn't ignore the expanding emptiness of the silent house, as the reality of my private teenage agony returned. Back in the world of the living, I had my own lies to contend with.

When my mother and I got home, not long after the sun had risen, we stood in the kitchen, listening to back-to-back messages left by my play director, Mr. DiNardi, who had no idea why I'd left rehearsal the day before. He asked where I was and why I wasn't in school today. I checked the clock and realized I was missing first-period English class, of which, not coincidentally, Mr. DiNardi was also my teacher. "It's your lucky day," he said, claiming that the part had nearly been mine in the first place. He went on about how the real lead—Julliard (the nickname by which I remember that prodigy now)—was in the hospital for the migraine. My heart sank and soared. "You'll be great," he said. "There's nothing to be nervous about. I'll feed you the lines." He had no idea.

My mother and I exchanged blank expressions. The timing of this good fortune could not have been worse, or so it seemed at first. Here was my chance, which under the circumstances I would have to forfeit. I began to cry. My mother pressed her palms to my cheeks and wiped my tears with her thumbs. She said, "You and me till the end of the world, right?" I nodded at the familiar words, which for months I had not heard, since the last time she'd said them and I huffed and turned away, another in a series of odd outbursts meant to prove my independence—or my desire for it. I blotted my eyes on my sleeves and took a deep breath. "The show must go on," she said, and I understood it wasn't exactly permission she was giving me. "It's your choice." My chest swelled with gratitude and dread.

Of course, the choice was already made. My grandfather's viewing would not be until Friday evening, the funeral Saturday. The two play performances would be held *today*, Thursday, one in the morning and one in the evening—the matinee performed for the school district's elementary-school kids; tonight's show, for families and friends, who would fill a few rows and pepper the theater with their polite presence. For a moment I considered asking my family to attend, or at least my mother, since I had never actually been the lead until now.

The phone rang. The young, untenured Mr. DiNardi, whose own reputation was evidently at stake, launched into a manic speech meant to be calming. He reminded me it was only children's theater, not Shakespeare.

"Are you willing to do it?" he asked.

"Yes," I said.

"I'll feed you the lines from the pit. The audience will hardly notice. They're a bunch of elementary—"

"I know my lines," I said.

"Really?" he said. And then, "How? Why?"

"I'll meet you backstage," I said.

"You're a lifesaver, Demos," he said.

I had not thought of acting until three months earlier, in those first days of school in late August, when Mr. DiNardi convinced me I was born to play Geppetto in the upcoming children's theater production of *Pinocchio*. In class we were reading *Death of a Salesman*, and I'd been hamming it up with an old-Greek-man version of Willy Loman: "*Now when-eh you kick off, boy, I want a seventy-yard-eh boot-eh, and get-eh right down-eh the field-eh under the ball-eh, and when you hit-eh, hit-eh low-eh and hit-eh hard-eh.*"

Little did DiNardi know, egging me on, that it was Sierra McCloud's approval I was after, with my heartbreakingly realistic version of the old immigrant protagonist—painfully lovely Sierra McCloud, who sat front-center and shot green-eyed smiles into the back corner every time I cranked up the Greek accent for comic relief. Meanwhile, for all of my many years of gushing admiration for her, I had no idea that Sierra was, among innumerable other impressive things, queen of the theater department, destined to play Pinocchio. I would also soon realize she was eyeing me up to play Geppetto, not to be her boyfriend, as I'd been fantasizing.

After the audition Mr. DiNardi told me I'd nailed it, and yet the next morning I discovered he hadn't given me the part, or any part at all, an embarrassing, confusing slight for which I could not forgive him. My stomach sank to the floor along with my eyes as I scanned the cast list posted in the hallway outside his classroom. I chalked up the mishap to the young teacher's lack of experience, despite rumors of his theatrical superstardom at a college I'd never heard of and then in a Shakespeare troupe he'd traveled with for two or three years.

The insulting sting was compounded when, after class, DiNardi invited me to be a stagehand, a word for which he kindly provided a definition. "You're behind the scenes, helping out, doing whatever I tell you to do." He added, "First rehearsal is today after school," and didn't wait for my answer.

When he gave me an approving nod in the auditorium that afternoon, I understood that I had passed my first real test as an actor, or at least as a devotee to the theater, where I wanted to be, as Sierra McCloud took the stage and awaited our teacher's direction.

After rehearsal Sierra secretly lingered by the rear exit, while I arranged and rearranged props on shelves, hoping any minute now DiNardi would pat me on the shoulder, impressed to see me working overtime. But it was Sierra who'd grown impatient in the empty wings and cleared her throat to get my attention.

"This year isn't the first time I've noticed you," she stated.

In the awkward silence that followed she must have understood that I could say the same thing to her and it would be the understatement of my life. And then, as if I were an actual actor playing a suave teenage boy, I delivered the line: "I could say the same thing to you and it would be the understatement of my life." Her cheeks flashed red, and I thanked the theater gods for the inspiration—and the revelation: How easy it was to be cool when I pretended to be someone else! A flash of sweat appeared at her eyes, perhaps residue from rehearsal under the hot lights, but it made no difference to me now.

"Don't you need a ride?" she said.

"How'd you guess?" I said and followed her into the student parking lot, where her car sat alone under a lamppost. The greatest moment of my life up to that point was soon to be surpassed, as she turned on the ignition, radio instantly blaring, and then, apparently overcome, twisted into the passenger's seat, which sank back and remained fully reclined until Bon Jovi's "Livin' on a Prayer" faded to a commercial and she unsealed her lips from mine.

For the next three months, I watched rehearsals from behind curtains, dressed not in gray beard but in black to make the stagehands invisible, waiting to haul the next scene's props, as Julliard's Geppetto danced with delight each time Sierra's Pinocchio came to life. I knew I was witnessing real talent. I'd never seen a high-school play before, so I couldn't have known what every other theater kid already seemed to know: Julliard had been the shoo-in for the male lead, and counterpart to Sierra McCloud, in every production since ninth grade. In addition, I learned that Julliard was continually fending off headaches, some chronic condition he'd learned to incorporate into his performances. I'd watched in wonder, not knowing whether this was his or Geppetto's agony.

Now here I was in a surprise performance, about to play a Geppetto who was suddenly delirious from lack of sleep, as the cast huddled behind the curtain. The anonymous buzz coming from the seats ceased at the first flicker of drapes. Mr. DiNardi assured us: "If you're even just kind of good, they'll sit there quietly the whole time." We were not thespians, he might as well have said, or at least there was no need to be. Still, butterflies turned to bees inside my hive-belly.

As I set my hammer on the masking-tape X just inside the hanging wall of velvet, I peeked through the slit to identify the source of a sudden burst of hooting. Filing into the side aisle was a cluster of varsity football players, my ex-teammates, whom I'd abandoned after three seasons of playing backup in a variety of increasingly unimportant positions—an embarrassing reminder that I was not rolling up my sleeves to play Stanley Kowalski. And there was Big, leading the way for these overgrown jocks ambushing the show: Big, whom I'd called an hour earlier to tell him I was the lead after all and to offer my apologies for the lies I'd told him. In turn, Big had offered me a last-minute ride to school and said he wouldn't miss the show for the world—or miss the chance to see me make a complete fool of myself. Now it appeared the whole offensive line was sitting down on the carpet near the pit, like toddlers eager to be read to.

As the curtain opened, I sat in the middle of the stage, pounding a wooden shoe. My mind blank, I could have gone on pounding all day. In a flash, I saw Big, my steadfast supporter, grinning, teary-eyed, while the crew he'd brought along with him appeared rabid, as if uncertain of their whereabouts or their purpose here. No doubt they'd sneaked out of math class or study hall on Big's command, blindly following their star running back wherever he might lead them, as they were wont to do, even into the auditorium to watch a play meant for eight-year-olds or, I feared, to heckle me now during my one chance at high-school glory. With a late crunch and *voom*, three white-hot beams lit me up, and I was blind as well as speechless. I wanted to rise out of the spotlight and into the rafters. To my horror and relief, the players exploded with a single clap-and-howl just at the sight of me. Then they settled back as I looked up, bearded and open-mouthed.

I thought of Papou, lying there, on the brink of oblivion, my mouth hanging open for eternity, and it was then that forgetting my lines became a blessing. Had I charged right into "These darn shoes!" I would not have felt the trembling, the nervous rush that paralyzed me in the wake of the team's raucous burst, nor would I have accidentally pulled off what I realized later was acting. I had the old hollow face of the man without a son—Geppetto's loneliness was mine, and so was the audience. Papou felt alive inside me. I could hear his

Bogart and Brando as I stared into the blazing white light and tried to breathe. I experienced at that moment what Big must have known for years, what might have been the equivalent of that terrifying, ecstatic crack of helmets against your ribs as you split the defensive line and score.

—

On Friday, in the strange, sad afterglow of the play, I didn't go to school but, instead, ran errands in preparation for Papou's viewing, while my mother took Yiayia shopping for a new black dress. At Papou's house I picked up a few framed photographs to display at the funeral parlor, rushing in and out of the living room and stopping suddenly in the family room. In a flash, I remembered lying on the copper shag carpet, warm in the afternoon sun, making those three-second animated movies you flip through with your thumb, Papou leafing through lap-sized *Life* magazines and looking over my shoulder, while I scribbled movie frames onto restaurant business cards, my tongue jutting furiously. Then I remembered the passport photo in Papou's bedroom, and something compelled me to go get it, as if it were meant to be mine and this would be my last chance to retrieve it. I walked hesitantly to the stairs. I crept past the elevator chair in its metal track, all the while recalling, just hours earlier, Papou's wrapped body descending the steps in the arms of Chad Taylor and his stone-faced assistants. I paused at the bedroom door, took a deep breath, and darted to the dresser, failing to avert my eyes from the white sheet in a swirl on the bare mattress.

Back in the car, my heart racing, I sat staring at the photograph and wondering at the world without my grandfather in it, puzzling over a future that, by another giant subtraction, had just become, like the sky overhead, a bright void I couldn't fathom. I found myself resorting to a secret talent I had cultivated since childhood, an ability to reel up memories in such vivid detail that something or someone I'd lost could seem for a while not gone at all and I could finally relax. In this way, I had been able to recall, or I had pretended to recall, my father.

All my life, in these memories of him, I hoped I might discover who I was, or who I was supposed to become, if only I could draw connections between me and the person I imagined my father to be. Time and time again, I returned to what I believed was my last, and possibly only, true memory of him, one not triggered by a photograph but simply remembered, of the two of us running on the marble floor in the hospital mezzanine, my father in jeans and hooded sweatshirt instead of the provided cotton gown, with an untamed puff of hair on his head and IV pole in hand, reaching for me as I raced away from him, both of us grinning ecstatically.

My mind became a kaleidoscopic blur of such painfully soothing images. I remembered being ten when my best friend, William, who lived next-door, moved to California. For months after he was gone, I kept him by my side, where he'd been for as long as I could remember being alive. My mother permitted my private mutterings to go on until one day she heard me whispering my own name to myself and realized that I was pretending not to *play* with William, but to *be* William playing with *me*. She was confused at first, then a little horrified, afraid she'd lost me, until she snapped, "William!" and I snapped out of it.

Staring at the small picture in my hands, I tried to imagine myself in Papou's skin, his whole un-lived life ahead of him. I listened for his voice and heard him saying, *Go ahead. Act if that's what you want to do.* I felt relieved for a moment, imagining going to New York, this dream that had been awakened in me weeks before Papou's death—a premonition, I wanted to believe. I had no good reason to trust this vision of the future. The restaurant had seemed, all my life, to be my destiny. In my brief experience in the theater, I envied the other actors—especially those veteran thespians Julliard and Sierra—who reminisced about their earliest performances at parties hosted by their families, exotic bashes populated with art lovers and connected socialites—all there to witness the dawning of genius. I wanted to brag that in my childhood I had been a one-man comedy show, blasting through the stainless-steel doors of the restaurant's kitchen and swaggering into the dining room, wearing wild sunglasses and my uncle's wingtips, to roaring applause. But the truth was that my early acting experience was limited to making prank phone calls with Big, soliciting buyers for our trademark Global Tires, and tape-recording radio commercials for feminine-hygiene products.

At eighteen, sitting there in my mother's car on my grandfather's driveway, I tried to picture myself at twenty-five, on stage in New York or in a studio in L.A., or just alive, anywhere. But I couldn't imagine myself even a year from now. Instead, I wondered when I was going to die. I wondered if it was worth the effort to pursue anything at all when death was coming sooner or later, at eighty-six, as it had come for Papou, who had welcomed it, or at thirty, as it had come for my father, who had fought it. I took out my wallet and slipped Papou's picture into the clear plastic pocket that displayed my driver's license. For a split second, looking at that smiling image of myself two years ago, I couldn't remember ever being sixteen.

My mother and I stood before an endless line of mourners. Across the dully lit funeral parlor, playing greeter, was the man I called Bates, though his name was Batistatos. My mother had recently dared to call Bates her boyfriend. His back to the room, Bates picked the pants from between his clenched buttocks—a move he attempted to disguise by swiping his hand first by his face as if for a fly, then following the pest behind him, where he quickly pinched again. This elaborate maneuver was the kind of character detail that in any other person I was likely to spot with amusement, but that in Bates I was inclined to sneer at mercilessly.

My mother peered at me to see if I'd spotted him, this unworthy suitor with pear-shaped hips, abominable combover, and mustache like a ferret trapped between his upper lip and pointed nose, his imperfections blown all out of proportion in my mind.

I coughed, signaling to her that Ted Manos, the wealthy, cleft-chinned, silver-haired widower, of whom I shamelessly approved, was approaching us. Manos touched my mother's shoulder with such grace that I thought she might swoon into his arms. Instead, she nudged my ribs, not indelicately, after he shook my hand and passed.

In the line of mourners nearing us was the Mitzakis family, among them my distant, and much older, cousin Mitch Mitchell, whom I strained to hear explaining to a bald and bespectacled man in a blue suit that he was working on a "feature film." I wondered if a *feature film* was different from the movies I'd seen in theaters. Mitch had recently caught a break with this current "project," I heard him say. "A *big* break," he said, seeming at once to invite questions and to imply his sworn secrecy. I felt a rush of excitement imagining Mitch in whatever movie he seemed to be promoting to these hometown Greeks, whom for years I'd overheard prattling on about how "the funny Mitzakis boy" still hadn't returned home to work in the family's construction business after "trying the acting." Often, I'd felt I was Mitch's biggest hometown fan, secretly rooting for him to prove them all wrong.

As I nodded politely at one after another vaguely familiar person offering condolences, I thought I heard Mitch say that the cast might include "Dante Saludo," a name that seemed to have the intended effect on the blue-suited man, who appeared as incredulous as I was. Dante Saludo was my idol. I'd seen all his movies. As of a few weeks ago, I possessed all of them on VHS, thanks to Bates, who, in a slightly successful effort to win my approval, had given me the only three Saludo movies not yet on the family-room shelf, two of them brand-new, shrink-wrapped in cellophane, and an early classic he said was from his personal collection, the cardboard case worn along the edges, the tape itself fragile from overuse—further evidence of Bates's good taste, his one redeeming quality, I decided. The posters of many of those movies adorned the walls of my bedroom, not to mention that for years people had been telling me I looked just like Dante Saludo. More than a few strangers had stopped me in public to ask if I could possibly be his son. Once, when I was in the supermarket with my mother, an old woman asked if I was Dante Saludo himself, as if time had stood still since he'd first appeared in *Runaway* and I somehow looked twenty-six, not sixteen, despite the bright lights of the produce section.

Mitch flashed a business card and encouraged the blue-suited man to invest "even the smallest amount, a thousand dollars if possible." I figured if a thousand bucks was a small amount, then Mitch was obviously on the brink of something amazing, home temporarily from a place I couldn't begin to fathom. He appeared to me suddenly as if in the distinguished uniform of a soldier on leave—Pacino in *The Godfather*, playing possum before taking over the empire.

And yet, I couldn't say I was surprised by any of this. I'd always believed Mitch was bound for glory—ever since the night of that singular church-talent-show performance. My mother had taken me to the New Year celebration, held in the church gymnasium, in one of her many well-meaning attempts to expose me to "real Greek culture," which I understood meant exposing me to Greeks outside the restaurant, where my Sundays were usually spent. I dreaded the hours-long event, dinner followed by the "entertainment," which turned out to be tiresome skits and Greek dance performances by the youth group. As a twelve-year-old unaccustomed to the Sunday-school scene, I'd had enough of dancing boys in *evzon* outfits—knickers kicking, vests flapping, tassels spinning on beanies—and had just begun begging my mother to make an early exit. That's when Mitch entered, bow-legged and blustering in a fisherman's cap, his sister in tow, the two of them hollering in Greek and chasing each other back and forth across the stage. I didn't understand a single word, and yet I understood completely since *All in the Family* had been unmissable, in syndication, for years now.

They were the Bunkeropouloses, Greek bigots, their dark-haired Gloria forbidden to date non-Greeks, least of all her blond-mustached boyfriend, not to mention the black neighbor; the place roared when Mitch marched across the living room, pillow in shirt, yelling, "*Kreas-kefali!*"—Meathead! and "the *mavri!"*—the blacks!—while his sister, in her screeching Edith voice, with trilled r, screeched, "Oh, *Arrrchie-mou!"* Words like "genuine talent" and "genius" fluttered from the mouths of the congregants, who seemed overjoyed to see these young Greeks improving on the versions of the actual sitcom. I believed I was witnessing history.

Now Mitch was surrounded by a mob of old ladies swathed in black, pinching his cheeks and gushing, "When we see you in the movies, Dimitrios Mitzakis," not quite a question. He replied, "Soon, soon," and gently reminded them, "It's Mitch Mitchell now." Some years ago, to the chagrin of many, Mitch had actually changed his surname to Mitchell, presumably because "Mitzakis" would ensure his failure as an actor, though the anglicized version hadn't yet worked any magic, as far as anyone knew. Long before concerns about marketing, he'd rejected the more common James or Jim in favor of the alliterative Mitch, which most agreed was at least better than Meat, the nickname preferred by a few other local Dimitrioses.

My mother hugged Mr. and Mrs. Mitzakis and each of the small, black-dressed women, all of them bobbing and huddling like penguins, frozen at the sight of Papou in his casket. Right behind them, Mitch was still at it, confiding to the blue-suited man that "it's a tough industry." I presented my face to be kissed by the women, barely able to hear Mitch beyond their sniffling. He massaged his whiskery chin, prematurely peppery, I noticed, his silver watch dipping behind his black silk cuff. When I heard him say that name again, "Dante Saludo," I nearly cheered from the receiving line.

The blue-suited man gripped Mitch's shoulder. "You keep working hard."

"I will, sir. Thank you," Mitch said.

"We'll look for you," the man said, and turned toward my mother.

I shook Mitch's hand and clenched my jaw to mask my excitement.

His silver rings clinked in my grip. "Your grandfather was a good man." He glanced at my mother, who was finally free from hugs. "My *papou* was friends with your *papou*," he said to me.

My mother offered Mitch a sympathetic smile. "When I was a waitress, your *papou* would come into the bar with his construction buddies."

Mitch kissed my mother on the cheek. "Sorry for your loss."

"I'm sorry for *yours*," she said.

Mitch nodded vigorously, his dark gelled curls bouncing like loose commas. "I'm home for his forty-day memorial this weekend." He reached for his hair and plucked sunglasses from their nestled perch. I anticipated the shades landing on his face to disguise his welling tears; instead, he stuffed them nervously into the breast pocket of his velvety sport coat. He set his teary eyes on me. "Now, remind me. We're *third* cousins? You're Lemondakis, right? My mother's mother was a Lemondakis—"

"Demos," I blurted.

"Johnny's father was a Lemondakis," my mother said. "Johnny's a Demos now. And an actor, too."

I was stunned by my mother's assertion. We exchanged grins.

"That makes *one* of us," Mitch said.

My smile sank. "You're not an actor anymore? In Hollywood?"

He shook his head. "Not in years. I'm a producer. In New York."

Mitch vanished from the big screen in my mind, leaving a perplexing blank.

"What have you produced?" my mother asked.

"Nothing you've seen yet, but we just got a *very* big break."

Dante Saludo, I thought, but I kept silent, as did Mitch, who appeared dazed, suddenly, his stare boring into me.

"What is it?" I asked.

His face seemed expressionless. "Nothing. I just … I was thinking …" Others began to pass behind him to greet my mother, as Mitch went on gazing at the space between us. "Johnny Demos," he said. "That's a good name."

"Thanks," I said, and my mind drifted to my father—and to that forsaken name—John Constantine Lemondakis, a high-school English teacher and fiction writer bound for fame and fortune, according to my mother, his lone reader of unpublished short stories. After he died from lung cancer when I was two, my mother, feeling angry, or lonely, or just drawn back to her roots, reverted to her maiden name, and at sixteen, I followed suit, becoming Johnny Demos, just like Papou and Big, whose nickname had distinguished us since childhood. My mother had finally accepted my claims that, like her, I'd never been anything but a Demos. As I studied Mitch's face, I wondered if he felt the same guilt I did for renouncing his father's name.

Returning to us, my mother said, "Did you tell Mitch about the play, Johnny?"

Mitch smiled dazzlingly, seeming to get his bearings. "What play?"

"Um."

"Pinocchio," my mother said.

"*Mom*," I whined.

"Yes?"

I shrugged. "It was just children's theater. I was Geppetto."

"He's a natural," my mother said, though she hadn't seen a minute of it.

I disguised my delight with a puzzled frown.

"People say you look like Dante Saludo?" Mitch asked.

I beamed. "All my life."

"An old woman at the Acme thought he *was* Dante Saludo," my mother remembered.

When his eyes rested on me again, I found myself filled with hope.

"You should see his bedroom," my mother said. "Covered with movie posters."

Mitch said, "It's uncanny."

My mother took my arm. "He's my handsome guy."

"We should definitely talk," Mitch said.

"About what?" I asked.

"Stop by the house this weekend."

Mrs. Mitzakis grabbed her son's arm, muttering something in Greek, then offering my mother an apologetic smile.

Mitch looked over his shoulder at me. "Summer internship."

"Seriously?" I asked.

My mother nudged me with her elbow.

"Definitely," I said. "In New York, you mean?"

"Of course New York," he said.

My imagination reeled as Uncle Nick received Mitch's hearty handshake.

"Your lucky day," my mother said to me. "*Someone's* looking out for you."

For a moment I thought she meant my father or Papou—as in, looking *down on* you, from heaven—but my mother was not one to soothe with, or be soothed by, ideas you had to *imagine* were real, like guardian angels, much as I might have longed, now and then, to hear her put forth such a notion. The thought had occurred to me yesterday—and I'd kept it to myself—that Papou had no sooner died than I stepped into the role of Geppetto. Pure luck? Or was someone looking out for me? When she smiled, I understood that she'd meant someone alive—namely herself.

"Thanks," I said.

A minute later, when Mitch ducked out the side door, Uncle Nick gripped my shoulder and I felt secure. He might have seen my gaze lingering under the red exit sign. For an extraordinary moment, I believed Uncle Nick was impressed with Mitch Mitchell and was about to impart wise words of encouragement, to tell me to seize such opportunities when they presented themselves and to create my own luck—a distorted version of the pep talks I'd received on matters close to home. The summer, and whatever "internship" might come with it, seemed suddenly close at hand, in a future that felt for the first time to be my own—until Uncle Nick said, "How many years he's been in New York and he has nothing to show for it?" It might as well have been my own life he'd just reduced to ashes.

The end of the line came and went. The room was empty except for Chad Taylor and Bates making their way toward us at the casket. Chad Taylor shook Uncle Nick's hand and hugged Aunt Helen. Uncle Nick told Chad, "You did a nice job." They nodded in agreement, looking at Papou. Uncle Paul escorted Yiayia and Aunt Dawn from their chairs along the wall to the head of the casket. Big took Hayden's shoulder and pulled him to his hip. When I turned to my mother, Bates wrapped an arm around her as she slipped a hand inside his sport coat. They embraced and shifted toward the coffin.

I thought again of my father, imagining him just weeks after the diagnosis, lying in a similar casket in the same funeral parlor, my mother holding me in her arms. My mother could joke with me now, as my father had with her in the days before he died, that he'd never smoked a cigarette, he was a runner of marathons, a devotee of the Mediterranean diet, and so this couldn't actually be happening.

I always wanted to believe that my father was looking down on me from above, as many adults other than my mother had assured me over the years, but I could never hold the thought for long. Instead, I always imagined him alone in a boat, being ferried across a mythical river. I looked at Papou, suited up in rugged rust-brown wool the color of his old Buick. Tomorrow, the big brown coffin would become the Buick magically transformed into a boat. I imagined playing ferryman, at the helm, until I saw the coffin fade from view, and I inched back, staring at Papou's folded hands, the peaked creases of his stiff slacks. I took my place among my family. Tomorrow, we would stand by and watch him leave us once and for all.

3
REBEL SONS

I drove home alone from the funeral parlor. Downstairs in the family room, I popped in *Rebel Sons* and prayed Bates's old videotape still had some life left in it. The movie seemed ancient to begin with, since Soro Martello had shot it in black and white to give it that Golden Age of Hollywood feeling. With all the lights off, everything in the room became part of that gray world. I fiddled with my old fedora as I dozed, imagining Papou hovering off-screen, offering his husky asides.

Upstairs, the front door thumped open. My mother said, "Johnny's still up." The stairwell flickered. She said, "Goodnight," and Bates asked if he could use the bathroom.

Dante Saludo, as card shark Jimmy Streets, and Paul Gabriel, as his best pal, Donny, were fiddling with a staticky radio when my mother appeared.

I set my fedora behind the leg of a chair.

"Hi," she said.

Bates snorted in the bathroom just above us.

"You okay?" she said. "That wasn't so bad, huh?"

The toilet seat clonked. The flush followed.

"Not so bad," I said.

Bates emerged from the shadows. "Hey there, Johnny. Is this—?"

Saludo muttered, "You wanna fuck my girlfriend?"

"*Johnny,*" my mother said.

I raised my open hands, exaggerating my innocence.

"How could you ask that?" Gabriel said. "We're like brothers."

"I haven't watched this in years," Bates said, peering through his thick frames, tipping back and forth on his heels and toes. He took off his glasses and rubbed the lenses with one side of his button-down shirt he untucked from his suit pants. "When did they make this one?"

"Get out of my house," Saludo hissed, and I reached for the TV.

"Sorry," I said, and turned down the volume.

My mother flicked on the lights so that I could see her sneering at me, her hand at the switch on the wall.

Bates squinted. "Well, goodnight, Johnny." He replaced the glasses on his face. "Your papou was a great man. Better yet, he was a *good* man." He turned for the steps. "I'll see you soon."

My mother flipped the switch and left me in the dark.

"'Night," I said.

My mother followed Bates upstairs, where he offered to pick us up tomorrow on his way to the funeral. He said he'd missed her in school today, and added, "So did the boss."

Bates was a history teacher at the city school, Tower High, where my mother had been a secretary for twenty years, and where she'd met my father. At the door, Bates quipped about the principal, supposedly a notorious philanderer who was suspiciously generous toward my mother.

She offered Bates a peck in exchange for his jealous teasing and said: "We'll see you at the church."

My mother returned and sat on the sofa behind me. We watched the silent screen. Saludo sat on the lone chair in the gray living room.

"You could be a little friendlier," she said.

"I didn't say anything," I replied.

"Exactly," she said and let the point sink in.

"Fine."

"Do I give you a hard time about *your* love life?"

"Yes," I lied, and continued staring at the TV.

"I haven't bothered you once about how much time you've been spending at Sierra's. I feel like I haven't seen you since school started."

I shrugged. "You don't have to worry about that anymore."

"What happened?"

"Nothing."

Her eyes narrowed. "We can stop talking altogether if you want." A long moment passed. "I lost my father, you know."

I shot her a look of stunned recognition. Her expression softened, apparently surprised herself at this unintended insight: we shared this loss, too, now.

I looked back at the TV, the gray screen an infinite blur. Papou materialized before me, fuzzy gray. *How much do you expect your mother to take? Give her a break, eh?*

"I'm not exactly Liz Taylor anymore, you know," she said.

"What's that supposed to mean?"

She smiled and batted her eyelashes. She understood that I'd meant to sound supportive, despite my tone. "That's what they used to say, you know."

I tried again, "Liz Taylor's not exactly Liz Taylor anymore."

"That's true. No one is safe from time."

"You're only forty."

"*Only.*" She yawned. "You must be tired." Her eyelids dropped, slowly at first, and then quickly. "Tell me about Sierra. She's so lovely …"

"Tomorrow," I whispered.

As she sank into sleep, I thought of the men my mother had allowed into her life over the years, men she only briefly enjoyed, for three or six weeks or, at most, three months. She'd always kept the private worlds of her relationships magically discreet, sparing me the shared burden of whatever sense of loss she might have felt after she let them go and they reluctantly acquiesced. Sometime later she would acknowledge to me, with mild disappointment, their vanishing—a landscaper, who'd lined the neighbor's adjacent yard with shrubbery, then trimmed our hedges for free; a biker, who'd worked on my mother's car at a nearby garage, then cruised into our driveway; a Sears salesman, who'd sold her a picnic table, then delivered it himself. The men who'd loved my mother had taken full advantage of their initial encounters. It had always seemed to me that the relative ease of these approaches was proportional to the unworthiness of these men, with the exception of my father, who, twenty years ago, invented some extracurricular business to attend to in the main office, appealed to the newly hired secretary for assistance, and married her less than a year later. In my mind, my father could do no wrong. He'd had little time to disappoint my mother, and, of course, even less time to disappoint me.

As for Bates, his method of seduction was the least worthy in my eyes. In the version she'd told me, my mother had politely declined his advances for much of her life. When they were teenagers, he could never track her down in church since she was always working Sundays, and so the best he could do was try to talk to her when his family came to the restaurant for lunch and she was busy waiting tables. They also went to Tower High School together, and not long after that, they worked there together—for a brief time right alongside my father. My mother had never denied my theory that Bates had had his heart set on her from the beginning and that my father had slipped in and stolen her from him—as if Bates had actually had a shot. Years after my father died, in an admitted attempt to jumpstart her social life, she returned to church, or, rather, she started going regularly and took me with her. Both of us felt out of place anywhere but at the restaurant, where on weekends I'd begun to bus tables and my mother had retired her waitress dress to help out with the clerical side of the business—organizing receipts, balancing the checkbook, calculating this or that, filing taxes—solitary tasks her father and brother had gladly entrusted to her, performed upstairs in one of the old, abandoned hotel rooms converted into the business office. But it was on our few visits to church that Bates had somehow made the inroads he hadn't been able to make at the high school, where innumerable times throughout the day, throughout the lonely years, he had breezed through the main office and by her desk, going to or coming from his distant classroom. Her first outings with Bates evolved from post-liturgy coffee-talks into lunches she refused to call dates. But then something she couldn't pinpoint—and I couldn't begin to understand—had taken hold.

Just months before my grandfather died, she'd said to me, "Your needs change as you get older"—a claim I'd been mulling over ever since, my confusion inflamed by Sierra's recent change of heart.

On the still-muted TV, Jimmy Streets was at the window, panning the street for Donny, who was gone from his life for good, though Jimmy didn't know that yet.

As I watched my mother sleeping, I thought of the photograph, on her bedroom dresser, of my father, forever alighting from a mint-green two-door, lean and young, in a black suit, briefcase in hand, beguiling smile flashing beneath horn-rimmed glasses. I thought of the lies I'd been telling for reasons I failed to understand. In addition to pretending that I'd been cast as the lead in the play, I'd also been pretending that my heart had not just been broken by my girlfriend of nearly three whole months. I had not yet told my mother that the beautiful, well-rounded Sierra McCloud—Homecoming Queen, future civil engineer, and exquisitely poised puppet in *Pinocchio*—had decided seemingly out of nowhere that she didn't want to be with me anymore. I was not yet ready to accept that she was off to Columbia University next year, "too young," she'd explained, "to get attached to someone I could see myself marrying." Her twisted logic had simultaneously raised and crushed my spirit, then left me secretly inconsolable, as I dreaded a future fraught with beautiful, complicated girls who retreated the moment they felt love for me. My own logic was that Sierra was too smart to be with someone whose presumed plan was to attend Wheatcroft College—the dumping ground for underachieving locals who maintained they were undecided and planned to transfer—a plan I had already begun to reconsider on the dark drive home from the viewing earlier tonight.

The TV screen was a static dark gray, the tape having run to its end. I popped in another Dante Saludo movie, *Runaway*, and lay back on the carpet, reciting the dialogue and fighting off arousing thoughts of Sierra. When my mother stirred, I shot up and pretended to be organizing, on the carpet, the numerous contents of my wallet—a ballooning nylon job secured by strained Velcro—spread out before me: my driver's license, along with my newly acquired passport photo of Papou; a tattered social-security card; a counted pile of singles, typical of busboy tips; an unused pair of tickets from *Pinocchio*; and my scissored-to-fit photograph of Sierra, from our secret day-trip to Philadelphia weeks earlier. I couldn't stop staring, at her turquoise tank top and tan shoulders, her sockless ankles and white canvas Tretorns, her index finger wagging at City Hall behind her, her raised eyebrows and mischievous smile—excruciating evidence of her delight to be with me, this unmistakable happiness captured by chance on the disposable Kodak I'd picked up minutes before at a newspaper-and-candy kiosk. I left the family room and returned minutes later, scrubbed-up and wearing sneakers, as if I'd just got off the phone and now had plans too vague to explain—such was life on a Friday night in late fall of senior year—though my mother, suddenly wide awake and sitting up, knew well enough that my nervous shuffling meant I was off to see Sierra.

"You don't want your lucky hat?" my mother said. She'd found it sitting somewhere and now was holding it out to me.

I shook my head and turned for the front door. On second thought, I grabbed the hat.

"A coat!" she called, but I was gone.

It was as if Sierra had been expecting me. No sooner had I turned from the car on the driveway than her dark sparkling eyes greeted me from the front porch. "What are you doing here?" I froze, taking in the view of Sierra in her pink gingerbread-man flannel pajamas and matching-pink wool slippers.

It had been right here, in that bedroom over the garage, where we'd first admitted our love for each other and then reclaimed it again and again. Right here in this house, time had seemed to slow down, stretch out, for three months of consecutive weeknights and weekends that had become a kind of eternity, an independent reality, which, I realized now with a rush of gratitude and regret, my mother had sanctioned through her silent acquiescence. Inside these walls, Sierra and I had scarfed down the dinners her mother had saved for us after rehearsal, spaghetti or chicken or fish or whatever, softening and hardening under cellophane domes speckled with water droplets; raced through calc problems and drafted essays for DiNardi, right there in the kitchen while her father tore through mail at the dining-room table and her little brother practiced the piano with her mother in the den; and finally, once the homework was complete, watched countless movies from the living-room couch, or pretended to watch them, sweating under blankets after her parents said goodnight—and, on weekends, the coast clear, dashed into the sanctuary of her pink bedroom, where I let myself believe I was the first boy to know her so well, despite her alarming expertise. Since the breakup, she'd somehow made herself absent, or at least invisible, in the hallways and even on stage, right before my eyes, her identity strangely altered as the boy puppet.

Now here she was, walking to meet me on the lawn, where I stopped and said nothing, hiding in the shadow of my fedora. She reached out and nudged the brim of the trademark hat so she could see my face. I returned her smile, anticipating her fingers interlaced with mine. In the dim lamplight she said, "I love you, but it's not what I want"—this outrageous contradiction I still couldn't make sense of. How freely she used the word love, which seemed haughty and punishing now.

She seemed to expect another argument, but all I could say was, "Why?" My sadness was matched only by my fascination with her clear-sightedness.

"Don't be so naïve," she said. "It can't last. We can't see each other anymore—like, at *all*, I mean."

I shook my head. "I don't understand."

But I did understand—that she intended this revised, ramped-up plan to spare us, especially me, from temptation and anguish. Driving off, I remained mystified by this unfathomable creature, who at eighteen could deny herself a pleasure for the sake of some larger mission she'd already formulated in her mind.

Determined to forget her, I found myself parked outside the Mitzakis house. *I'd show her.* My spite was short-lived. I sobbed in the car, trying to control my imagination, which was a tangle of twisted plot lines involving her growing happiness and my everlasting despair. Eventually, I got control of myself, remembering that whatever tears I couldn't hold back would not seem out of place here, where the Mitzakis clan was still in mourning themselves.

I left my hat in the car, lest I be mistaken for a prowling gangster. From the dark porch, I could see through the window that Mitch was literally the center of attention in the bright living room, rotating to face each member of his rapt audience. It was easy enough to gather that Mitch was imitating his deceased grandfather, apparently a notorious farter; each time Mitch struck the old man's relieved expression, his relatives rocked in their seats, wiped their tears, and settled back to quiet the rude thump and crunch of the plastic-covered furniture. Mitch's sister dabbed her cheeks with a napkin while bouncing her baby. Mitch went on ranting in Greek, taking hectic swigs of beer, as the room wept and laughed.

When I knocked, Mrs. Mitzakis opened the door and seemed unsurprised by the sight of me. "Ahh, Yianni Demos," she said, as if it was about time I'd showed up. She led me to Mitch, who lit up. "Geppetto!"

I said, "I remember the Bunkeropoulos skits." I peered left and right, feeling surrounded.

Mitch shook my hand. "You're here sooner than I expected. I wasn't sure if I should expect you at all."

"I wasn't sure either," I said, immediately regretting my uncertainty—and, worse, revealing it. I was determined to seem more committed.

He turned for the kitchen. "Something to eat?"

I followed him. "Are you still acting?

"Not tonight." He sipped his Miller Light and set the bottle on the counter. "Show's over."

"I mean, at all? In New York?"

From his pants pocket he plucked a mangled pen, a white tube flattened at the end by vigorous chewing, and stabbed it between his lips.

I was prepared to sign a contract.

He leaned back against the counter and crossed his arms, making fists. "Trying to quit smoking."

"I didn't mean to interrupt your performance earlier." I glanced into the living room. "You really had them going."

He took a drag off his mangled pen. "You did me a favor." He let out a long stream of invisible smoke. "Their questions get tiring. If you haven't been on the cover of *Time* magazine yet, you haven't made it." He grabbed a can of Coke from the counter. "No one here understands what it takes, or how long it takes." He cracked open the can and handed it to me.

"You like New York?" I asked.

"Yeah. It's home for now." He removed the pen from his mouth. "But it can be tough."

I sipped my Coke, then offered my own deep sigh—the appropriate reaction, I believed—identifying with Mitch's frustration, two struggling artists commiserating.

He told me about his life in the city. He lived above a diner, he said, in the downtown section of Manhattan that, "you know," Dante Saludo had virtually taken over through his real-estate investments. I nodded, stifling my incredulity, as Mitch went on about how "Dan" had bought several buildings and a few years back "Dan" had started his company, the Ferrara Film Group, named after his hometown in Italy. "You've heard of it?"

I nodded. "Dante Saludo," I said, just to be sure.

Mitch casually relayed these facts as if any sentient being, even someone from Kornfield, Pennsylvania—even the most devoted Saludo fan, who knew none of these things—would be unimpressed by them. I tried to demonstrate a certain nonchalant curiosity. But when Mitch slipped in that he happened to work ("part-time, you know, between projects") at the most famous of Saludo's restaurants, I finally failed to disguise my awe. "Saludo owns a restaurant?"

"Three of them. He's not just an actor anymore. He's a businessman."

I couldn't believe Mitch's good fortune. I set my Coke on the counter and crossed my arms in deep contemplation as Mitch went on to paint a picture of a tycoon in a penthouse, overlooking his empire—restaurants, warehouses, apartment buildings, and his own production company housed in a renovated factory where other filmmakers rented space. Saludo was creating a new movie capital, a *film* capital, Mitch said, where *real artists*, like Soro Martello and Paul Gabriel, and up-and-comers like the Avellino brothers, were all working together and inspiring each other, "unlike those hacks in L.A." This was a community of creative spirits, like *family*, Mitch said, and they were going to change cinema.

"Change cinema," I repeated, amazed by the concept, which I couldn't begin to comprehend.

"You should come visit," Mitch said. "See if it interests you."

"Absolutely. I'm definitely interested."

"We've got a dozen college interns on the staff. You could help on the set—"

"Of the Saludo movie?"

Mrs. Mitzakis suddenly appeared. "He's in high school, Dimitri," she said to Mitch. "What are you saying to the boy? Aren't you in high school, Yianni?"

I nodded.

"We're cousins, Ma," Mitch said. "It took me five years to learn what I could teach the kid in a week."

"Don't listen to him," Mrs. Mitzakis said to me. "Go to college."

"I'm not suggesting he not go to college." Mitch turned to me. "You going to college?"

I shrugged. "I guess."

"We're shooting in June," he said. "You can stay as long as you want. I'll get you a busboy job."

"Are you serious? At Saludo's restaurant? That would be amazing."

Mitch shot me a puzzled look, my enthusiasm for bussing tables striking him as out of proper proportion with working on a film set. I wondered how I might explain to Uncle Nick how I was leaving one restaurant to work in another.

"Education …" Mrs. Mitzakis waved a finger, just as Mr. Mitzakis entered the kitchen and finished, "is *everything!*"

"There's more than one way to get an education," Mitch said.

"*Skohlio,*" Mr. Mitzakis said, then translated, "School, is the only way. That is why it is called"—he enunciated, as if to clarify the etymology—"edz-you-*cay*-see-on."

Mitch nodded, "Okay, Pop," and Mr. Mitzakis hissed something in Greek.

This conversation wasn't about me, I finally realized.

"*Ti kaneis,* Johnny?"—How are you?—Mr. Mitzakis said.

"He's good," Mitch said.

"The boy can't answer the question for himself?"

I looked up, unsettled by thoughts of my own education, trying to picture myself on a stage at Wheatcroft College and then wondering if Wheatcroft even had a stage.

"Look at this guy," Mitch said. "If I looked like this guy, I'm telling you—"

"You're blaming your looks now?" Mr. Mitzakis said.

"He's very handsome." Mrs. Mitzakis beamed at me.

I smiled politely.

"Not just *handsome*." Mitch glared at his mother. "Dad, who does Johnny look like?" Mitch shifted his eyes to me. "You must be sick of this."

I returned his grin, not at *all* sick of this.

"He looks like his father," Mr. Mitzakis said. "Now *there* was a handsome man."

"Okay, we've established the kid is handsome. Who else? Think movies."

Mr. Mitzakis studied my face. "I don't see it."

"Dante Saludo," Mitch announced.

Mrs. Mitzakis shuddered. "So what he looks like Dante Saludo?"

"Never mind." Mitch waited for the silence to escort his parents back into the living room—a cue they ignored—unless he was waiting for someone to ask what exactly he was thinking about.

I, for one, couldn't resist: "Never mind *what*, exactly?"

Mitch's parents hadn't budged. Their scowls settled on him. "Forget it," he said. "I just had an idea for the film I thought I'd share. That's all. Not a big deal."

"The *film*," Mr. Mitzakis mocked. "Whatever happened to the *movies?*"

"What's your idea?" I asked Mitch.

Mrs. Mitzakis tossed her hand in the air. "That's all we need now—his mother calling, saying, 'What did your son say to my son?'"

"*Your* son," Mitch said, "is a producer of independent films. You still don't understand what that means."

"You got *that* right!" Mr. Mitzakis said.

"*What film?*" I asked.

Mitch's parents hissed and walked away.

Mitch sat at the kitchen table and looked up at me.

I leaned back against the counter, returning his stare.

He studied my face, then pondered the twisted pen in his hand. "There's a part I have in mind for you."

"You're kidding."

"I'm just thinking out loud here, so don't get your hopes up."

I shook my head and frowned vehemently, as if *not* getting my hopes up were my forte, which I was beginning to understand was the opposite of the truth. I crossed my arms, a fortress against any and all delusions.

"Remember, I'm not the director. I'm a producer. You know the difference?"

"Of course."

"It's just an idea. You can't tell anyone."

"An idea, that's all."

"It's not my decision to make."

"Got it."

"On the other hand …" His eyes trailed off. "You don't want to wake up and realize you missed your one shot. Right?"

"My one shot to do *what*, exactly?"

His fingers formed a square between us to frame the shot. "Picture this. Saludo sits at a bar. His only scene in the whole movie, but it's a crucial one, believe me."

"He's only in one scene?"

"Right now, the plan is to shoot it all in one shot, no cuts. Close-up. You don't see anybody else. Just Saludo. He's our only star, you know, so they want to milk the scene. Milk the shot—of him alone."

"Who's *they*?"

"*They* is the Avellinos, Joe and Mike. They're producers, like me, but also the director and co-writers. They want it close up on him the whole time. That's how they see it. Nothing else. No bartender. Nobody. Just his face. That was fine. Until now. *My* idea—as of tonight—is: *You're* the bartender. And it's as if Saludo's character is talking to himself—his young self. His best self. He's down and out, you know. An old drunk. Giving advice, how bartenders do. Only, tonight, he's the one giving the advice—*to* the bartender. And we see *you*. Because *you're him*, as a young man, before everything turned to shit."

Mitch's eyes were scanning me up and down again—waiting for my reaction, I realized. I'd been swept up in the fantasy.

I uncrossed my arms. "It's beautiful."

"Thanks."

"Would I have any lines?"

"No, you wouldn't have any lines. You're an *idea*."

"That's fine. I wouldn't want any lines." I didn't know what I was saying. I found my Coke on the counter and took a long slug. I was in a far-off room drenched in bright light, face to face with Dante Saludo.

"I don't even know if you *exist*," Mitch went on. "You could be a complete hallucination. It doesn't matter, you see? You're a symbol. A figment of the imagination. *Angelo's* imagination."

I swallowed hard and set the Coke back down. "But I'm *actually* the bartender, right? In reality. I mean, I would *be* there, behind the bar, and he's talking to me, and I'm just listening."

"Yes, you'd be a *real* bartender—and a *real symbol*, too. That's what a symbol is. It's a real thing that also represents something or *someone* else."

I licked my lips and nodded approvingly. "His best self."

"That's right."

"So … would we *both* be in the scene? Or just me? Originally you said it was just going to be all close-up on him, so now would it be all close-up on me?"

Mitch laughed. "Getting greedy! You think I'm going to have Dante Saludo in my movie and not show his face? Of course you'd both be in the scene. A traditional two-shot, and we'll drop in close-ups."

For a moment, every unfulfilled desire in the universe had been replaced by this one possibility. "I can do it," I decided. "I'm a bartender at my grandfather's restaurant."

"But only *you* can play *this* bartender. Understand? Now I just have to talk them into it."

I blew out a breath. "Okay. Wow." I shoved my hands into my pants pockets.

"I shouldn't have told you. You've already got your hopes up."

"No, no." I couldn't stop grinning.

"You've got to promise me you won't tell anyone about this. Nothing to anyone. Nobody in the business has read this script, which, I'm telling you, is like nothing you've ever read or seen before. It's got to stay top-secret. Nobody knows about Saludo being involved, either. The twist in the end is going to blow people's minds. Would you please stop smiling? I need you to promise me."

"I promise. Sorry. It's just—" I pressed my smiling lips together. "This is incredible."

"It's a long shot, Johnny, and we'll do our best to make it happen." He paused, seeming to fight back a smile. "But I have to admit—hah!" He clapped his hands and stared at me, beaming. "It's a great fucking idea, and you're literally the one person on the planet that could play this part."

"This is fucking awesome." I stuffed my hands into my pants pockets and made fists. "Everything's been so terrible lately." I was nearly hopping in place. "But not anymore."

In a flash I thought, ridiculously, of Physics class and Newton's laws of motion—positive and negative forces fighting for their places—my recent grave losses now suddenly offset by the luckiest stroke of luck I could ever imagine, and I wondered if this was evidence that the universe actually was, as I'd learned, always in the process of balancing things out, working within its fixed sums of matter and energy.

Mitch was gnashing at the mangled plastic between his teeth. "The other thing is," he said, "Saludo's in Italy all spring, at least through May, shooting some James Bond wannabe action heist remake. I've seen the script. I don't know why he bothers with that garbage." He balled the twisted pen in his fist. "Then midsummer he's in L.A. doing a Flintstones movie. Can you believe it? The greatest actor of our time is playing Fred fucking Flintstone. Anyway, there's, like, a two-week window he might be able to shoot in New York. That's half the reason we're waiting till June. The other reason is interns—college students free for the summer. Otherwise, we're ready to go."

"I'll be there, even if I have to miss graduation," I said, my vision clouded, already summoning up Saludo as a young man. "I'll quit school if I have to."

"Let's not get carried away," Mitch said.

4
JUST BUSINESS

When my mother and Big's parents announced they might all go to some distant cousin's wedding in Harrisburg on the following Saturday, I started making secret plans for New York City. First, I called Mitch, who said, "Sure, come up. I'll show you the script," which was good enough for me. Then I told Big that I was going to New York to check out the movie set. Since Mitch had sworn me to secrecy about his plans for me to play in a scene with Dante Saludo, all I told Big was that this could be my one shot and left it at that. Big didn't question a thing. He didn't care much for details. But he did insist on playing my agent, on the condition that I pay his train fare. He was still waiting for a written commitment from Joe Paterno, and he blamed the delay on poor representation, namely our football coach, who was notoriously lazy when it came to promoting his talented players. At first, I laughed at his offer, but by week's end frightful thoughts of me lost in the city made me grateful to have an escort of Big's stature. I did my research to find the cheapest pair of roundtrip tickets—first to Philly on Amtrak, then to Trenton on SEPTA, and finally to New York on Jersey Transit—which I would purchase with busboy tips.

In the meantime, Aunt Helen was attempting to pull off a miracle, trying to convince Uncle Nick that, in the wake of his father's death, he needed time away from the restaurant, if only for a night, even though he was the only one capable of running the show—his untested claim, for which no one could supply evidence to the contrary. Finally, Uncle Nick acquiesced, suggesting that Aunt Helen was the one who needed the vacation, terms she was happy to accept. And, incredibly, for the first time anyone could recall, the restaurant was closed for the day—and night. A Saturday, no less.

Once our parents left for Harrisburg, Big picked me up in his mother's bright white Oldsmobile, which we parked strategically behind the Kornfield train station between a trailer and a freight car, for fear a family friend might see it and inquire. This trip remained top-secret—less because our parents would have forbidden us to go to New York on our own than because I wasn't yet ready to go public with my newfound career aspirations, or even to break the news of my "internship" plans to Uncle Nick, who was counting on me to tend bar all summer. As the train began to move, an ache of disloyalty turned in my gut. Seconds later, that guilt mixed with a rush of family pride as we skirted the back border of the Old Kornfield Inn and I questioned if I could ever truly leave this place.

The Kornfield-to-Philadelphia line traced the restaurant parking lot and dozens of acres of low-lying stables—the largest stockyard this side of Chicago, Uncle Nick bragged. There had been a time when livestock was unloaded daily, slaughtered on the premises. When Papou bought the Old Kornfield Inn, it was a watering hole for truckers, who in the stories Papou told were real cowboys, in their hats and boots and dirty dungarees, hauling all those cattle from out West. In the fifties and sixties, those early patrons feasted on not only burgers but, thanks to the new proprietor, *souvlaki* and *gyros*, Papou's trademark sandwich. The rear corner of the kitchen was adorned with glistening meat rotating on vertical spits by the fryers, those giant frozen pink cones brought in by the truckload from some Greek mogul's company in Chicago. In the seventies, Uncle Nick refined the menu, despite the clientele, or because of it. After closing time, he would mimic them entering from the back porch, as if through saloon doors, bow-legged, head tilted, straddling a barstool: *Hey, Johnny, gimme a Bud and a jah-roe.* The real reason Uncle Nick eighty-sixed the *gyro* might have been to spare himself those grotesque midwestern mispronunciations. "It's pronounced *yee*-rroh," Uncle Nick would say, trilling that "r," breaking out of cowboy character and sipping his cold Bud.

On the Amtrak train, Big stared out the window at the horizon, where brown fields met sky, this line only occasionally interrupted by a farmhouse or grassy hill, until we reached the Philadelphia suburbs and finally Thirtieth Street Station. As the river and skyline came into view, Big mused, "Why don't we ever come here?" I looked up, tipping the brim of my fedora, as if to get a fresh view. I didn't tell him that weeks earlier I'd sneaked away with Sierra McCloud to catch *Death of a Salesman* at a theater off Broad Street.

In Trenton we transferred trains, bound for New York. On my thigh I flattened a pencil-drawn map of Manhattan I'd sketched days before while on the phone with Mitch. Alongside street names and subway lines was Mitch's address—at the corner of Hudson and Franklin—and the name of the joint, the Acropolis Diner, where we'd planned to meet at four o'clock.

"How do we know where the subway is?" Big said, pointing.

"Mitch said everything's marked. Look for red circles with 1 and 9 and go till you hit Franklin. He said don't take the Uptown, or you'll end up in Harlem." I tapped my finger on the circle where Franklin met Broadway. "Here. Easy."

"Ask this guy to make sure." Big gestured toward the conductor punching tickets. "I don't want to end up in the ghetto."

"Ask what?" I said. "Mitch said just look for the red circles."

"Mitch said…" Big mocked.

I rolled my eyes just as the train approached what we assumed was New York.

"I thought it would look bigger," Big said.

Amid phone lines and parked cars, the train rested at a concrete island lined with benches and advertisements patching a wire fence. The muffled voice of the conductor announced the stop, and we exited. Big and I stood side by side under the pavilion as our train receded into the distance, leaving us to gaze beyond the tracks at an unimpressive city marked by a sign that read "Newark."

"Fuck," Big said.

Beyond the platform, our train was sailing towards a magnificent cityscape, an endless band of points and notches spanning the horizon.

"Oops," I said.

"Now what?" Big was sweating under his puffy, nylon Eagles jacket. He tugged at his zipper for ventilation. Steam poured from inside the collar. "We're such hicks," he said.

"Speak for yourself," I said, and he shoved me toward the tracks.

"Asshole," I said, and lunged at him.

We fake-wrestled for a few moments, until he got me into a half-nelson, I elbowed his ribs, and we caught our breath while taking in the view.

"It's unbelievable." Big put his hands on his hips. "I had no idea."

I was speechless, gripping my knees, hunched over and head up, my eyes locked on those two impossibly tall buildings at the end of the island, that pair of perfect silver columns against the sky.

A half-hour later, we caught the next train, and, of course, I coughed up the cash for the tickets. As we approached our destination at last, it appeared as though the city went on forever, perhaps as deep into the horizon as it went wide.

"So listen, kid." Big gazed out the window. "Be careful with this Mitch character."

"What are you talking about?"

"Think of my dad, at the restaurant. If he's not careful, distributors will sell him bad fish for double the price, guys he's been doing business with his whole life—*especially* those guys."

"Are you serious?" I said. "This isn't *business*."

"*Not business?* You have something to offer this guy, or else he wouldn't be bothering. Trust me, kid. This is just business."

"What's with the 'kid' bit? Are you Humphrey Bogart or something?"

"I'm your agent. I'm lookin' out for you, kid."

"Mitch is our *cousin*. He's trying to help me out. He wants me to meet the Avellino brothers."

"*Whose* cousin? Who the hell are the Avellino brothers?"

"The producers—and also the director and the writer. They're the next big thing."

"*Tshhh …*" Big shook his head as the landscape vanished and we descended once more into blackness.

After our Newark-New York confusion, we were careful to exit at Penn Station, then to zigzag through the mob in the underground maze of bright light and white tile, rushing past magazine racks and pizza peddlers, and to take the 1/9 south to Franklin Street, which was announced clearly in colored ceramic squares on the subway wall. My map guided us to Tribeca and to the smaller marked area Mitch had called Ferrara, which to our disappointment, and maybe also to our delight, seemed more like Kornfield Central Market than some booming film compound. The streets and sidewalks crisscrossing before the Acropolis Diner were pleasantly unpopulated, serene as the surrounding red brick buildings, which appeared to be converted warehouses with loading bays that might have been used for fruit and fish deliveries.

Bells jangled above our heads when I opened the door. We were surprised to see that the diner, like the streets, was nearly empty at four-thirty on a Saturday. I hadn't imagined that there were down times or down places anywhere in New York. Mitch appeared to be dozing in the third booth, his head against the window. He lifted his coffee cup, about to sip. He gestured for us to sit, at the same time indicating *two*—an unlit cigarette in the crotch of two fingers in a V—to a waitress who delivered two cups of coffee, before we even reached the booth. Big slid in and glared out the window. I sat across from Mitch and smiled as if Big didn't exist.

"I like the fedora," Mitch said to me. "That your grandpop's?"

"It *was*," I said.

"We had a chance to visit Newark," Big said. He nudged his saucer to the center of the table, coffee splashing, and caught the waitress's attention. "Coke, please."

"That's why we're late," I said. "I'm really sorry."

Big peeled off his coat and slugged his Coke the moment the waitress set it down.

"I hope you don't mind I brought my cousin," I said.

"We're all family," Mitch said.

I braced myself for Big to set him straight. But Big's attention had already wandered to the counter. Attending to the stoves and ovens were three fat Greeks in T-shirts worn and stretched nearly translucent-thin. "Look," Big said. "They need three guys back there. What a waste."

Mitch jabbed his cigarette between his lips and reached inside his black leather jacket. "Unfortunately, I don't have much time. Cigarette?" He pulled out a box of Marlboros, flicked the top open, and presented two cigarettes over the lid's edge.

"I don't smoke," Big said.

"Neither do I," Mitch said.

"*Thank* you." I took a cigarette.

Big flashed me a wicked glare. He used to take lickings for hiding his father's cigarettes; it took a heart attack a few years ago to get Uncle Nick to finally quit cold turkey.

Big looked again over his shoulder, mesmerized, as if the cooks were emptying the cash register into the garbage disposal. "Do they take turns flipping the hamburger?"

"It gets busy in here," Mitch said.

"They don't even know busy," Big said.

I smiled weakly at Mitch. "We're used to the restaurant getting *very* busy."

Mitch glanced at his watch. "I gotta get to a thing—"

"Yes! The movie set!" Big blurted. "Let's go see this thing."

Mitch gazed dully at Big. "No." A floppy book bound by two brass brads emerged from his lap.

"You write that?" Big asked.

"I've had significant input." Mitch leaned toward me over his empty cup, hand spread across the title page. "You ever read one of these?"

"A screenplay?" I said.

"What's Johnny's part exactly?" Big said.

Mitch glared at me.

I assured him, "I didn't say anything, I swear."

"Let's—" Mitch looked at Big. "Not get ahead of ourselves. Okay?" He looked back at me. "This is going to be great exposure for you. No matter what role you end up playing—in front of the camera or behind it."

"The kid's gotta be in the picture," Big said.

Mitch shot Big a long, crooked stare.

"He's very loyal," I said. "He looks out for me."

Mitch nudged the script toward me, as if it were a confidential document, letters peeking from between his spread fingers. "We've been in pre-production for years, raising capital, re-writing, casting, and we're finally ready to go." He paused. "I think I mentioned, our PAs are mostly film students—another reason we're shooting in the summer, when school's out."

"PAs?" Big said.

"Production assistants," I said.

"Helping the gaffer," Mitch said, "sound crew, basically whatever needs to be done around the set."

"*Gofer?*" Big said.

"*Gaffer*," I said. "Chief electrician. Does the lights."

"How do you know this stuff?" Big asked.

"Been studying."

"Since when?"

I mirrored Big's scowl, unlit cigarette drooping from my lips.

"You gonna light that thing?" he hissed.

Mitch said, "I talked to these guys, and it's cool."

"The Avellinos?" I asked. "You talked to them? About your idea?"

"About you being an intern," Mitch said.

Big didn't catch on. He was busy glaring at the cooks.

Mitch continued, "You can stay with me. My apartment's right upstairs from here. The Ferrara Center's right around the corner. We shoot for a month. Come as long as you want. A week or the whole summer. There'll be plenty more to do in post. It's all about networking, getting to know the right people. You never know what could develop."

"Wait a second," Big said. "You only shoot for a *month?* And you said *summer?* It's November. That's—" He counted them out on his fingers: "Seven months from now."

"You're very pushy, you know that?" Mitch released his hand from the screenplay. "Take a look at it," he said to me. "I'm entrusting you with this thing."

"*I'm* pushy?" Big set his hand on the screenplay. "I've got the kid's best interests in mind."

"*Do* you?" Mitch held my anxious stare. "Because you seem kind of … in the way."

I anticipated Big's fist in Mitch's face.

Instead, Big said to me, "Did you know about this? Not shooting till summer?"

I shrugged.

"You said we were coming to see the set!"

"Learn what you can from the script," Mitch said to me. "You can't show it to anyone or talk about it. People steal each other's ideas in this business all the time."

Big scooped up the screenplay. He flipped through it aimlessly. "Why you so interested in Johnny?" He set his eyes on Mitch.

"Relax," I said.

"So, there's no movie set?" Big said.

I pried the pages from his loose grip.

"What are we doing here?" he asked. "Why did we come all this way?"

"Just—" I gestured to the script. "We're talking."

"Talking," Big huffed.

"In June there will be a set." Mitch crushed his undamaged cigarette in the aluminum ashtray. "You're both welcome to come back."

"June's no good for me," Big said. "I'll be at football camp at Penn State."

I offered Mitch a puzzled shrug.

"I'll be here," I said.

"Sorry I gotta rush off," Mitch said, "but at least you have the script. You understand, it's a really big deal I'm letting you go home with this. Protect it with your life. And don't forget—*top-secret*."

Holding his belly with both hands, Big let out an exaggerated high-pitched laugh.

Mitch zipped up his jacket and slid out from the booth. "Check out the neighborhood before you head back. That's Saludo's place ..." He pointed toward the restaurant across the street, a row of bay windows glowing bright orange from the light inside. "The warehouse next-door is where we'll shoot most of the film." Mitch squinted and aimed a finger toward the sky. "He lives right over there. That's his penthouse." Mitch made these pronouncements as casually as he might describe the weather. Beyond the intersection a row of money machines sat encased behind glary glass spanning the sidewalk.

"He lives in a *bank?*" Big said.

"Top floor—*above* the bank. He's supposed to be at this thing I gotta get to."

Big said, "You *know* Dante Saludo?"

"Johnny didn't tell you?"

I shook my head furiously.

"Tell me what?" Big demanded.

"I thought he was in Italy," I said to Mitch.

"I thought we weren't going to talk about his *unknown* whereabouts, either," Mitch said.

"I didn't tell anyone anything. Honest."

Big shoved me nearly out of the booth. "You knew he knows Dante Saludo? Why didn't you tell me?"

"He made me swear."

Big sat up straight and got his bearings. "Don't even tell me … Is Saludo going to be *in this movie?*"

I shrugged, still playing ignorant.

"I'm going to make sure of it," Mitch said, "if it's the last thing I ever do."

The secret was out.

"Are you shitting me?" Big sank back in the booth, eyes out the window. "You're going to be in a movie with Dante Saludo—and you didn't tell me?"

"He leaves for Italy in March," Mitch said. "He'll be back here in June for one day of shooting. One day. That's all we need him for. I'm going to the office right now to discuss all this. If things go as we hope, this movie could be huge."

Big smirked. "You mean, *if* you get Dante Saludo."

Mitch beamed, apparently welcoming the challenge. "Dante Saludo is going to be in this movie." He stood up and rolled crumpled dollar bills like dice on the table. "And if I get my way, which I plan to do, our cousin Johnny here is going to be in this movie, too."

"*Our* cousin Johnny?" Big smacked his palms on the table as if he were about to drive it through the floor.

I put my hand on his shoulder. "Easy, boy."

"Until June, gentlemen," Mitch said.

"The day after graduation," I said.

He hesitated before walking away. "Not a day sooner," he said. "I don't want to get in trouble with your mother—or with mine. We'll talk." He winked and flashed a thumbs-up.

I raised a thumb in the air and repeated, "We'll talk."

Mitch waved to the Greeks behind the counter. "Okay, Mitch!" they called.

The bells on the door jangled. Big and I were alone with the cooks and waitresses.

When Mitch passed by the window outside, Big shouted, "Thanks for the hospitality! Cuz!" He put his hand like a phone to his ear. "Our people will call your people."

"What's your problem?" I said.

"*My* problem? You lied to me. *Again.*"

"I didn't lie."

"You *forgot* to mention Dante Saludo?"

"Mitch swore me to secrecy."

"Oh, I see." Big pinched my cheek hard.

"Ow. What was that for?"

"I'm your agent. What else aren't you telling me?"

"Nothing."

"How can I serve my top client if you're keeping secrets from me?" Big eyed Mitch turning the corner in the distance. "You believe this guy?"

"You think *he's* lying, too?" I riffled through the pages of the screenplay.

"I believe he wants you to come up here and live with him for the summer."

"What's that supposed to mean?"

"*We'll talk.*" Big shoved a stiff thumbs-up in my face. "You better watch your back."

"Why?"

Big made flirty eyes.

"You're crazy," I said.

"He's an *actor*. What do you think?"

"So what? *I'm* an actor!"

"Oh, one play and now you're an actor? You sound like you're joining a cult."

"Like the football team," I said.

"*You* played football."

"I was on the team, but I never *played football*. I wore a uniform and watched *you* play."

Big laughed and jabbed my arm.

"You're fired," I said.

Big glared at the Greeks behind the counter, one of them in an apron thumbing through a deck of cash, not counting, apparently, just sparring in Greek with the other cooks and waitresses, all of them passionately smoking and pointing their cigarettes at each other.

"Maybe they're arguing over who gets to take the next customer," Big said.

"Not telling something is not a lie," I said.

Big studied my face, before his eyes fell on the screenplay under my splayed fingers. "We came all the way to New York for *this?*"

I lifted my hand slowly and uttered the two words at the center of the page: "SHADOW KING."

His eyes brightened. "Good title."

I slid the script reverently toward him.

He hesitated. "Holy shit."

"What?"

"You're going to be in a movie with Dante Saludo."

I mirrored his growing smile. "You can't tell anyone, I swear to God. I'm sworn to secrecy."

Big put a conspiratorial finger to his lips, then began paging through the script.

We lingered, grinning, in the sacred silence for a while. I blew invisible plumes of smoke, before tamping out my unlit cigarette.

When we left the diner, Big said, "You want to stroll around the big city now or what?"

"If you do," I said.

Big started for the subway and, faithfully, I followed him, crossing toward the bank across the street and gazing up.

I had not thought of time or home. I took off my hat and faced the darkening sky. I imagined Dante Saludo up there, cross-legged on a couch, testing voices and faces, having just read the script lying open on his thighs, the same top-secret script I held tight against my hip—and then I let it hang loose, as if this were one of any number of scripts I might be lugging around with me on any given day in this city. I imagined myself on the day of the shoot, the whole script committed to memory, anticipating every word. The crew would hush, and I would get as close to him as possible to witness the transformation, to see the trademark squint, hear the sad whisper. I imagined hauling heavy electric cables on my shoulders, arms and hands ludicrously entwined with hot rubber wires that connected directly to the camera, as I followed the gaffer at the perfect pace. What did I know about film production? I'd gotten my definition of gaffer from my newly purchased *Movie Buff's Dictionary*. I imagined aiming some big round light at the perfect angle, doing my job as PA but secretly studying Saludo's twitching wrinkles and shadows.

5
SNAPPER SOUP

Come December, Uncle Nick was becoming obvious about keeping me in Kornfield for good. With Papou gone, he would need a new right-hand man, a Demos, of course, and he reminded me that now I was even technically a Demos, thanks to the name change I alone had chosen to make. It went without saying that once Big strapped on a helmet in Happy Valley, with his limitless potential, his future was impossible to foresee—while my future was predictable, if not inevitable, at least in the eyes of Uncle Nick, who assumed I would live at home, attend Wheatcroft College, and work at the restaurant in some growing capacity for an indeterminate length of time, probably forever. As winter set in, there wasn't much I could do in the way of laying claim to that other path, aside from picking up a few more books on the finer points of acting, watching classic movies, and setting my mind on June.

On Christmas Eve we were closed for lunch to prepare for the early dinner crowd. Reservations alone promised over four hundred customers. I'd arrived early to help in the kitchen. In exchange, I got another in a series of Uncle Nick's career-planning lectures, which I routinely provoked for reasons I failed to comprehend myself, but once again instigating the very confrontation I pretended to be avoiding.

"I'll probably spend the whole summer there," I said to Big. I was shucking oysters while he was making coleslaw. "Then who knows?" I tacked on for good measure. When at first Uncle Nick failed to look up from the butcher block in the corner, I went on about the movie project, dropping names—Saludo, Martello, Avellino, Ferrara.

Finally, Uncle Nick cracked, "You sound like you're joining the mob."

Big offered me an encouraging nod.

"I could see myself living in New York," I said.

Uncle Nick raised a hand in disgust. "We're restaurant people, not bums. You go to school, study business."

"Papou started there," I said.

"Papou didn't have a *choice*. That's where the boat docked." He swept his meat cleaver in the air as if for flies. "He left that city as soon as he could—and now you want to go *back?*"

"Not forever," I lied.

Uncle Nick tucked the virtual machete under his armpit and shifted to see the TV, set atop the cold-seafood counter, next to a pile of ladles and trays. "What you have to do before you just go running off and do something stupid is ask yourself: How talented am I? I mean, okay, you're a little talented. Your mom says you're talented."

The television flashed and murmured quietly.

"He's talented," Big said.

Eyes on the screen, Uncle Nick organized on the butcher block neat rows of snapper turtles, each one uniquely patterned in brilliant gold and green. "Penn State," he said. "Franco Harris. Look at him back then." A fierce thump was followed by the sound of ripping leather. Then the wet, clean scoop of blade against shell. Uncle Nick was making snapper soup. His hands were thick, his fingers short stumps of muscle that moved through animal flesh without thought. He stacked shells on his right, pulled meat into a tub set at belt level, and to his left he pushed wrinkled brown heads into a trashcan, not shooing them like flies but rolling them slowly to the edge until they fell. He worked alone at that wooden table, hammering and chopping and slicing, steadily, all in organized quick movements, stopping only briefly now and then to sip some Coke and check the TV.

The sun filled the kitchen, bouncing off plowed mounds of snow in the parking lot, each window a blur of radiant white, chrome countertops gleaming with silvery incandescence.

Big was now mixing the coleslaw and simultaneously concocting crabmeat *au gratin*, each arm elbow-deep in separate plastic tubs.

"*Yo, Johnny*," he hissed, a cream-coated arm emerging, a dripping finger pointing like a gun. In our inspired unoriginal dialogues, every character was named Johnny.

"*It was you, Johnny*," I returned—early Brando, his voice like gravy, thick and dark, not the gravelly whisper that came later: "*My own cousin. You said, 'You ain't ready yet.' Rememba dat? You told me, wait this one out, Johnny. So I did, and what happens? You go become a national hero, and I get a one-way ticket back to Kornfield. You're my cousin, Johnny. You shoulda helped me get outta here. I coulda been somebody.*" And so on.

Big fed me cues while I went on splitting oysters and improvising my own version of *Waterfront* until Uncle Nick slammed his machete into the worktable.

"You don't think everybody in New York is talented?" he barked. "He wants to be goddamn Marlon Brando!"

I took it as a minor victory that he recognized my Brando during old Franco Harris clips.

Again, he raised his weapon. Another thwack.

I jutted my chin and frowned like a fish. "*I knew Johnny was going to have to go through all this—and maybe your cousin Johnny, too,*" I choked out, extending my hand with tragic lament.

Uncle Nick and Big swapped identical looks of amusement.

"*But I—I never wanted this for you, Johnny.*" Knife in hand, I contemplated the Godfather's motivation for shucking oysters: by now, I had devoured Stanislavski, my paperback *Actor's Handbook* curved like a wallet, in my back pocket. I faked a sneer and tore into shells.

"He's going to New York," Big said. "He's a great actor."

"You keep your eye on the crabmeat," Uncle Nick said.

I nearly launched into another monologue, not from a Brando flick, but from that top-secret screenplay I'd begun to memorize, the speech meant for Saludo, a brilliant meditation about starting over after losing it all. But I stopped myself, faithful to my confidentiality agreement with Mitch—my loyalties divided.

Uncle Nick met me at the walk-in fridge. "You have to ask yourself how talented, is all I'm saying."

I presented a full tray of shucked oysters. He took the tray and went inside.

"Lock him in there," Big said.

When the door thumped open a moment later, Uncle Nick glanced at us suspiciously and went back to his turtles. Big and I swapped furtive grins and got back to business ourselves.

For a while, I kept an eye on him, half-hoping he might catch on to the deeper meaning of the *Godfather* monologue I'd just performed, at least as I'd intended it—the golden son destined, or doomed, to take over the family business. But he seemed oblivious to my intent, and for a moment I hated him for it. I wanted him to know that I was gearing up for something unpredictable. Something all my own. At the same time, I was satisfied to know something he didn't know. Even if it was only about myself. All my life it had always been Big who seemed to know about things I never would.

—

As twelve-year-old busboys, Big and I cooled down in the walk-in fridge, first signaling to each other with a wink or wave. Our sweat bled through crimson, polyester busboy sport coats that seemed reminiscent of the 1920s, when Papou came to America. When we barely raised our arms, reaching for boxed ketchup or stretching for whipped-cream cans, the coats rose inches above our belts, our white oxford shirts ballooning from the gaps at our sides. They were *French-cut*, Uncle Nick said. They were *classy*, which was no comfort.

The first time we got high off whipped-cream cans, I was curious about Big's knowledge of such things and wary of his confidence. When had he made this discovery without me? Though behind soundproof enamel walls, we were still only a door-swing away from being sent to military school, as I saw it.

"You empty your lungs first …" Big exhaled, the cylinder's white, plastic tip resting, ready, on his lower lip. "Then—" He tilted the small tube with his thumb and found that small area where nitrous oxide crept out alone, cold and quiet, without the interference of whipped cream. The air settled into him, and he peeked up, grinning, eager for me to take my turn.

"It's like sucking helium from a balloon," he gasped, handing me the can.

I waited for his voice to jump up an octave.

"It's like fixing a light switch between on and off," he exhaled, "and you can feel the buzz in your fingers." He tipped the nozzle, my thumb on his, as I felt for that in-between place. The quick burst of wind surprised my insides, filling me up like an exhalation in reverse, a soft snowball floating up and into my brain, coating my ribs and neck and face.

"Isn't it great?" Big said, mirroring my smile.

The door opened, and that snowball sank into my stomach as quickly as it had risen into my head. Even though the door was heavy and swung slowly, giving me ample time to hide it, my hands and fingers froze, gripping this whipped-cream can as if it were somehow my last hope and not my doom. Big was frozen, too. Imagine Uncle Nick, his stained oxford shirt in a patchwork of sweat, kitchen heat simmering beneath his forehead, opening the door to the horrible sight of us, his son and nephew catching a quick fix between buttering tables and getting croutons for the salad counter. He would reach into our throats with a vacuum and scrub brush and wash out our insides, then suck our lungs out through our ears to make sure he hadn't missed anything. *This is it*, I thought. *This is our death. Two whipped-cream junkies, dead at twelve.*

We watched the door open, forever. Nylon legs. A black skirt, white padded shoes. A voice.

"Johnny, where're the lemons? Here they are—" And she was gone.

Big leaned into me, laughing and heaving and grabbing the can from me, his lungs catching air again.

"Holy shit," he said. "My dad would kick my ass."

Recently, not long after Big's high-school football career had come to an end and the curtains had closed on my theatrical debut, Big and I smoked pot together on the bike trails behind Apple Grove Pool. I didn't tell him that I'd taken a dozen such treks with Sierra McCloud, after rehearsals, on the weekends, into the same dark woods, where she exposed me to her latest discoveries. The joint had been a gift from that soon-to-be-ex-girlfriend, whose varied and fleeting interests never ceased to amaze and bewilder me. Big and I rode our red and brown ten-speed Schwinns to a mulchy plateau that looked over the city of Kornfield. "It's just like sucking in those whipped-cream cans," I said. "You let it fill you up and you just hold it." The pot was hot, burning our throats and stomachs, smoldering and bubbling into the strangely sweaty late-November air. "Let it go. Just let it all out." We blew out thick smoke, emptying our lungs, a gray film dimming the sky and dissipating, Kornfield's tar-topped flat roofs reappearing below, dark and sticky. The fire in our heads took us somewhere else.

With whipped cream, though, we stayed right where we were—in the restaurant with Papou and Uncle Nick, yet away from it all, behind the big white door that separated us from the world.

When the waitress left and the door latch clamped, we laughed and punched and pushed each other like young tough guys.

"This is the best part of working here," Big said, with an authority I never questioned.

He took another hit and, leaning back, blew clouds straight up, watching his breath get trapped in corners. Steam thinned above him, reaching out across the ceiling and disappearing behind cakes and fish.

—

The TV whispered a distant roar as Penn State came onto the field. Uncle Nick gazed up at the screen, arms crossed.

I announced I was going to set up the bar.

"Don't forget to visit us back here." Uncle Nick's face flickered as the brass rang out.

In the lobby, Aunt Helen stacked menus at the hostess station.

"Yiayia's here," she announced pleasantly, and I understood that this was a kind of warning, a reminder that we would have to fill in for Papou now. Tonight, Aunt Helen had played chauffeur.

I nodded. "Okay."

In the barroom, I kissed Yiayia, sitting alone, swaddled in black.

Ordinarily, I would step past Yiayia at this point, duck under Papou's hat brim and kiss his damp, half-shaven cheek.

Still here? he would say, grinning.

I could still hear him placing his last order: *My wife will have the pork chops.* And then, *I'm not hungry anymore, Dotty. I'm too old. Maybe a little rice pudding.*

Months ago, when he took off the old brown fedora and set it on my head, I was sure I'd never leave here. He puffed an invisible cigarette and said, *Here's looking at you, kid.*

Tonight, Dotty arrived with a cup of snapper soup.

Yiayia sneered at it and then at Dotty, shaking her head.

Dotty looked at me, apparently distressed. I shrugged.

One time, years before, Yiayia had said in Greek, "I don't like her," thinking Dotty had walked away. Papou and I had laughed. Yiayia hated indiscriminately.

Now, Dotty leaned in toward Yiayia, unconvinced that she still had all her faculties. In her froggish, smoker's voice, Dotty shortened her vowels in an unhelpful attempt to make her words sound Greek-ish: "*What—can—I—get—you—tu—day—Mis—sez—Dee—mos?*" Dotty's sprawling pink-lipstick grin and blue half-moons for eyes must have appeared devilish to Yiayia, whose hand froze midway to the pretzel basket.

I braced myself for whatever pent-up fury Yiayia might unleash.

But then she smiled and said, "Pork tsop, maybe little rice pudy," as she swiped her pretzel at a pad of butter—evidently all faculties intact.

Maybe it comforted Yiayia to see the familiar face of the old leathery-skinned waitress, whose signature makeup combination apparently hadn't changed since the sixties, when Papou had hired her.

"Coming right up, Mrs. Demos," Dotty said, and turned for the kitchen.

The windows began to darken to a cold purple. A man I'd never seen before entered the barroom, beating the reservation crowd. He wore a wide-brimmed cream-colored cowboy hat with a soft dent where his right hand had pinched the rim. He nodded and took the corner barstool, as if he were one of the old regulars, though he didn't seem to notice Papou's absence, let alone recognize the coincidence when he ordered, "Old Grand-Dad on the rocks."

Dotty returned with Yiayia's rice pudding. "Pork chops'll be out in just a minute, Mrs. Demos." She stepped quickly toward the hatted man at the bar, flashed her toothy, smoky smile, and handed him a menu.

Yiayia called out, "*Yianni,* where the pork tsop?" She dipped a spoon into the rice pudding.

"Not ready yet, Yiayia," I said.

When she turned only vaguely toward me, I choked up, realizing I wasn't the Yianni she'd been addressing.

"I'll just be drinking this and heading out," the man said to Dotty.

"*Thelo cafeh!*"—I want coffee!—my grandmother cried, her English suddenly failing her.

As Dotty turned away, I blurted, "Bring the man something to eat, Dotty," and I heard Papou's voice in mine.

"The man don't want nothing, Johnny," she said and disappeared in a rush.

I glanced at the man and saw that he'd been watching me.

"Sorry," I said, and swiped at my teary eyes.

"It's all right," he said.

The man's eyes were green and forgiving, and for a moment I let myself believe he'd been sent from above, or from the past. After getting Yiayia's coffee, I found a washcloth and pretended to be busy behind the bar, drifting toward the man as he nursed his bourbon.

I kept thinking about how Papou had adored these old cowboy types and his crew of rugged waitresses, spewing their smoke and bad English. *The man don't want nothing, Johnny.* Dotty had been here for over thirty years now. She was the heart of this place, or what remained of it. She'd been here long before snapper soup *au sherry* and crabmeat *au gratin* replaced *souvlaki* and *gyros*, when the clientele had been made up of the same livestock truckers and cattlemen that brought the meat now on their plates. As soon as he could afford to, Papou had changed the ambiance to complement the cuisine, replacing the tarnished mint-tiled walls with scenic wallpaper depicting cowboys rolling into small towns in parades of coaches and covered wagons and telling stories of gold miners, from the barroom entrance to the authentic cattle horns immortalized above the back kitchen doors. For years, a glass-encased, barely yellowed *Kornfield Times* front page hung beneath crisscrossed Remington rifles in the Wild West Room: *Old Kornfield Inn Brings the Spirit of the West to Town*. Beneath the newspaper headlines, a black-and-white Papou and Uncle Nick, bow-tied and beaming, shoulder to shoulder in white host jackets, like New York maître d's, held with outstretched arms a silver platter piled high with steaks and prime rib. They smiled before the restaurant's new double-door entrance, above which hung the new logo, the silhouette of a hatted cowboy. Now the framed article hung just above the lamp at Papou's table, where Yiayia sat alone, sipping her coffee.

Papou had reveled in the success, donning his fedora, looking, as much as a Greek immigrant could, like his cowboy customers, who still filled the barroom, while Kornfield's wealthiest herded into the dining rooms, ordering New York strip and filet mignon, and, not long after, lobster and swordfish. Meanwhile, the cowboys and truckers began to seem exploited rather than immortalized by the decor, isolated in the barroom, hunching over hamburgers and Papou's once-famous gyros. The rich widows and businessmen, not to mention the lobster and swordfish, seemed as misplaced among cattle horns and stories of the dustbowl as the cowboys and truckers seemed to be among pearls and pinstripes. Uncle Nick was biding his time, seeing that The Old Kornfield Inn was due for its final facelift. The Wild West was dead, and so was the gyro.

When Uncle Nick took the reins for good, he adapted to the new clientele, redecorating with rich blues and tan molding, white Doric columns and mahogany banisters, complementing a stained-glass backdrop to a brassy, streamlined bar. Customers still left happy, often admitting you couldn't buy a better steak, but now they were country club women with madras-shirted husbands, tipsy on martinis, not red-faced cowboys hunching over beef-and-beer-filled bellies.

"Thank you, young man," the cowboy said to me, punctuating my daydream, just as Dotty returned with Yiayia's pork chops. He reached for his hat, which sat on the stool beside him. He pinched it in a farewell gesture, and it sank into the crease in his forehead.

I called out, "Dotty, bring the man a nice sirloin, and tell Nicky to add some shrimp and a little crabmeat." I turned to the cowboy, who appeared stunned, as I was. I didn't recognize my own voice: "Please, eat. It's Christmas."

—

I had never felt as devoted to the restaurant as I did at that time, even as I understood that it was the nostalgia of the holidays distorting my vision, as it had been for weeks now, confusing my sense of destiny, of my very identity. Since Thanksgiving, and events surrounding that holiday, Big's fate had been finally sealed, while mine seemed increasingly in limbo, as my star turn in *Pinocchio* receded into the past and my future role in *Shadow King* felt more and more like a pipe dream. When I thought honestly about our respective paths, I had to admit that Big's had always been directed away from this place, while mine had been designed to remain local by default. By the time we'd reached high school, and for most of the time since, I'd never imagined ending up anywhere else but here.

As a freshman, Big was already playing linebacker on the varsity. He hit Tower's fullback so hard in the season opener that the kid's helmet popped off like a dandelion flower flicked from its stem, and with the grinding finish of the tackle his shoulder pads stretched over his head, leaving his face somewhere near the bottom of his numbers. College scouts were already curious. Wheatcroft's coach handed Big a pamphlet one night and said, "We have a nice program." Uncle Nick had gone to Wheatcroft. He could have played at Penn State, but Yiayia had gotten sick his senior year of high school. Franco Harris had gone to Penn State that same year. They'd played in an all-star game together near Philadelphia. Uncle Nick had sat with him on the team bus, even shared half his lunch, having noticed Franco's eyes on his fresh-cut roast beef sandwich.

After tearing his Achilles tendon and sitting out his junior year, Big returned as a senior to break county records for touchdowns and yardage, as well as records for tackles. With every sack, Uncle Nick came closer to his dream. In late November, when the official offer from Joe Paterno finally arrived, Uncle Nick had opened the envelope before Big got to it. He must have ripped it like an early Christmas present and left the letter for Big on the stainless-steel dessert counter. The mangled envelope lay nearby. Big read the letter without picking it up, his chest expanded and frozen. He blew out something between a *whoa* and a *wow* and just stood there looking at that piece of paper.

On Thanksgiving night after closing, the family ate in the back dining room, as always. Uncle Nick reviewed the spreads of upcoming games, and, at one point, with empty Bud bottles lined up before him, raised a stainless-steel bowl of steaming sweet potatoes above his head and announced that P-S-U was Number One. This would turn out to be true. In two months the Nittany Lions would be ranked on top. As that sweet-potato steam rose above Uncle Nick's head, his own unfulfilled prayers and dreams seemed to be rising and vanishing once and for all. Big was going to Penn State. Everyone smiled, admiring Big's modesty, as he stared at his turkey. The whole room seemed to be shining and warm, reflecting the orange glow that might have started in Uncle Nick's chest, rushed through his arms and fingers, and heated the silver bowl.

We were all looking at Uncle Nick when all of a sudden he turned teary-eyed and said, "Big's going to play at Penn State, Pop." Aunt Helen took Uncle Nick by the shoulders and guided him back into his chair and that bowl back onto the table.

Later, with Budweisers in our coat pockets, Big and I walked out through abandoned stables behind the restaurant's parking lot. That week, winter had arrived. Days before, we'd been riding our bikes in T-shirts. Now, we were walking in the newly snow-filled neighborhoods that lay blocks from the restaurant. Big held his stare at the black sky above us that seemed so strangely to be the source of this vast white surrounding us down here. We lifted our legs above snowbanks, thumping and crunching our way through this maze of white as if the weather had masked these houses, their fences and their lawns, and made it all our own. At the edge of a back yard, we covered our faces with our arms and backed into a dense wall of evergreens, tucking the mouths of our Bud bottles into our armpits, wedging our rear ends and wriggling past bending wet branches like cars through a car wash. When our bodies passed through, we turned and saw the restaurant, though it was far below now, a hundred yards from the base of this hill we stood upon. We had made a giant U.

"You think he'd sell it?" Big said.

As if presented to us so that we could see it perfectly, the restaurant was a thing disconnected from the world, surrounded by white like the last stamp on a sheet.

"My dad said if I bust my ass next summer I could start as a freshman."

"You could," I said.

He leaned his head back, opening his mouth to the wet, black sky. "Four more years of fucking school," he lamented.

"Penn State," I said. "Are you kidding me?"

Big slugged his beer. "Either way, I end up back here."

"You'll get drafted."

"Get real." He shot me a cruel grin. "I'm gonna be *nobody* there. And what if I tear my Achilles again? Then what?"

I glared at him, and he turned his eyes back toward the darkness.

"After dinner I told him I might not go," Big said.

"Where? When? *What?*"

"Penn State—" and before I could interrupt, he said: "I wasn't serious. My dad's drunk. You saw him. He says if *you* don't stay, he doesn't know what he's going to do."

"If *I* don't stay?" And I caught myself before I said it: It's *your* family, not *mine*.

"He can't run the place on his own, you know."

I remembered the time last year when Big was injured and I filled in for him at work, picking up most of the kitchen tasks he ordinarily did. I stared at the restaurant and pictured myself and Uncle Nick quietly stirring soup.

Big sipped his Budweiser, then reached back slowly and launched the bottle in an arc toward the street. The black dot rose and disappeared. We watched for the landing, the angry crash and spray, but it vanished at the bottom of the hill, thumping like a cork.

I asked, "If you could do anything you wanted …?" The infinite night and silence called for such questions.

"I don't know," Big said, but he sounded as if he did know.

We started down the hill, my beer bottle dangling, pinched at the neck, Big's hands in his pockets. As we walked into the parking lot toward the back kitchen doors, the long brown Buick appeared, dark and soulless like a hearse, its headlights spilling a giant, lemon-yellow V onto our path. In an instant it seemed as though Papou had returned to take us with him, before I realized that my uncle had exchanged his own car for his father's, which handled better in the snow. The door swung open, and Uncle Nick got out from the driver's side. Big leaped into the tracks we'd just left, ran the few steps out of the lot and high-stepped into deep snow, heading up the hill again. Uncle Nick followed, calling out for him to stop, expecting him to come to his senses, but then, seeing him continue to run away, he started after him. Midway up the hill, Big stopped and turned around.

Maybe he'd heard Uncle Nick gaining on him and knew he could never get away. I always believed that he'd had his chance when he leaped into that first footprint heading back where we came from, that he'd had the right idea even when he turned to face Uncle Nick after all. But maybe when you looked down on your approaching father, there was nothing you could do but let him take you down.

I could only imagine.

From the parking lot, the tackle looked soft. The two of them fell together. I stood before my grandfather's Buick. Its lights were on, the door was open, and the car bell chimed lightly. Big's footsteps and Uncle Nick's footsteps converged in the distance from where I stood, the shadowy holes meeting where my uncle and cousin lay covered in the snow and, it appeared, embracing.

—

Early Christmas Eve customers ordered drinks while waiting to be seated. The cowboy, filled with steak and crabmeat now, sipped coffee, the commotion of the crowd bubbling around him. Aunt Helen said she'd pull the car around and take Yiayia home. I got Yiayia's pale peach fur from the coat rack. At her table, I held the coat while Yiayia reached for the armholes.

A waitress called out an order.

"Wait here, Yiayia," I said, and slipped behind the bar to make martinis.

"*Yianni* …" Yiayia was saying—to me or to Papou, I wasn't sure. I imagined Papou donning his fedora and extending his arm for her to take. "The wrestling, the wrestling," I heard her muttering.

"Okay, Yiayia," I said. "Aunt Helen's coming. She'll take you home now in time for the wrestling."

Happily, Yiayia nodded.

The wrestling would sustain her, I thought. Even in her grief, this passion of hers was unquenchable. For years she had awaited the return of Bob Backlund, the crew-cut, pink-skinned champion who'd been made obsolete by flashy newcomers, costumed bodybuilders with nicknames like Hulk and Superfly and an influx of black wrestlers, *the mavri*, who represented the beginning of a much larger kind of takeover. It wasn't the violence that drew her to wrestling, but the ongoing and inarticulate human drama of it all.

Aunt Helen returned and took Yiayia by the arm. The cowboy stood up, and for a moment I thought he was rushing off. I nearly blurted, "Wait!" until I realized he was opening the door for the ladies. Yiayia nodded, and the man tipped an invisible hat. "Thank you," Aunt Helen beamed and called to me, "Get the gentleman some rice pudding for dessert."

The cowboy returned to his stool, pulling his wallet from his back pocket.

"It's on the house," I said, and surprised him with the bottle of Old Grand-Dad.

The cowboy's eyes were bright green above the glass.

"Best meal I ever had." He lifted the drink in a modest toast.

I returned his smile, knowing in my youthful heart that, here, behind this bar, in this restaurant my grandfather had built, I was involved in something lasting and significant. As I cleared his plate, I was filled with a rush of gratitude, along with the unexpected sense that order had been restored in the wake of my family's sadness. We go on, I thought, and believed that this revelation marked a defining moment in my life, a moment that extended into a kind of calm living reverie. Christmas sounds, Crosbys and Coles, seeped through the swelling sea of customers—gray-haired ladies with holiday hairdos, hunched grandfathers, their arms filled with babies, blond boys with parted hair and gold-buttoned blue blazers …

I reached back with my left hand, grabbed a draft glass and pulled the tap handle. I felt the tilted glass against the nozzle, looked up, said, "Next," poured gin, plopped straws, rocks, pushed trays into waiting hands. Here was where I was most comfortable. This was what I did best. This was the kind of talent that Uncle Nick had been talking about. It was not about making drinks or being familiar with the few square feet that boxed me in. It was about being so good at something that your mind rises up and out and lets your body go on alone. Your body never doubts a thing. Your hands and hair fling and spray and you realize that your brain has divisions, each one operating simultaneously: one works your hands, one hears, one speaks, and one, maybe the part that dreams in sleep, floats separately—a spattering of outside sounds nicks the surface but doesn't disrupt this clearing of space. And *because* of this absence of thought, this part of your mind, much like your hand unconsciously reaching for olives, isolates a single idea and gives it total attention. Tonight, it was a question that remained unanswered, the question that, out there in the cold, a month ago, I'd been asking not Big, but myself. It hovered there still: *If you could do anything …?*

And then suddenly I saw myself in that city, on some dark stage. I looked up, startled, my fingers in maraschino syrup.

"Take care of yourself, young man," came the voice.

The last cowboy, I thought, ridiculously, as he tipped his hat and turned away. *Follow him.* My eyes were salty and wet. *Follow him right out of here.*

"Your rice pudding!" I called out.

He paused, and I ran back to the kitchen.

A line of waiters curved around the salad counter and faced the chest-high pick-up ledge, the back side of a stainless-steel island that housed, on the far side, cutting boards and heating bins for vegetables and soups. Behind the silver wall, Big, head down and shoulders taut, twisted left and right, reaching for carrots and steaks.

"How is it out there? Lobby full?" Big asked.

"Packed. Just need a rice pudding for a guy at the bar."

Next to the dessert refrigerator on a clean, wiped butcher block, a small mountain of chopped snapper, resembling crabmeat, sat beside one turtle. Uncle Nick, the walk-in door thudding shut behind him, laid a gray plastic bus tub centered between his straddled feet and surrounded the turtle meat with extended arms. His forearms, now a short wall on the far side of the meat, pulled toward the table's near edge, and the snapper bits fell in one rainy thumping sheet, leaving a clean surface and a single turtle in its wake.

"Hey," Uncle Nick said, looking up and pushing his workshop glasses against his face with a wrist. "What brings you back so soon?" His lenses and grin flashed. He ran a thumb down his inner forearms, shoveling white meat from his skin. The restaurant—this kitchen, the bar, the lobby, *everything*— was teeming with adrenaline, and Uncle Nick and Big were moving and chattering back here like synchronized players, executing their parts perfectly, and I felt drawn deeper into this place.

Uncle Nick raised his cleaver, just as one of the cooks stepped back from a burst of fire that bubbled quickly into a yellow cloud above the stove. Big reacted to the popping sound immediately, grabbing a plastic tub of flour, a kitchen's makeshift fire extinguisher, and in one quick toss, replaced this fireball with a mass of white powder, the flour cloud now reaching out across the ceiling.

Uncle Nick stood back from his worktable, wrapping an open hand around what seemed to be a bloody fist, perhaps the remains of a turtle that had not been struck cleanly and evenly. But the blood kept covering his forearms, and we were slow to realize what had occurred because he was more surprised than hurt. The awkward whisper of cheering fans from the TV was all we heard until he said, "My thumb." Big, white-faced from powder, stepped out from behind the stove area, where fire and flour were settling. In command, he called out to servers and cooks. Keep things moving. Everything is fine. Get wet rags. Pull up the car. Big wrapped dish rags around his dad's hand. Uncle Nick, it seemed for the first time ever, was waiting to see what would happen and let Big do all of this. Big finished wrapping what could have been a volleyball onto the end of Uncle Nick's arm. He handed me keys and said go. *His thumb*, I thought. I grabbed a Styrofoam to-go box. His thumb was there, perfect, lying beside the turtle head like a twin brother. I ran for the back steps to catch up with them but had to slow down. Big was walking Uncle Nick down those steps so slowly that, in the rush, I nearly shouted hurry up.

When Uncle Nick and I were in the car, it was quiet. I could not think of what to say to him. Hunched over and wincing, gripping the rags with a fist, he just kept looking down at the carton in his lap. His whole face was plum-colored and clenched. His exhalations were fierce—short, thick grunts, as if from a punched stomach.

"You'll be okay," I said as we drove toward the hospital. He was holding his breath, pursing his lips as if he were dying to tell me a secret. "No matter what happens."

He cradled the carton and un-clicked the Styrofoam tab with his wrists. His lips ducked into his mouth at the sight of the thing, inside this foam carton, a cold white casket for severed fingers. His thumb could have been a damp French fry that leaves a thin skin on your plate. As he stared down, his head bowed and shoulders caved in and knees came up, all aiming for the open container. Finally, he breathed, making a faint sound that came from his throat. A whimper.

It started to snow.

"They'll sew it back," Uncle Nick said. "They do that now."

"Sure."

We believe what we need to believe, I thought. Big was back there at the restaurant, running the place as if it were the only thing he ever wanted to do. The next day, Christmas, he would tell Uncle Nick not to worry—he wouldn't go to Penn State right away but stay home and run the restaurant for a while. For now, Uncle Nick wouldn't argue.

Steadying the wheel, I pictured that cowboy in front of our long brown Buick, turning his green eyes to me and ignoring the cold.

6
WRONG DREAMS

The winter trudged on. In the weeks following Christmas, everything was a blur of meaningless classes and heartbreaking brushes with Sierra McCloud, who, with her own plans for New York, embodied everything I longed for. In my mind, there was nothing but June, which would not come soon enough: June, when I would be heading to New York to work on *Shadow King* with Mitch—and, with any luck, be *in* it. I secretly hoped to stretch a few weeks of shooting into the whole summer, and then the summer into forever, though I promised my mother I would attend Wheatcroft in the fall while living at home.

I told myself that this promise was not a lie, because over and over again the future had proven to be unpredictable, despite my most reasonable assumptions. For better and for worse. The only lie was to say that this or that was *definitely* or *never* going to happen. And so, while steeling myself for disappointment, I envisioned myself in a film career that would begin with a scene in which I appeared opposite the greatest actor of our time. I kept my dreams to myself, and without anyone else's skeptical input, I soon discovered just how bright my future promised to be. My lucky break would allow me to skip all the usual steps. I had no need for high-school theater or the girl who starred in its plays. I managed to convince myself that Sierra had done me a favor when she cut me loose. In my mind, I was already out of there. Graduated and gone. I forged ahead with my self-education in film studies, putting Stanislavski on the shelf and picking up, in addition to *The Movie Buff's Dictionary*, *Teach Yourself Movie Making*, and other such industry tomes I was stunned to find at the Kornfield Shopping Center bookstore.

My bedroom became the set of *Shadow King:* the streets of New York, a Park Avenue penthouse, a dump in Hell's Kitchen, a bar called Heaven. I played all the parts, including Ray, the tortured middle-aged hero. I also played the film's director, who called "action" from behind the camera I imagined set in the corner or on the cinematographer's shoulder, tracking my every nuanced and intentional gesture. "Quiet on the set," I said, and then acted as if I were so deeply in-character that I didn't notice my mother, in the hallway, following the script in her lap, sitting with her back to the wall, and chiming in with an occasional line from a supporting character.

"Take five," I said, and, in the course of numerous such breaks, summarized for my infinitely patient mother what I believed was a "brilliant, genre-bending screenplay, a sci-fi psycho-thriller fantasy about a super-rich guy named Ray, who's battling a condition called omnesia, which is worse than *am*nesia because it *prevents* you from forgetting anything. It *causes* you to remember *everything*. No one has ever survived it because it makes you go insane. Ray's worst memory is the car accident that killed his wife and son and put him in a coma and then in this incurable mental state. The pain is so unbearable because he was the *driver*, see, and he blames himself for being distracted by the affair he was having. So, he quits his job as a lawyer defending white-collar criminals and tries to drink himself to death. He wakes up in a bar, sitting next to a guy named Angelo—Dante Saludo's character—and you think Ray's dead and the bar is hell and Angelo is the devil, but soon you realize Angelo is an angel—*Angelo*, right?—Ray's guardian angel, when he tells him in this amazing monologue about his *own* downfall, all the bad stuff he did, and how he woke up in heaven and was shocked to discover that he and everyone else there were remembering their whole lives all at once, in every moment, just like Ray is. But it's okay, Angelo says, once you stop resisting the memories, and that's the difference between hell and heaven—if you can just let go of the past, then time just disappears because nothing lasts. You're just living in the moment—that's *eternity*, see? Ray suddenly realizes he's not dead but alive, and he's so happy that this is his life—not the *afterlife*. He walks out into the bright sunshine, and it's heaven on earth. Get it? That's the name of the bar—remember I told you? It makes you wonder about heaven, you know? If maybe this is it, this is all there is."

"Sounds wonderful, Johnny," said my mother, getting to her feet.

"It is, it's incredible, and it could end right there, but it goes on. Ray—"

"Johnny—"

"It gets better, Mom. Ray goes back to his mistress and their secret love child and says he's going to take care of them from now on. He moves into an apartment and goes to work as a public defender because now he wants to defend the rats, you know, and save them from the death penalty. And then the final twist: they discover a cure for omnesia, but Ray refuses to take the drug because the pain from his memories makes him stronger and nicer to people. It's like his superpower. He experiences everything differently now. He sees time as circular, not linear. He's actually *living* in eternity. You know? Do you ever think about that? Time? As circular and not linear? Do you think about eternity? Mom?"

My mother wiped her sleepy eyes. "I'm proud of you, honey. Did you do your homework?"

When Mr. DiNardi asked me after class one day in January, "Why haven't you signed up yet?" I replied, "For what?" He frowned and directed me to the classroom door. Hanging from a single piece of scotch tape was a flyer with a list of dates below a photocopy of that familiar cover of the book we'd read back in September, *Death of a Salesman*. Then he led me into the hallway, where an elaborate display featured Arthur Miller memorabilia, including vintage posters, Broadway ticket stubs, a pile of books, and a black-and-white shot of the playwright with Marilyn Monroe, along with, thumbtacked to the case's rear wall, candid shots from *Pinocchio* I'd somehow passed by without seeing but now stayed gazing at despite an oncoming wave of sickening nostalgia, my forehead thumping at the glass.

"You all right?" DiNardi asked.

"Sierra sign up?" I asked.

"She sure has, pal," he encouraged, somehow misreading my slowed breathing and crumpled shoulders.

"I'm sort of more into film these days," I said. "But thanks."

"Uh-huh," he said, and then, "One of the reasons I chose this play, in spite of its difficulty, is because of your excellent readings in class."

I took a deep breath and held it.

He said, "This is your chance to do some real acting."

In one grainy close-up, Sierra, her mouth a surprised "O" despite the battery of lies the little bastard puppet had told, frowned cross-eyed at the cardboard-cone nose that had just sprung ridiculously from her face. I let out a long sigh. Big schnozz and all, she was still beautiful. In a nauseating flash I regretted for the thousandth time the meticulously crafted Hail Mary pass of a mix tape I'd made for her weeks earlier, the chronological soundtrack of our three-month romance, from the Bon Jovi that accompanied our first kiss to the Def Leppard that marked the last time I'd entered her bedroom, some two dozen titles—"Pour Some Sugar on Me," "Hot for Teacher," "Love in an Elevator"—in two neatly penned columns, "SIDE A" and "SIDE B," on the plastic case's cardboard liner—one song after another—by Van Halen, Aerosmith, Mötley Crüe, Poison—that I both loved and loathed for their pleasures and their pointlessness that would forever remind me of Sierra.

I said, "She's gonna play the wife." When DiNardi didn't respond, I looked him in the eye. "I can't be her husband. You have to promise me. I can't play Willy."

He studied my serious face. "Sure, pal."

Our agreement probably wouldn't have made a difference. Playing Willy Loman, Julliard proved why he was bound for that elite school in Manhattan. Biff seemed just the right part for me, though playing Sierra's underachieving son proved no less a challenge than the one I'd feared in playing her doomed husband. The first real acting I ever did, I quickly realized—not including my successful channeling of Papou, fueled by personal sorrow, into my Geppetto—occurred when

I had to pretend *not* to feel what I was feeling every second I was onstage with Sierra, in rehearsal after painful rehearsal, and then in three consecutive evening performances and one Sunday matinee. Four times we brought the house down, and with each thrilling success came an increased and unquenchable longing, as I failed to distinguish my passionate feelings for Sierra from my feelings inflamed by the theater, never more so than in those final moments before the curtain fell, when I announced, "He had the wrong dreams. All, all, wrong," and then, at last, to my brother, Happy, "I know who I am, kid," and, finally, when I called for her, "Let's go, Mom," and, as I escorted her from the grave, she buried her teary face in my arms and cried, "We're free, we're free …"

By the weekend, word had gotten out. Attending Saturday night's show was the popular four-term mayor, Wilton Samuels, in his gold-buttoned blue blazer and with his bright orange combover, accompanying the ancient, shrunken, still-elegant matriarch of the Stedman family, owners of Kornfield newspapers, which the next morning featured a close-up shot of the Loman family—Willy, Linda, Biff, and Happy—hand in hand and taking a bow, on the cover of the *Sunday Times*. And finally, as if such acclaim and coverage weren't enough to make me feel like a legitimate player, the matinee's audience included my actual family—Mom and Bates, Big and, incredibly, both Aunt Helen and, yes, Uncle Nick, who had recently, after a grueling holiday season, punctuated by the severing of that most crucial digit, acceded to his wife's pleas to close the restaurant on Sundays; this concession freed him to rest for a day and also, as it would turn out, to attend his nephew's play, which he called "good" and then elaborating— unoriginally but no less pleasingly to me, quoting verbatim from the front-page article published that morning—"not just for a *high-school* play, but for *the greatest American play.*" The best review of all came from Mitch Mitchell, who traveled all the way from New York City just to see the show, and who declared (back at my house during the after-party, for the whole family to hear, most crucially my mother) that I had "the instincts of an actor, a real flair for the stage—and maybe the screen, too. We'll see." In my mind, my fate was sealed.

Agreeing to attend Wheatcroft had won me some bargaining power with my mother, at least for the short term, and she'd cautiously approved my very humble request to stay with Mitch for just two weeks after graduation. But now with Biff Loman under my belt, it seemed I had some real footing. As I began to talk more openly about my plans for the summer, testing my mother's temperature, she became quietly encouraging, snipping from newspapers and magazines and leaving on the kitchen table vaguely relevant articles, with snapshots of Dante Saludo or New York City. My promise to go to college crystallized in my mind as a lie I could live with, exposing my flawed philosophy that promises could never be lies because no one could predict the future—even one's best-laid plans. Here's all I knew for sure: Come summer, I would be working on a movie in New York City. Beyond that, anything was possible.

But then, at the tail end of a long and tiring Memorial Day weekend, Big had gone on a new-recruit visit to Penn State University and I was left alone in Kornfield with Uncle Nick. I was arranging bottles of beer in the refrigerator under the bar when I looked over my shoulder to find him standing behind me, contemplating the cash register or his own asymmetrical hands gripping its sides. You couldn't blame him for being paralyzed by the sight of that nub, and there was little you could say to comfort him. *Thank God it wasn't your right hand* was a tired bit of consolation.

It was late Monday afternoon, my favorite time at the restaurant, in that serene period when the sun warmed the drapes and tabletops and lazy lunchers lingered in the Black Stallion Room, adjacent to the bar. Their distant conversation and the sporadic clink of silverware, along with the voice of Harry Kalas narrating the late innings of a Phillies game on the TV overhead, provided me soothing company while I stocked up and tidied up. The hours ahead promised a modest dinner crowd, and, at this time of the year, especially on a holiday like today, when the usual customers would be home cooking on the grill, the whole scene was a prelude to the warm steady rhythm of summer.

When Uncle Nick squatted at the half-empty case of Budweiser at my ankles and said, "Look at me," I was already staring straight into his dark, foreboding eyes, which seemed to warn of the worst possible news.

"What is it?" I braced myself for news I couldn't fathom— *Big on the long drive back from State College … a tractor-trailer crossing over the median … a sheer drop off the shoulder …*

I saw in Uncle Nick's gaze both sympathy and dread, though I soon realized he meant to convey confidence and a kind of ceremonial earnestness.

"I want to be clear," he said. "Your cousin is quick on his feet, but not up here." He tapped his forehead with a finger.

I blurted, "Yes he is," then caught my breath, not relieved, exactly.

"Don't play dim. Listen to what I'm saying. He doesn't have the ability. For this." He tossed a finger into the air and gazed at the ceiling. "Not like you. He'll play ball for a few years—if he can cut it in the classroom. Maybe he gets picked up by some team. But with his Achilles, you never know …"

"What are you saying?"

He checked his watch and glanced over the edge of the bar toward the door, as if Big might enter any second. "Eventually, he winds up back here. In the meantime, I teach you the business. This summer. Before you start school. Everything. Paying the bills, insurance, stocking liquor, hiring and firing."

"Big can do whatever I can do—*better*." I meant it.

"Papou understood what I'm telling you," Uncle Nick said. "He always said so. Look at this." His thumbless hand, four fingers, shot up between our faces. "I'm half what I used to be … It's hard enough running the show alone now."

"What did Papou say exactly?" I stood up straight.

Uncle Nick reached for the bar top and pulled himself up. "He wanted this for you."

"I'm going to New York."

"When you get back … By the time you start classes at Wheatcroft, you'll be able to run this place in your sleep, or at least on the weekends. Then we'll take it from there."

I leaned back against the bar.

"Your mother is proud of you. Papou would be proud of you—he *was* proud of you. You know— You *understand* …" He smiled gently. "Your grandfather saved all his money. You'd never know how well he did, but this place has made us all … *comfortable*. Did your mother explain to you? Papou's will?"

I shook my head. "His *will?*" The concept was foreign to me, and evidently it was a topic unlikely to be brought up by my mother.

"He left the restaurant to his three children. Your Uncle Paul agreed to sell his third. But your mother didn't want to sell. You understand?"

"My mom is half owner?"

"No, she kept her third. I bought Paul's share. So that's how it goes for now. But changes can always be made down the road. You need to know, things have worked out very well for this family. Papou made sure of it."

I was frozen.

He went on, "People work a lifetime to achieve this, and you're stepping right into it. This will be yours and Big's one day. That's how it's going to work. Equal partners. Your mother and I have talked about this, too."

He extended his hand for me to shake. Instinctively I took it.

"I don't know what to say." I really didn't. I hadn't meant to sound grateful, or ungrateful. I kept thinking about this secret my mother had been keeping from me—and wondering why.

Uncle Nick strengthened his grip. "You're welcome." He scooped from his pants pocket a jumble of keys and presented them to me. "*You* close up tonight."

I was eighteen, and I'd just been granted keys to the kingdom.

"We're just going to have to make do," Uncle Nick said. "You and me. Until Big gets back."

In twenty years?

He grinned and winked, while my wild mind raced into white space.

Big did soon return, safe after all, and a few hours later the two of us would close the restaurant together. Uncle Nick had left early, evidently making good on his promise to bequeath the more privileged responsibilities as soon as possible. He'd instructed me on stashing bundled cash in the safe, bestowing, in addition to the keys, the combination to the lock in the office behind the barroom.

Big was cleaning up back in the kitchen. I was wiping down the bar. I kept seeing myself in that brown Buick, Uncle Nick hunched over in the passenger seat, the two of us drifting not toward the emergency room, as we had months before, but toward my own preselected grave.

I imagined Papou alone at his table, staring at his folded hands. He materialized in a light gray suit, not in the thick brown suit he'd departed in.

Hello, he said, barely shifting his eyes toward me.

Now I was sitting across from him. He took a pink packet from a glass container. An untouched soft-boiled egg sat in a vegetable dish between us.

Well, he said. *Now what are we going to do?*

I shrugged.

How about a little cup of coffee? he said, flipping the Sweet & Low slowly in his fingers. His hunched gray shoulders bounced as he chuckled.

I brought a filled cup on a saucer. Steam rose into his face.

Very nice. He slurped. Coffee rippled at the cup's edge under his lip, his pinkie pointing to the ceiling.

What if I went to New York for good? I wasn't any kind of actor—*yet?*

The cup slipped as he set it down on the saucer. Coffee spilled onto his fingers and splashed onto his white cuff.

I handed him a napkin.

He salted the egg. The crystals sparkled.

He pushed the dish toward me and stared at his hands.

One thing is for sure. If you don't try, you'll never know.

I felt a deep dread. Big was in the kitchen working while we were out here making plans.

What if I never came back? What about this place? I loved this place.

Papou shut his eyes tightly.

Big entered the barroom. He wore an apron with straps over his shoulders. He looked like a butcher. He sat down across from me, taking Papou's place.

"Just talked to my mom on the phone," he said. "Dad's already asleep." He let out a long, satisfied breath. "I have to tell you about Penn State. You will want to go there, too. Wait till you visit—it's amazing. It's called Happy Valley for a reason."

I slurped coffee.

"All set?" he said, gazing at the clean bar. He slapped his apron on the table. "What's with you and coffee now?"

"Nothing. Just tired."

Big gestured hungrily toward the egg in the dish before me. I smiled, okay, and he scooped it up and chewed, oblivious.

Out on the back porch, I plucked Uncle Nick's keys from my pocket. After locking the door—for the first and the last time, I decided—I returned the keys to Big and we set out into the dark parking lot.

7
JUST CREW

After graduation, Big drove north to Penn State for training camp, while I was on a train to New York. By now I believed my own fantastic visions of how a stint as production assistant would evolve into a life in the movies. These visions involved Oscar award acceptance speeches for roles I couldn't imagine, though my mind drifted now and then to the thought of me as Hamlet, sliding along the edge of a stage, musing about existence. My fantasies were probable only in that each provided refuge from any future involving me in Kornfield. In my private formulations, I was prepared to do anything if it meant an alternative to the life I'd inherited. I kept my dreams a secret from everyone, including my mother, even after she told me of her plans to quit her job as secretary of Tower High School and instead "to become more involved" at the restaurant—a vague and surprising twist I couldn't help reading as part of some larger design to keep me close. How could I ever express to her or to anyone that, for me, a life in Kornfield would mean the very death of my precious, inspired, artistic (if a bit untrained) soul?

The moment Mitch welcomed me into his apartment, I stood paralyzed behind a couch wrapped in a pink paisley tapestry—fedora snug on my head, duffel-bag straps wedged into my shoulders—as if unsure about settling in. Beyond the couch were a wooden coffee table and an amazingly funky, gigantic blue-and-green upholstered chair. I disguised my awe with a critical gaze, my eyes traveling from one movie poster to another. There was *Touch of Evil* and *Vertigo*, which I'd read about but hadn't seen, and *Persona, Breathless, La Strada*—titles and images that were dizzyingly unfamiliar, the names of directors prominently displayed—Welles, Hitchcock, Bergman, Fellini, Godard, Coutard, Tarkovsky, Truffaut—progressing from the vaguely familiar to the foreign and unpronounceable. Mitch's apartment undermined my pride as movie connoisseur. I had seen every Soro Martello movie and in the last six months had learned by heart not just the *Shadow King* screenplay but also the industry classic *Teach Yourself Movie Making*.

Every observable detail of this place, every odd knickknack and tattered book, every deformed candle and half-dead plant, seemed emblematic of its inhabitant, my host, who was suddenly marvelous beyond words—his black boots, with their silver buckles, the unbuttoned cuffs of his tousled shirt, the rings bulging from his fingers like extra knuckles—his persona as exotic as the objects that surrounded and adorned him. The prospect of living in such a place, let alone outfitting oneself in such a way, a style that was so identifiably one's own, seemed to me the highest level of artistic cool, and in an instant I set my mind on that goal—the hat on my head suddenly an embarrassing reminder of my complete lack of originality. At the same time, the impossible fact that Mitch, too, had come from Kornfield filled me with hope. My imagination formed pathways and shapes that would mark my future. In a rush, I removed my hat and then quickly returned it to its proper place on my head.

"Somethin' to drink?" Mitch stabbed a cigarette into his mouth and went into the kitchen.

"Whatever you're having."

I hovered by the couch. Impulsively, I started working Mitch for a "real job," which in my mind meant at a restaurant—"Maybe something downstairs at the diner," I said, a modest first proposal, I figured, not yet ready to reveal my secret plan to drop anchor here for good and land a job at Ferrara's—Saludo's place, where Mitch worked.

"Are you nuts?" From the kitchen counter he retrieved an open can of beer whose green-and-yellow label I didn't recognize. "You're here to make a movie, not bus tables."

I shrugged, intuiting that with a non-paying internship in the movie business, I needed to establish my roots—and fast.

"You need to be unencumbered, bro …" He took a swig and reached into the refrigerator for what I expected to be another beer with the green-and-yellow label. "Besides, *nobody's* getting paid on this movie. You're lucky. You have no expenses. Take advantage of it." He pulled out a can of Coke and presented it to me.

Mildly humiliated, I shook my head, no thanks, too emphatically communicating the sting I felt.

"Let's be clear." He stood firm in the kitchen doorway. "I'm responsible for you. I've talked to your mother, and we have an understanding."

"You talked to my mom?"

"We're going to have fun, but this is serious business. I'm in charge of you. We're not going to be sitting around slugging beers together."

"You're in *charge* of me?"

He lifted the can toward my face. "Do you want the Coke?" I shook my head again, and he returned it to the fridge.

The cigarette wagged up and down as he spoke. "You need to *network*. That's how things get done, especially independent films. Don't forget that—you're doing *them* a favor, too." He inhaled, plucked out the unscathed cigarette, and sipped his beer.

"Are you still *not* smoking?" I said, delighted by my own wit.

He looked up, faintly grinning. "Very clever, Johnny." I watched, curious, as he studied the thing between his fingers and took a long, satisfying drag. He squinted behind the invisible smoke he spewed. "You never know what opportunities might come up."

I played it cool, wishing he'd say something about a certain part he'd nailed down for me. I couldn't understand why he would delay telling me the one piece of information I cared about more than anything else. But asking about it seemed rude—unprofessional. Instead, I tossed out, "What am I going to be doing?"

I slipped my thumbs under the duffel-bag straps that were digging into my shoulders.

"Helping with lights and stuff." He took another fake puff.

I could no longer resist. "What about … *you know* …?"

"What?"

"Me being in the movie."

Nodding, he filled his lungs again and exhaled. "We'll see."

"Did they say that? *We'll see?*"

"Not exactly. I mentioned you. Look, I know it seems like a big deal to *you*, but to *them* whatever you end up doing for this movie is very small potatoes. They've got bigger fish to fry right now."

"What fish? What do you mean?"

"Let's just say there's no Johnny Demos in the movie if there's no Dante Saludo in the movie."

"No Dante Saludo? What happened?" Suddenly I was not the least bit concerned with my own possible role in a movie without Dante Saludo in it.

"I told you he's shooting a movie in Malta. We think he's on his way."

"You *think? Malta?* You never said Malta."

Mitch finished his beer and set his empty on the kitchen counter. He walked into the living room and sat on the oversized blue-and-green chair, draping a leg over one of the armrests.

I said, "He *has* to play Angelo. The whole story hinges on that scene. On that *concept*—of Angelo as guardian angel."

"You read the script I gave you?"

"It's amazing. I memorized it."

He smiled. "I'm glad you like it."

Despite the chair's enormous size, Mitch looked larger than life, leaning back into a pair of giant pillows, fingertips pointlessly tracing the piping that lined the armrests.

I said, "Do you still like the idea—*your* idea, I mean—of me as his best self and all that?"

"I love it. I want to see it happen."

"Me too," I said.

Mitch nodded thoughtfully. "You can put your bag down now."

"Oh." I'd been standing inside the doorway this whole time. In the next room, a bed was fixed with smooth red sheets below a window. I pointed. "In there?"

He thrust his chin toward the couch at my hip. "Right there." He stood up. "Let's stay optimistic, all right? Tonight we're going to a party down the street. You'll meet the other producers, the DP, the PAs—" He went back into the kitchen and cracked open another beer.

"What are *you* going to be doing?" I asked.

"Introducing *you*."

"I mean for the movie—on set."

He walked back to his chair. "I do everything—or everything the Avellinos don't think of. Which keeps me busy. Are you going to sit down?" He sipped and sank back, kicking his black boots onto the low wooden table half-covered with dry candle wax, yellow and red nubs melted onto magazine covers. "You want something to eat or something?"

"No thanks."

I let out a deep breath and bowed my head in a panic, doubting everything Mitch had ever told me about this so-called Dante Saludo movie. What exactly was Mitch's role in all of this? Even after all I'd read about moviemaking, I still didn't understand what a producer was, or at least how Mitch was functioning as one.

I asked, "Why aren't you acting anymore?"

He chuckled. "What?"

I drifted toward the window, drawn toward the restaurant across the street, the arched windows bordered with lights and ornate molding. Three thin women in assorted-candy-colored dresses and high heels walked into the place.

"Hey, bro …" Mitch got up, walked toward me, and peered under the brim of my fedora. He followed my gaze out the window. "You looking for something? Or *someone?*"

I shrugged. It seemed too obvious to bother saying out loud. And slightly insulting. Then I said it anyway: "If *you* couldn't make it as an actor, how can *I*?"

His eyebrows shot up. "I wasn't as good as you think."

"You were incredible. The Bunkeropouloses are legendary."

"Your memory is playing tricks on you," he said.

"Everyone thought so."

"You know, bro ..." He waited for my attention. "If you stand there long enough, you'll see him eventually."

Only then did I make the connection: "That's Ferrara's? Saludo's restaurant?"

He nodded. "That's it. On the same block as the office building he owns on the corner, where we run the business, and right next to the warehouse where we do most of our filming."

A wave of envy ran through me. Mitch was the luckiest man on the planet. It seemed to me the whole universe existed on this one city block. This was all I would ever need in life, I decided. The summer night was coming on, a powder-blue sky falling into the crags of the buildings. I could see myself in five years, ten years, waiting tables in this town while pining for roles. I sank my hand into my pocket and clutched the familiar cash, bartending tips, which reminded me not just of home and of the restaurant but of a sense of security that was suddenly more potent, and more remote, than ever.

Mitch was reading my mind. "You can wait tables when you get back to Kornfield—for the rest of your life if you want." He leaned toward the coffee table and mashed his pristine white cigarette on a hard wax puddle, dry tobacco fragments crumbling ridiculously. He stood up. "Lose the fedora, grandpa. And drop the bag already."

I let the straps skid down my arms. The lights across the street glowed bright orange above the sidewalk. I remained mesmerized.

"Who's playing Ray?" I asked. "Anyone I know?" I was trying to get into the spirit of the night or pretending to be. "Will he be there tonight?"

"It's not a cast party, bro." Mitch drifted toward his bedroom. He slipped behind the half-open door and said, "Just crew."

It was too late to disguise my disappointment. I reminded myself that this was my one shot—to make it in the movies. And yet, even as Mitch went on about tonight's esteemed guest list—"the interns, a few of our favorite investors …"—I couldn't take my eyes off the restaurant across the street. I felt as if I should be strapping on an apron and scraping gravy from plates. I couldn't help myself. It's what I knew best. I didn't feel like an actor. I felt like a hick.

8
BRONX BREW

"You an actor?"

I looked up from the ice bin, where I'd buried my face, pretending not to feel already pathetic and abandoned.

A pretty woman who looked vaguely like my mother, dark hair clipped in a twist, taste-tested the cocktail she was concocting in a blue plastic cup.

I was thrilled I might be putting out such signals, even without the fedora. "How could you tell?"

She set down the giant bottle of gin. "I assumed you weren't a producer since you're too young to have failed at everything else already."

I returned her sly smile. "What do *you* do?"

"I'm a producer."

"Hah." My smile froze.

"Don't worry," she said. "I was a terrible actress. It took me about a week in this city to realize it. So what have you done as an actor?"

"I just got here." I surveyed the liquor options. "I played Biff in *Death of a Salesman*."

"That's lovely," she said. "Where?"

"Uh, a theater in Pennsylvania."

"Anything else?"

I fumbled the ice scooper. "I played an old man in search of his son."

"A prodigal story," she offered.

"Exactly." Geppetto and Pinocchio danced ridiculously in my mind.

Mitch approached us, swigging a beer—the same brand, with the green-and-yellow can, from his apartment. He said, "My cousin the prodigy."

"I can see that," the woman said.

I scooped ice into a blue plastic cup, hoping she was referring to my self-evident talent, not my vague resemblance to Mitch.

Before she could elaborate, he said, "Excuse us, Mary. He's yet to meet our illustrious hosts." He cracked open a can of Coke and handed it to me.

I set the can on the table half-covered with giant bottles of booze. In a rush I brought a handle of rum to my ice-filled cup; torrents tumbled in. I topped it off with the Coke.

As Mitch scooped me into an anonymous circle of minglers, I glanced back at Mary, who raised her cup in a toast. I gulped my drink, which went down like caramelized fire.

I was beginning to develop my cocktail-party repertoire. I was a bartender with a background from Mitch's hometown. I'd scored a short list of acting credits.

"How old are you?" someone asked, and, before I could answer, a man with a blue beret on backwards popped open another one of those familiar cans of beer and said he wished he'd started so early.

"What are you drinking?" I asked him.

"Bronx Brew. Sip—" he insisted.

I took a good swallow. "Holy shit," I beamed. The beer was rich and spicy, like nothing I'd ever tasted.

"You've got to meet Ed and Steve." He pointed to two shaggy-haired guys in sweatshirts. He read my puzzled expression and explained that those were the dudes who'd created the beer in their basement two years ago and that they'd just picked up another gold medal at the Great Northeast Brewmasters Festival.

"I guess it hasn't made it to Pennsylvania," I said.

"It's coming," he said.

I pictured the golden brew dripping through glass tubes into beakers, under lightbulbs hanging from basement beams. I was stunned by the notion that any human beings outside of a corporate brewery, let alone a pair of friends, had formulated beer in their home then transformed their experiment into a full-fledged business—all in the time since I'd taken Algebra II. Now they were collecting awards and attending parties where their own smartly designed cans filled the ice tubs, not to mention the shelves in Mitch's refrigerator two blocks away.

"How old are you, did you say?"

A sense of urgency was suddenly pressing in on me. "Eighteen—"

Mitch whispered, "Follow me," passing me in a flash and then circling up with a crew of slick-haired talkers in the corner. I retreated anxiously toward the salsa. While I recognized the enviable fact of my youth—nothing but potential stretching out on the sparkling clean slate before me—time seemed to be racing by, these partiers all chattering hungrily, intent on making another leap in their rapid progress in the film business. From across the room, Mitch mouthed,

"Av-e-*lli*-nos" to me while I piled tortilla chips on a napkin. He made a furious flick of his hand, directing me to join him. I remained paralyzed by doubt that the producers of *Shadow King* wanted anything to do with Mitch's teenage cousin from Kornfield—a hometown name that needed no ironic substitute. Mitch frowned at me then turned his back. I found the rum and filled up.

Nearby, a ceiling-high window made a violet-sky backdrop to the bereted man and a sharply dressed woman speaking nearly chin to chin. I imagined a love scene, as she turned gruffly and he pleaded.

I can't go on like this, I imagined her saying.

This is New York, he replied. *We've been through this. It's what I am. I can't leave. You can't leave your self.*

He ducked his head, trying to make eye contact with her, boyish in his army pants and blue beret. She poked a straw at the ice in her glass. She wore a black suit with three gold buttons in front. A lawyer or a banker. She shuffled and stirred. When she turned away from his gentle touch, he reached for her, then whisked off his beret and worked it in his hands—

"You Mitch's cousin?"

My reverie of sorts had been interrupted by a strapping blond-haired guy in an NYU sweatshirt. He swiped a bottle of beer from an icy plastic tub under the snack table and awaited my reply.

"Yeah," I said. The lovers held their positions by the window.

"Working on the film," he said, not quite a question.

"You, too?" I set my chips on the table.

"Bill." He swigged his beer, and we shook hands.

"Johnny. You go to NYU?"

"Just graduated," he said. "You in school?"

"Finished," I said.

"Cheers." He clicked his bottle against my cup.

Again, I impressed myself with my twisted honesty. In Bill's eyes, I might have been a fed-up theater student, tired of theory and ready for action. I took a sip and gestured to the NYU on his sweatshirt.

He said, "Film production major. Assistant director—for now." He smiled. "More of a waiter than anything else, though."

"Me too! And an actor."

Bill's eyes shifted toward a burst of laughter in the corner—Mitch and his cronies, tipping back bottles. "Gotta hand it to them," Bill said. "These guys are about to finish their first film."

I nursed my rum. "A Dante Saludo film, no less."

"Hopefully," Bill said.

"You think he'll get here?"

"They've changed the schedule for him a dozen times already."

I shook my head in genuine disbelief. "What will they do if he doesn't show up?"

"You know Jay Kauffman? He's here somewhere. Not as famous, but just as good."

"As good as Saludo?"

"Maybe *better*. Listen—" Bill hesitated. "I think something happened. Something no one's talking about. Everyone's in the dark. Except for *them—maybe*." He gestured to Mitch and the Avellinos.

"If no one's talking, then how do you know something happened?"

"I pick up bits and pieces. Something during the shoot in Italy. He was doing his own stunts."

"Isn't he, like, fifty?"

"Even at Ferrara's, everyone's talking, but no one knows anything—or no one admits to knowing."

"You work at Ferrara's?" I strained to disguise my absurd enthusiasm for his place of employment—not to mention my spontaneous and irrational loss of interest in the physical welfare of Dante Saludo.

"Did Mitch say anything to you?"

"About Saludo?" I shook my head, no, then steered our conversation back to the more pressing matter at hand: "At the restaurant—they need a waiter? Or a busboy?"

Bill laughed.

"Dishwasher?" I was in shameless pursuit. "I can do anything. I'm from a restaurant family."

"Greek, right? You guys have the best food."

I felt a rush of pride, and a sudden leg up. "I'm a bartender mainly."

"Have you met Steve and Ed from Bronx Brew?"

Just then the lovers by the window were rushing toward us, the man trailing the woman. She huffed, "I can't believe you," and the man watched her slip away into the crowd.

Bill said, "Everything all right, Jay?"

"Stay single, fellas." He made a cartoonish stressed-out face, neck muscles taut, eyes bugging. "Just kidding. Where would I be without her?" He reached past me for a pretzel. "Dead in a ditch somewhere. That's where. Excuse me—" He turned and followed his wife's trail into the kitchen.

"That's Jay Kauffman," Bill said.

"Saludo's understudy?"

Bill laughed. "He's no one's understudy. If I were him, I'd be on the beach in L.A. right now, reading the script Spielberg just sent me."

"Why isn't he?"

"Beats me. Lifelong New Yorker. Started a school here. Better acting teacher than any prof I had at NYU. Does a play now and then. Writes." Bill shrugged. "Guy's a total enigma. I studied with him two summers. I feel like I hardly know him. Consummate professional. Oh, also"—he grinned—"very rich wife."

Just then Jay returned. "Handsome Bill, how are you? Sorry about that. I left the coffee maker on. Whole way over here, she's letting me have it, like I'm gonna burn the place down. Thing turns off automatically."

Up close I could see the gray in Jay's sideburns. I'd pegged him as young and struggling. I was disappointed to learn that he was settled in, a supposed genius content to be arguing with his wife about small household appliances. His beret, I could see now, was a Mets hat, clenched in his hands.

Handsome Bill introduced us. "Johnny's an actor."

"And a bartender," I said, "or a busboy, or whatever."

"Jack of all trades." Jay grinned. "You taking acting classes?"

"Thinking about it," I said. "I mean, definitely. I will. Right now I'm sort of in between—"

In the distance Mitch waved me over again.

"I run a school right around the corner," Jay said.

"Yeah, Bill was just saying …"

"In an old church. Converted it into a small theater—along with a few other noble thespians. And some even nobler patrons." He grinned. "You can see it from here." He moved toward a window. "Look." I followed him. "Pews still in there and everything. Perfect acoustics. You can see the domes and crosses."

"I see it."

He plucked a pen from inside his sport coat. On a round cardboard coaster he swiped from the table behind him—a Bronx Brew coaster—he wrote, in the white band that encircled the green-and-yellow logo, his phone number and the address of The Annunciation. "We kept the church's name. You should check us out."

I was studying the coaster as if it were a priceless collectible, a signed baseball card of some future Hall of Famer, when Mitch arrived. "Gentlemen." He nodded considerately to Jay and Bill. "Gotta introduce Johnny here to the boys—*finally*." He shot me laser eyes.

"Thanks," I said to Jay, and stuffed the coaster into my back pocket.

"I'll see about a job for you," Handsome Bill said.

Mitch dragged me away. "You can't help yourself, can you? I'm trying to get you *inside* here, and you're trying to find restaurant work."

"You didn't tell me about Saludo's understudy."

"He's not an understudy, bro. Let's hope we don't need him." We approached the circle of important people. Mitch lit up, "*Heeere's* Johnny!" grinning devilishly, invoking Ed McMahon or Jack Nicholson.

His movie cronies beamed impressively: "So, this is little Dante Saludo."

"Didn't I tell you?" Mitch said.

They extended their hands to shake: "Mike Avellino, how are ya …"

"Joe Avellino, what's goin' on …"

While they went on grinning thoughtfully, I guzzled my rum. No one was saying anything. I lowered the cup and rattled the ice. Then it occurred to me that I might be in the midst of my own audition. I felt my eyebrows rising and lips loosely puckering, not quite unconsciously willing myself to resemble the young Dante Saludo—in that classic moment in *Rebel Sons* when he's leaning out the window and panning the empty alley. I went on mugging for the producers when, all at once, a thousand frantic birds seemed to be fluttering in my otherwise empty skull. I wanted to find the nearest couch.

"Take it easy," Mitch muttered, and I found my footing. His grip on the back of my arm held me steady.

"Uncanny," someone said.

The Avellinos were nodding, apparently pleased, as those birds multiplied and nearly filled my vision. I was too drunk to smile, but not too drunk to realize that maybe I'd just gotten the part—unless I'd just lost it. Whatever my prospects, as Mitch whisked me away, my mind drifted back to that longer-term plan involving my new friend Handsome Bill landing me a busboy gig down the street at Ferrara's.

9
BROOKLYN BRIDGE

When I woke to find Mitch staring down at me in the dark, I shot up on the couch, assuming something had gone terribly wrong, a feeling precipitated by the ominous rumbling in my stomach. I thought of darting to the toilet, then thought better about darting anywhere. I lowered myself back down and closed my eyes, not sure if I was dreaming, drunk, or delusional. It seemed only minutes had passed since returning from the party and crashing on the couch.

"This is it, bro," Mitch said. "Rise and shine."

I strained to open one eye. Beyond Mitch, the kitchen light was on.

"Is he here?" I said. "What's happening?"

"Is who here?"

"Are we filming?"

Mitch took a sip from a mug. A cloud of steam rose between us. "Are you still drunk?"

"Dante Saludo."

He went into the kitchen. "Let's go. We're shooting the bridge."

I stood up. "What does that mean, shooting the bridge?"

"It means we spend money we don't have on shots we don't need while we wait for Big Dan to get here."

"You mean Dante? That's what you call him? Big Dan?"

He emerged from the kitchen, whipping something in a bowl with a fork.

"Get dressed. We've got to beat the sunrise."

I rubbed my eyes and trudged toward him.

"What time is it?" I groaned.

"Almost five." Beads of water dripped from thick strands at his forehead. "City that never sleeps." He dipped back into the kitchen and popped open the microwave.

"What are you making?" I stepped back to give him space.

He handed me a glass of orange juice. "Gotta feed that hangover."

"I'm not hung over." I slugged the juice.

"What the hell were you drinking?" He put the bowl in the microwave and started it. "Avoid the booze, bro. You need to be ready when the universe calls."

"Don't producers need to be ready when the universe calls?"

The microwave hummed. Mitch stared at me smugly from the kitchen's doorless doorway. "I lay off the hard stuff, Johnny. And, believe me, I'm ready when the universe calls."

I handed him my empty glass. "Those guys really started their own brewery?"

"Our biggest investor. In two years, they'll be in every bar in America. It's nice to have rich friends who like movies."

My mind was spinning. "Everyone in this city is amazing."

Mitch sang, "*If you can make it here, you'll make it anywhere …*"

The microwave beeped.

I said, "You're microwaving *eggs?*"

"You didn't know you can do that? I thought you were restaurant people."

"Exactly."

In seconds, Mitch slid a puffy golden moon onto an already toasted English muffin garnished with ketchup, cut the sandwich, and handed me half. When I donned my fedora, Mitch insisted I lose it once and for all—we were headed for manual labor, not office work.

We set out into the dark morning, munching and hustling toward the intersection where Greenwich met Franklin. Under a streetlamp on the sidewalk up ahead, one of the Avellino brothers, along with Handsome Bill, holding a clipboard, and a half dozen new faces, cradled steaming cups and stared like tourists at the top-floor windows of the Ferrara Center across the street. I raced after Mitch, following everyone's gaze.

Mitch wolfed down the last of his sandwich and called out to the group, "What's going on? Where's Joe?"

I whispered, "Which one's Joe? Who's this?"

"*Mike*, obviously."

Mike Avellino shushed us with a thick finger to his lips. "We're waiting for Dan."

"Dante?" I said.

Mitch scowled at me, just as Joe Avellino alighted from the black Saab parked at the curb. The production team formed a huddle in the middle of the street. I sidled up to Mitch.

Mike asked Joe, "You call Dan again?"

That the Avellinos owned a car phone seemed a promising sign—of something, anyway.

Joe said, "*Yes*, I called Dan again. *And* I left a message again. Where the hell is Buddy?"

"Who's Buddy?" I asked.

Mitch poked me with an elbow. "Don't interrupt."

Mike and Joe were staring at me, or at the space I occupied, as if tracing the sound of my voice to the source, only to discover the body of an eighteen-year-old boy they'd never seen before.

Mitch said, "Sorry," apologizing on my behalf.

When Mike said, "Johnny Demos," and Joe said, "Little Dante Saludo," I felt a surge of relief and hope—until Joe added, "You get home all right last night?" grinning wildly while Mike cackled.

"I'm fine," I said, hardly covering for my poor performance at the party.

Mike said, "Buddy's getting bagels."

Joe turned to Mike and snapped, "We do *not* need bagels right now, Mike. We need Dan!"

I took a step back.

"No shit we need Dan," Mike said. "What'd you find out?"

Joe shook his head. "What do you want me to tell you, brother?"

"I want you to tell me where the hell he is! The warehouse is costing us daily. The bar is built. The set is ready. We rewrote the monologue, so now—" Mike paused for air, his neck veins bulging. "I want to shoot the fucking scene and get this movie in the can!"

Joe sighed deeply. "First of all, calm the fuck down. Second of all—oh! *You* want to shoot the fucking scene?!"

Mitch patted me on the shoulder. "Johnny, wait over there." He shooed me away, directing me toward the crew of young strangers—four shaggy-haired guys and two girls, who were shuffling in quiet circles near a white van parked across the street.

I didn't move.

Joe said, "We've got to get going here, Mike. It's time for Plan B."

"Plan B?" I let out.

The Avellinos glared at me.

Mitch put his face directly in front of mine. "Would you *please* go over there? With *them*—"

I inched toward the white van, where the interns sipped from their coffee cups and grumbled things I couldn't hear. The van's rear doors were open. A dim interior light shined on giant lamps, silver poles, and mysterious black boxes. I looked back at Mitch, who got his hands on Handsome Bill's clipboard and penciled notes while flashing nervous glances toward Broadway and the building where Saludo lived. I wondered how much it must have pained Mitch to be hustling as a producer rather than contemplating whatever lines should have been his, at least in the ideal version of his life as I imagined it.

Mitch checked his watch and joined the anxious producers at the front of the Saab. They kicked at stones, folded their arms, and leaned on the hood. They pressed their fists to their hips and gazed at the horizon. Joe Avellino walked away, as if for a moment of privacy, into the silent street that narrowed in the distance, and then, startling all of us, or at least me, unleashed a guttural yowl that seemed to fill the space between us and the edge of the island: "*Where the fuck are you, Dante Saludo!*" As he walked back to us, I felt a connection with Joe, both of us aching in some primal way for the return of a man we believed was crucial to our destinies.

One of the interns said, "Here we go again." Another added, "Morning meltdown mode."

Just then a pot-bellied man in a baseball hat appeared in the middle of the street.

Mike yelled, "Buddy! What the fuck?!"

Not the man I was expecting to see. His belly bulged behind a button-down Hawaiian shirt; his bare legs, pink from the sun, protruded from the fringed ends of cutoff jean shorts, his thin shins in striped, white socks. Unfazed, he raised both arms in apparent triumph, a cup of coffee in one hand and a stuffed paper bag in the other.

"You'll thank me for these!" he announced. "Who's hungry?"

Joe said, "Minutes till sunrise, Buddy."

Buddy said, "We got nothin' but time, chief," and walked to the white van parked nearby.

In unison the Avellinos clapped their hands, indicating no sweat, and shouted, "Plan B!" as if this were welcome news.

Mitch marched toward me at the rear of the van. The interns dispersed to other cars.

"You're coming with me," Mitch said.

"What's Plan B?" I asked.

"It's what I told you." With outstretched arms, Mitch grabbed the rear doors and examined the contents of the van. "The bridge."

"I thought that was Plan A."

He flashed a hard stare at me. "Johnny boy, listen: Plan A is Saludo. Every day, Plan A is Saludo. Every morning, since day one, we start out talking about Plan A, Joe has a nervous breakdown, and then we go to Plan B." He slammed the doors shut. "Just— You need to be patient, all right?"

"Jeez, sorry," I said.

Mitch did a quick pan of our surroundings, then once again locked eyes with mine. "I don't mean to be rude, okay?"

"Okay."

"But you need to just watch and listen and not ask so many questions."

"I'm just trying to learn."

Mitch looked across the street. The Avellinos were chatting with Buddy. Joe had his hand on Buddy's shoulder. Mitch said, "Things don't always go as planned when you're making a movie. Sometimes nothing goes right. Sometimes things go very wrong. Understand? Very rarely do they all go right. In fact, that never happens."

I nodded, oblivious—and hopeful he would elaborate on the curious situation at hand if I showed him I could keep my mouth shut. The strategy worked.

"Can you keep a secret?" he said. "Tell *no one*. Top-secret, okay? Saludo is back in town, but there was an accident. His face got fucked up or something. Our luck, right? His face, the only thing that matters for the scene. He couldn't have broken his leg."

"What do you mean, his face got fucked up—*or something?*"

The Avellinos hollered, "Let's roll!", sank into their car, and zoomed off.

Mitch said, "Buddy's coming with us. So, no more questions."

Buddy shuffled across the street toward us, carrying his coffee and giant paper bag. He greeted me with a tip of his cap and shifted his toothpick from one side of his mouth to the other.

"Buddy Klein," he said. *Klaahn.* "DP. Know what that is, young man?"

"Director of photography." I was glaring at Mitch, wanting more details.

Buddy tapped my arm. "I'll be damned. You may know more about making movies than these fellas."

I climbed into the van, pleased by the compliment, despite its implications for the movie and my role in it. Buddy sat beside me and closed the door. Mitch circled the van and got behind the wheel. He started the engine and mouthed the words, "Top-secret."

I managed a smile, thrilled to be on the inside.

"What's your specialty, young man?" Buddy asked, as we raced across town to beat the rising sun, his black Chuck Taylors tucked under the dashboard.

"I'm an actor," I confessed.

"New Yawk City …" he mused.

I looked up from Buddy's sneakers and followed his gaze out the windshield, giddy at the newness of everything.

"How about that," Buddy said, as if seeing this view for the first time, as I was. Buddy wore a mesh fishing cap with a silhouette of a marlin on front, a paper license safety-pinned on the inside. Under the brim of the cap, his ice-blue eyes seemed to float off toward the dark sky, or the dark sea I imagined beyond the island, toward wherever home was for him.

"Johnny's here to help," Mitch said. "In whatever capacity."

"Today that makes you best boy," Buddy said.

"I don't know anything about lighting," I said.

"Damn, son! That's right—best boy is a light man. Now listen, we got to work together on this. Today I'm DP, gaffer, grip, and God knows what else, so that makes you—"

"We're never gonna make it in time." Mitch gassed it.

"—best boy."

We roared through yellow streetlights turning red, shadowy buildings flashing to our right as we skirted the edge of the island, the moon a white disk in the dark blue sky. I wondered about Plan B, with no idea what part the bridge played, nor could I guess what purpose all those lighting accessories in the back of the van might serve—on an outdoor set?—not to mention what role each of the interns might play. And what role I might play, if any. I wondered how many times Plan A had been dashed, shaken by the thought that the promise of a Dante Saludo cameo might be a ploy devised by the producers to motivate the staff—or, worse, it might be the product of their own self-delusion.

Either way, it had always seemed too good to be true, and I should have known better. Shouldn't have let myself get my hopes up—to work on a movie with Dante Saludo, whose face was now supposedly so disfigured that Plan A might be canceled for good—maybe another invented story, come to think of it, so far-fetched that of course we would all believe it and go on hoping for the best until the end of production.

"Brooklyn Bridge, son," Buddy announced, and my suspicions vanished the moment I saw it, majestic and menacing, lights glittering in the cool morning.

With a few quick turns of the wheel, we had descended into its shadows and come to a stop. Almost instantly the scene turned into a whirl of anxious urgency, with hardly a word uttered, everyone preprogrammed, it seemed, hauling tripods and poles and heavy cases into a grassy area where interns unclamped, arranged, and assembled, while I tried feebly to insert myself in some helpful way. I picked up a pole, which was promptly removed from my hands. I opened a toolbox, which was promptly shut.

Buddy tapped me on the shoulder. "Watch over the crew here, son, while I go see what these art*eests* got in mind."

He winked, and I stood tall with folded arms, watching him huddle up with the Avellino brothers on a stony path near the base of the bridge. Not far from them, Handsome Bill sidled up to Mitch, who clutched a clipboard.

The half dozen interns—college grads, only a few years older than I—appeared preternaturally skilled in their execution of the tasks they performed in the grass nearby. In a flash, huge white disks, six-feet wide—stretched sheets of nylon or silk, girded by circular metal strips—sprung one after another from the quick hands of the pony-tailed girl in gray sweatshirt; the black-haired girl, in construction boots, swiftly arranged them on their sides, leaning them against a large, buckled-shut black case. Then, as if one task were no less important than the next, and no less familiar, the two girls moved briskly to assist the four guys fastening heavy poles to erect a scaffold.

Feeling useless, I kicked a stone, my mind drifting toward home. I felt the urge to find a phone or dash off a quick letter addressed to everyone in the family, the living and the dead, to tell them, with trumped-up enthusiasm, that I had arrived, that my dreams were at last coming true, without the slightest fear of regret. My mind drifted to Happy Valley, where Big plowed into a rock-hard wall of varsity linemen. I imagined Papou almost a hundred years ago, standing where I was standing now, thinking what I was thinking: that the Brooklyn Bridge seemed strange and contradictory, as I felt—rooted and sluggish, yet somehow free and soaring.

Buddy returned and climbed the finished scaffold. "Let's make some love!"

The interns continued to move with daunting efficiency, understanding precisely what to do next and how and where to do it. Each of the guys wore cargo shorts with big pockets their hands sank into and emerged from, gripping screwdrivers and wrenches they wielded with athletic ease. The camera had emerged from somewhere and found its way to the top of a tripod, which had already been situated on top of the scaffold.

I sank my hands into the empty pockets of my khaki shorts. Just then, an intern handed me one of those enormous white disks and positioned me next to him at one corner of the scaffold. "I'm Josh," he said. Two other interns matched our positions at the opposite corner. "Just do what I do."

Buddy said, "Aim her that-a-way, fellas."

I studied the interns, brandishing their disks, whose purpose remained a mystery to me.

Joe Avellino began running along the bridge's pedestrian path, waving his arms and pointing wildly as if at attacking ships on the still-dark-blue horizon, Handsome Bill in tow. Mitch wasn't far behind, pages curled over the clipboard. Mike Avellino scaled the banks below, barking into a walkie-talkie, when in unison, the brothers shouted, "Action!" and we hoisted our shields toward the bridge—or toward the sun, just now rising on the distant horizon.

"Beautiful!" Buddy twisted his hat around and leaned into the camera. "Give me that white-hot love! You are gorgeous this morning, baby!"

I laughed, exuberant, and locked eyes with Josh, standing next to me. "Buddy is crazy!"

"He's got his own style," Josh said drolly. He examined my technique, his own arms outstretched, his body an elegant T, which I tried to imitate. "Do you understand what we're doing here?"

"No idea," I beamed.

Beyond the bridge slivers of yellow light shot across the black water.

"We're reflecting light onto the bridge," he explained. "So the bridge shows up on the film. The focus is on the sunrise, but we want to see the bridge, too. Joe's a genius. He's going to be famous."

"Shine on me, baby!" Buddy shouted. "Don't stop! You're sizzling hot!"

"Where did they get him?" I asked Josh in a low voice, as Buddy went on roaring overhead, "Scorching, baby! Burn for me!"

"He actually came out of retirement to work on this project."

"He probably thought it was going to be a Dante Saludo movie."

"It might *still be* a Dante Saludo movie. Buddy has a shitload of experience. He's shot literally hundreds of adult films."

"*Pornos?*" I blurted.

Josh exaggerated a frown, all too disappointed that I should sound derisive toward Buddy's achievements. "He knows what he's doing with the camera, is the point."

"I don't doubt it," I said. My elbows sagged. "Seriously, though? Pornos?"

Josh ignored my question. "Everyone's working for free on this project. It's costing them practically nothing. Everyone just wants to be a part of this."

I offered a puzzled smile, not sure if this news was meant to make me feel grateful to be involved or to confirm my earlier suspicions that this Brooklyn Bridge footage would never appear in a movie featuring Dante Saludo, who I couldn't imagine reducing himself to such a no-budget project as this one, no matter the future greatness of the director or the brilliance of the script. I aimed my disk at the indefinite light and kept silent, as the minutes passed and sun rose into full view. Buddy had piped down; I looked up to see him alternating between glances through the viewfinder and down at his curled fingers, apparently at a nagging hangnail he kept bringing to his mouth. Josh maintained his impeccable form, while my biceps burned.

Near the base of the bridge, just outside the shot, the Avellinos teamed up with Mitch and Handsome Bill. I imagined them contemplating the next scene on the day's schedule, though they seemed in no hurry, content to be watching from the shadows as the sun's hot rays encroached on the water and on those of us shielding ourselves from it on the grassy banks.

When I saw that Josh was now wearing a pair of stylish Ray-Bans—and so were the other well-prepared interns wearing sunglasses—I closed my eyes, took deep breaths, and thrust my shield like a gladiator, once again willing my thoughts to Big, coolheaded and ferocious, on some open plain in God's Country, ramming his helmet into the ribs of one stunned recruit after another.

When Mike Avellino appeared in our midst, I straightened up, arms quivering. "Good job, guys," he said. I wondered what obscure movie credit they'd grant me for my pains. It took me a moment to see that my intern cronies had ditched their reflector disks somewhere and were heading toward their cars. Mitch was already at the van; he unlocked the passenger door and tossed his clipboard inside. I tossed my shield onto the grass and let out an audible groan.

Buddy climbed down the scaffold. "She's a beauty, all right!"

Joe approached. "Great light, huh, Buddy?"

Buddy removed his cap and wiped the sweat from his face. "A perfect ten."

Everyone was converging on the scaffold. Mitch carried Buddy's paper bag. The interns followed. Mike and Joe swapped high-fives. I returned a high-five from Handsome Bill.

"What's next?" I asked.

"We wait," Handsome Bill said.

For Dante Saludo? Here?

Buddy said, "Bagels for everyone."

Mitch held the bag open for the interns.

Joe studied his watch and looked up. "We'll set up around nine-thirty and shoot again at ten. Then we'll keep at it every hour. We couldn't have asked for better weather. Right, Buddy? The sunset should be spectacular."

"Dazzling, baby."

"*Sunset?*" I said. "We're not done?"

"Montage," Handsome Bill said, "when Ray's in Heaven. The bar? You read the script?"

I nodded.

"He's in there all day," Handsome Bill said. "So now Joe wants to cut away before Angelo enters. Show sunrise to sunset in fast motion. Then go back inside the bar."

"So today …?"

"We're here all day." Handsome Bill grinned. "Fun, huh?"

I pointed to the top of the scaffold. "Why not just set up the camera and let it—?"

"Film's expensive. Only need about five minutes of footage. If that."

I blew out a long breath. "Five minutes?"

"Probably end up being ten seconds in the movie."

I stared at the reflector disk on the grass and shook feeling back into my hands, stretching my fingers and making fists.

Mitch said, "Whoa, man, pick that up."

I picked it up, and he swiped it from me. He handed the bag of bagels to Handsome Bill, then turned and twisted the reflector disk down to the size of a large frisbee. "You know how much this thing costs?"

"How much?"

Mitch glared at me. "You really have no idea, do you?"

I shook my head.

"It was a rhetorical question, Johnny." He began to walk away. "Eat a bagel. You're going to need the energy."

Handsome Bill offered me the bag.

"What's he mad at *me* for?" I asked.

"He's not mad at you," Handsome Bill said. "These guys are under a lot of pressure. Trying to make the impossible happen."

Alone, I sat in the grass and ate a bagel, contemplating the varying dimensions of the impossible.

As planned, and with increasing ease, the bridge was filmed throughout the day and into the evening, every hour on the hour, as the sun peaked overhead—at which point the reflector disks were returned to the van for good—and descended behind us. By mid-afternoon, two of the interns had, with Joe's permission, gone home. The other four performed random tasks and ran errands, one of which was to deliver pizza that we consumed slice by occasional slice from boxes lying open on the grass. In the long stretches between shots, Joe hunkered down in the air-conditioned Saab, where, in the passenger seat, Mike or Mitch or Handsome Bill joined him for brief meetings—and he made phone calls. Meanwhile,

Buddy, sensitive to the sun, took catnaps in the van between shots, while I stood guard over the scaffold, or, *under* the scaffold, in its shade.

As each hour approached, Buddy welcomed me onto the elevated plane. He educated me on the finer points of natural light versus artificial light, the relative intensities of sunlight reflected off water, stone, or reflector disk, and the proper adjustments of aperture, influenced by these variables. I asked him if he expected Dante Saludo to show up tomorrow, and he said, "Who?" then chuckled, "It makes no difference to me who shows up. My job is to make that man's vision come to life on film." Joe Avellino was once again alighting from the Saab and making his way, one last time, toward the scaffold. Buddy said, "We met on the set of another movie he directed but didn't produce. That one had a smaller budget than this one, and this one doesn't have enough to cover the bagels. Joe makes it happen by sheer will and talent. I think he's got a hell of an artistic vision, and a hell of a future ahead of him, which is why I agreed to shoot this baby."

I was impressed by Buddy's sober description of Joe, whose talent I'd never thought to question. The mere fact that he was making a movie had proved his greatness in my eyes, at least until now. I was about to ask Buddy if that earlier film had been a porno, when Joe called out, "Some days everything goes right!" I followed Joe's satisfied gaze to the sky, which was a swirl of golds and pinks and blues. He beamed like a satisfied painter, and in an instant, I wanted to see through Joe's eyes, with that artistic vision Buddy had praised. Despite the beautiful landscape, I also wanted to believe that Joe had just made a phone call to confirm that tomorrow we were on for Plan A.

10
SHADOW KING

After the scaffolding and equipment had been packed into the van, we all gathered around Joe, the moon a white disc in the dark blue sky. "Big day tomorrow shooting the bar scene. Lighting and sound are going to be crucial—I mean, uniquely challenging. We all have to be on our toes. So everybody get your rest tonight. All right? Any questions?"

I looked around, hoping somebody else would ask the obvious questions: Did "shooting the bar scene" mean that Saludo would be there? Had this fact been confirmed once and for all, or would we once again be skipping Plan A and going right to Plan B—shooting the scene without him? And, why were lighting and sound going to be *uniquely challenging?*

Joe went on, "We got something really beautiful on film today. I have a feeling we're going to end up making much more use of it than originally planned." He gazed out into the darkness, still lost in artistic reverie, toward the bridge now lit up with flashes of passing cars. "Anyway"—he clapped his hands—"tomorrow, the grand finale!"

Even though I understood we'd just received our cue to go home, I steadied myself, still expecting an update on Dante Saludo. I figured you couldn't call it *the grand finale* if he wasn't going to be there, right?

But then, instead of providing the latest health report, Joe said, "Buddy, let's chat a minute?" and walked away.

Mike said, "Great job, everybody," and followed Joe and Buddy toward the Saab.

For a moment I expected some kind of revolt, a mini-uprising, at least—some demand from the crew, for an explanation, for a detailed plan for tomorrow morning. Instead, they all bobbed their heads like agreeable ducks before marching off. I stood there with slumped shoulders, scowling at the unreliable world, convinced that Dante Saludo was not going to be in the movie and so there would be no need for the young lookalike.

"You don't look happy," Mitch said.

The Avellinos sank into their Saab and skidded off, vanishing quickly into traffic.

Buddy called to Mitch from the van, "What do you say we *vamoose?*"

Handsome Bill approached Mitch, squinting at the cloud of lingering dust. "Working tonight?"

Mitch shook his head. "Too late now. Gotta be ready for tomorrow. You?"

"I'll jump behind the bar for a few hours. Gotta pay the rent."

Their hands met—their secret shake, I imagined—the two of them bound not only by their vague roles on the set of *Shadow King* but by their enviable positions at Ferrara's, where apparently they had earned the privilege of coming and going as they pleased, working at the restaurant only when their movie-life permitted—one of the perks, I inferred, of being a starving artist working for a fabulously accomplished artist.

Handsome Bill dipped into the car with the other interns.

I rubbed my shoulders and groaned, broadcasting my general irritation.

Mitch jabbed my arm.

"Ow." I shot him a scornful glare.

He held the van door for me. Mitch poked Buddy, dozing in the passenger seat. "Buddy! You driving or what, bro?"

Buddy scooted over behind the wheel. "Well, I'm not letting *you* drive. You think I'm crazy?"

I sat sandwiched between them.

Once we were on our way, Mitch said, "So, you don't want to make movies anymore?"

I was staring at his reflection in the passenger window. "Why do you say that?"

"You made it clear you weren't very happy about the work today."

I turned toward the windshield and the dark road ahead. "It is a lot of standing around."

"Uh-huh. You just want to be *in* the movies."

I shrugged. "Sort of. Yeah."

"Let the rest of us do the real work."

"I don't mind it for now, but long-term it's not what I want to do."

Mitch burst out laughing before he turned abruptly silent. He twisted in his seat to face me. "You're completely serious, aren't you?"

"Yeah." I mocked his exaggerated, confused expression. "What'd I say wrong?"

"You *really* think you know what you want to do for the rest of your life."

"I *do* know what I want to do for the rest of my life."

Mitched laughed again, and then he kept on laughing.

I said, "I want to be an actor."

He seemed genuinely delighted, and sort of amazed. "I'd tell you you were crazy if I didn't actually believe you. I mean, I believe you're going to become one—a really good one." He paused. "What's crazy is I think you might actually already *be* one."

I understood that from *his* perspective it might be incredible that someone at eighteen might already know who he was—but I *was* eighteen, and I just knew. The fact that my self-knowledge might be impressive to Mitch or anyone else because it was *unusual* made no difference to me. This was my life, and, for all my ignorance, I also understood that knowing what you want to be when you grow up—or even being good at whatever that is at eighteen—guaranteed nothing for the future. All at once, I felt a chill at my ears, my face flashing white, and I felt exposed, my confidence replaced by a profound and unfamiliar fear: The only thing I knew for certain was that I was completely and utterly alone in the universe.

Immediately, Mitch seemed to sense the change in me. "*I* know what you want to be," he beamed in a corny, TV-commercial voice, trying to change the subject by feigning some pleasant revelation: "*You* want to be a busboy at Ferrara's—and maybe even a waiter someday!" He meant for me to return his ridiculous smile, but I'd grown sullen.

I kept my eyes on the gray windshield. "I'd probably have a better chance of meeting Dante Saludo there."

Mitch cocked his head in mock contemplation. "Oh, now we're back to the moody-ingrate routine. Is that the only reason you came here? To get an autograph?" Mitch waited for an answer I couldn't provide. "Do you think this whole drama with Saludo is a big lie that the Avellinos concocted to get you and the whole crew to come work on the movie for free?"

"I just want to know if he's okay."

"Right," he said skeptically. "You're so concerned for his welfare. Maybe you should demand to see a medical report. Tell Joe you're splitting unless he provides you with Dante Saludo's hospital records."

I was unrelenting. "What if his face is fucked up, like you said, and he can't do it? What are we gonna do?"

Mitch shook his head and smirked. "I thought you came here to learn about making movies." He was back to staring out the window, where my eyes met his reflection.

"I did. I do," I said, though I was doubting if this were still true, even partially. "But you also said … You know—about *me*, acting. Did you ever really tell them about your idea?"

"You think I lied to you about that, too? Damn, bro …" He shook his head, a gesture of pity and disappointment, trying to spark or instill a sense of shame I didn't feel. "I also told you to be patient—timing is everything."

"Time is up, Mitch! The scene is *tomorrow*. Don't we need to rehearse?"

"Take it easy, Johnny. I've mentioned it, okay? People only hear what they want to hear when they're ready to hear it." He sighed. "You're eighteen and you already know what you want. That's good. But you have to be prepared for disappointment. Always. We all have our own personal interests. That's how it is. *You* have *your* interests. *I* have *my* interests. *Joe* has *his* interests. *Buddy* has *his* interests."

Buddy cleared his throat, reminding us of his presence. "I may be the one exception to that rule."

Mitch lifted his voice: "Welcome to the conversation, Buddy."

"Thanks for having me." Buddy held the steering wheel with loose grips, grinning straight ahead all the way.

"But we're all working *together*," Mitch said.

"Hear, hear," Buddy said. "Separate but together."

"It can get complicated," Mitch said. "So you need to stay cool."

"Stay cool, Johnny boy." Buddy's yellow grin stretched wide into his fleshy, bristly cheeks.

Mitch said, "If you push too hard, you'll get shoved out of the way. But you also need to be ready to jump when opportunity presents itself. There are a lot of selfish pricks trying to make it in this business, but *you* don't have to be a prick. And if you do ever happen to make it, you don't have to *become* a prick. There's no reason for it. Isn't that right, Buddy?"

Buddy groaned under his hat, "You do not have to be a prick to make it in this business. Just look at me."

"You learn to live with disappointment," Mitch said.

We stopped at a red light. "I've been disappointed since I came here," Buddy said, "when I was twenty-one."

"Thank you, Buddy," Mitch said. "Let's not get too depressing here."

"Depressing's not even the word," Buddy said. "More like dee-moralized."

"*Thank* you."

"Devastated." He hit the gas. "Demolished, destroyed—"

"At a certain point," Mitch said, "you begin to *feed* on the disappointment because you refuse to let it beat you. It makes you more creative. It makes you a better artist. Because if you're really meant to do this work, you just go on doing it because art's the only thing that matters to you anymore. It's the only thing that means anything. And so you do it, you make art, because there's no longer any choice in the matter, if there ever was."

"Amen, brother," Buddy said.

I was a convert who hadn't needed conversion. *Art's the only thing that matters …*

Mitch wasn't finished. I didn't see how he could improve on the message.

"Your disappointment becomes so familiar that you don't even remember what it's like *not* to be disappointed. You might think the most important thing in the world is that Dante Saludo appears in your movie—not because he's the greatest actor in the world, but because you have dumped *a lot* of money into this thing. I'm talking practically every cent you have—or *had*. You understand what I'm saying? And having this man's name attached is the only way this movie has a shot. Your career is banking on it. Everything you've done in the past ten years, every investment in time and money, every failure and success, has culminated at this point. And so you are going to do everything in your power to make sure he agrees to be in this movie and you do not care if his face looks like fucking ground beef."

Buddy and I swapped understanding, concerned glances.

After a moment, I tried to be encouraging. "Why not just shoot the scene a month from now, or in two months—when he gets better?"

"That would be an excellent idea, Johnny, if this weren't the last week of shooting. People have lives and schedules and careers, especially Saludo, who has to be in Los Angeles to play Fred fucking Flintstone. So, we need to get this thing *made* and *move on*."

"Preach," Buddy said.

"What do you mean, *if this weren't the last week of shooting?*" My mind went white with distress. "Didn't we just start?"

Mitch narrowed his eyes.

"You mean you shot the whole movie already? Before I got here?"

He took a deep breath, realizing this was all news to me. He offered a sympathetic stiff upper lip.

"Why didn't you tell me?" I was breathing hard, trying not to cry or hyperventilate, or to stifle whatever sense of the apocalypse was bubbling up inside of me.

"Your mom said you had school. She wasn't going to let you miss finals or—"

"My *mom?* You *both knew* I was missing practically the entire shooting of the movie?"

"She didn't want you to miss your graduation. And guess what? I agreed with her! You shouldn't miss those things. We had a twenty-day shooting schedule, Johnny. You're here *now*. For the big scene, bro. That's what matters."

"This is terrible," I said.

"This is *not* terrible. You're getting a few days of shooting in. The grand finale is tomorrow. I promise, I will remind them about my idea. There was never a reason to push it until Saludo was locked in."

"So he's locked in now?"

"He's supposed to be here in the morning. Yes."

"He *is?* Why didn't you *say so?!*"

"Because anything can still happen. Even if he shows up, you never know …"

"Truer words," Buddy said.

"You always have to be prepared for the worst- *and* best-case scenarios," Mitch said. "And don't forget, there's still months of post-production work to do. These are all crucial parts of the process. You're going to learn a ton. It's going to be a great summer—or however long you stay."

Buddy pulled the van over to the curb. We had arrived back where we'd started so many hours—a seeming lifetime—ago. The engine rumbled. Nobody moved.

I followed the headlight beams into the gray distance. I pictured myself with a pair of scissors in a red-lit darkroom, in stifling August heat, strips of film hanging from clothespins. I said, "I'm never going to make it here."

"That's a bullshit song lyric," Mitch said. "It's not about *making* it. It's about, do you feel alive in this city, more than anywhere else, when you're *not* making it?"

I released a long, uncertain breath.

"Fucked up but true," Buddy said. He killed the engine. The street went dark. When he opened the door, his face glowed, a peppery-bearded ghoul in the shadow under his fishing-hat brim. "I've felt more alive here every day since I got off the bus fifty years ago. It's like I'm growing younger."

I mirrored his wry grin. Then I realized he wasn't kidding. "Fifty years ago? You're *seventy?*"

"Seventy-one years young, son. Impressed?"

I nodded. "You seem fifty. Or forty."

"At this rate I may never die." Buddy stepped out of the van, keys jangling on a ring, and shut the door behind him.

Mitch and I sat in the dark. He seemed to be waiting for me to say something, as if there were a question that had gone unanswered.

Outside, a ghostly Joe Avellino approached Buddy, who handed over the keys and walked down the street and out of sight. For a moment I believed New Yorkers must know a secret about cheating death, and I was drawn once again toward the mystery of this place.

Mitch could read my mind. "What's the alternative?" he asked. "You want to go back to Kornfield?"

11
FALLEN ANGEL

Cocooned in an afghan on the couch, I was flying in a dream above the city, above phone wires, taxis racing through puddled night streets, a telephone ringing in the distance. At first, I mistook the answering machine's beeping and clicking, followed by Mitch's—and my mother's?—muffled speech for dream sounds sneaking into an otherwise noiseless sky, the two of them, airy figures, dancing and bickering in the fog. I hovered over rooftops, dipping down to meet glowing windows, translucent, with ominous silhouettes moving about.

"Your mom."

Mitch set the phone right in front of my face and walked away. My arms bound in the blanket, I stared at the pinholes, tiny black pits emitting nothing. The dead silence stirred me. I blurted, "Hello!"

Mitch said, "She's not there, genius. She left a message. I was in the shower."

I squirmed free and sat up. I contemplated the phone at my hip. In a daze, I pictured Papou draping seersucker pants over a chair and pulling a sheet up to his chin.

"What'd she say?" I asked.

"She said call her back. Thus the phone in your face."

I twisted to find Mitch standing in the kitchen doorway, dressed, with mug in hand, frowning at me.

I dragged myself to the duffel bag across the room.

"Wear something nice. We gotta be ready for anything today."

I balled up yesterday's T-shirt and shorts and hurried into a pair of khaki pants. "What's she calling so early for?"

Mitch presented the phone in one hand and a banana in the other.

I took the banana.

"Probably wants to hear about your first day—all that exciting standing around you were doing."

I dug through my duffel bag for shoes, a pair of stiff suede bucks I displayed for Mitch's approval.

"It won't make a difference what you wear on your feet."

I stepped into my old suede Pumas instead.

He tossed me the cordless phone. "Call your mother."

"I'll call later." I set the phone on the coffee table and donned my fedora.

"Seriously?"

"My lucky hat," I said, and led the way out.

—

Mitch led me through the concrete warehouse, which resembled a large barn. We approached a small crowd of flannel-shirted men standing cross-armed beside Buddy and the Avellinos. "Grip crew," Mitch said. They all appeared deadly serious, contemplating the set, a dimly lit bar lined with stools. I skirted the periphery, beginning to believe that the Saludo cameo might not be an invented carrot on a stick after all, though there was no sign of the movie star—nor of Jay

Kauffman, whose absence I decided was an encouraging sign. At once I stood paralyzed at the sight of this makeshift bar—evidence that, with or without Saludo, there was at least this one scene yet to be filmed, a fact I found suddenly thrilling.

Meanwhile, Joe Avellino appeared increasingly distressed, which seemed to be the director's only emotion until it swelled to a breaking point and ended in relief or a heart attack. Mitch looked over his shoulder to find me spying on him from behind the far end of the long bar. He waved me over and pointed at Joe, who was standing next to him.

"*Now?*" I mouthed. My heart sank in a swirl of hope and dread. *This is it,* I thought. Mouthing again, "Are you talking to him about *the idea?*" as if he could possibly read my lips despite the distance.

"Lights!" Mitch hissed at me. He jabbed his finger demandingly, again in the direction of Joe but *past* him, I realized, at a few familiar interns testing various positions of a tall lamp at the other end of the bar.

I shook my head, reminding him with a scowl that, after yesterday, I was finished with lights—no matter the source. Whatever problem the interns seemed to be deliberating about would not be solved by the rube in the fedora. I was ready to try my hand at something new. I gestured randomly to the two women working quietly near me, indicating that I was being of some use to them. Mitch kept staring at me, apparently waiting for me to prove it.

I approached the two shorthaired women testing sound equipment, the one in a Yankees cap, speaking in varied tones, the other in headphones, nodding with raised thumb.

"One more time," the woman in the Yankees cap said. "I'll whisper this time. The man mumbles."

The woman sitting at the soundboard noticed me lurking. She adjusted her headphones and swapped glances with her partner. The woman in the Yankees cap worked her glasses up her nose and squinted at me.

The woman wearing headphones said, "Hello there."

Mitch suddenly appeared next to me. He nudged me with his elbow. "You want to say hi?"

"To Saludo?" I said. "He's here?"

"To *Sue*," he said. "Say hello."

"I'm Sue," the woman in the Yankees cap said. She stood and gave me a firm handshake. "This is Patty."

"Our new intern," Mitch said.

"Know how to work a boom?" Sue said.

"Looks like an actor," Patty said.

"You can say that again," Sue said. "Take your hat off a second."

When I did, Patty said, "Anyone ever tell you—"

"—you look like a young Dante Saludo?" Sue finished.

I looked warily into the dark corner, where Joe was still standing with Mike, both appearing increasingly agitated.

Mitch said, "This is Johnny Demos."

"Does he talk?" Patty said.

"Kid's a prodigy," Mitch said.

I said, "Hi."

Mitch took the hat from my hands. "We need to see your face."

"Good idea," Patty said.

Sue said, "Johnny *Dee*-mose. Good name, too."

Mitch gestured toward the dark corner. "Let's go. I want you in on this."

I said, "They don't look happy over there."

"Not *them*." He pointed toward the bar. "Meet the gaffer."

"I'm boom operator."

Sue laughed. "We could use a third man."

Patty directed me to a black plastic chest with belts buckled in front.

I inched toward the chest while eyeing Mitch.

Sue announced, "Johnny Demos joins the sound team."

Mitch sighed and put my hat on. "I'll secure the fedora in the back room."

At once, huge lamps burst to life. The wooden bar gleamed golden brown. I wanted to take my place behind it.

"Donuts for breakfast over there." Mitch slipped a cigarette between his lips and went back to the men now drenched in white light.

"The really big microphone," Patty said to me. She smiled when she saw that I was already lifting the boom out of the box, ready to go. "What kind of prodigy are you, Johnny Demos? You work in movies?"

"I just graduated high school. I did theater."

Patty put her headphones back on. "They're getting itchy over there."

The Avellinos were unfolding metal chairs and arranging them in a tight circle.

"What's happening?" I gripped the boom like a fishing rod at my waist.

"Hold it like this." Sue pushed an invisible barbell over her head.

While the light crew set up tripods and arranged lamps and reflectors, I held the boom at my chest and Sue grumbled incoherently at the bar.

"Is he here?" I asked.

Patty said, "Higher, Johnny."

Sue got up from the stool and reached for the boom. "Let's switch."

"I can do it." I stepped back, committed to reeling in some stubborn fish. "Have you seen him?"

Sue took the pole from me. "No, we have not seen him. But our job is to be ready when we do see him."

Patty said, "I think he's in the back room, rehearsing."

"Really?" Again, I stared into the dark corner.

"You play Saludo," Sue said to me.

"He's in there?"

"Grab the script in the pile next to the chest."

"I know it." I took Sue's place on the stool.

"You know what?"

"I got the script months ago."

Sue grinned. "You memorized it?"

Patty set the script in front of me, leaves open. "Just in case."

Two dense columns of text mirrored each other on facing pages. "They changed it," I said. "The monologue's longer than it used to be." I cleared my throat.

Patty said, "Not too loud, Johnny Demos. It's not like being on stage. The microphone catches everything."

I sat on the stool and propped my elbows on the bar, shielding the script from the camera I pretended was filming. The Avellinos must have gotten greedy, I figured: this expanded two-page speech could be milked for a five-minute cameo, justifying the prominence of Saludo's name on all the ads I imagined in newspapers and on posters under glass displays outside movie theaters.

"Pretend you're alone," Patty said.

Sue smiled and gestured toward the script, gripping the boom pole above my line of vision, the oversized mike hovering out of sight. I cleared my throat and stared up at the makeshift shelves filled with bottles. I began skimming the monologue, these matching monoliths of ink spanning two pages before a "CUT TO" finally silenced Saludo's character. I peered into the corner where Mitch and the Avellinos now sat hunched over the scripts lying open on their laps, each anxiously flipping pages and scribbling with a pencil. I pictured Saludo pacing furiously behind the nearby door, reading through this speech that, since he'd agreed to play the part, had grown to the length of four Shakespeare soliloquies.

"Give me a few lines," Patty said to me.

I began to read aloud Angelo's revised story of how his life had gone off course. It was a hodgepodge of original and added material—newly inserted sentiments that were uncomfortably familiar or cliched, plagiaristic echoes of voices I couldn't trace. *I coulda been a better person on this God-given green earth* … As I read on, I wondered if Joe and Mike had taken to heart criticism that their once-grand finale was too subtle for a mainstream audience, that its meaning—and Angelo's purpose, as provider of salvation—needed to be clarified, all of the subtext raised to the surface. *Listen to what I'm telling you, Ray. You think I just happened to come in here today and sit next to you? There's a reason God sent me here.* Angelo was no longer simply a wise old drunk, an unlikely symbol of grace who happened to be in the right place at the right time, but now a divine messenger who spoke in cliches and who might as well have been wearing huge white wings that would carry him through the rafters when he was finished preaching. *I'm a fallen angel. You're a ray of light, and you've still got work to do.*

I felt sick to my stomach. For a rare, unselfish moment, I hoped, for his sake, that Saludo had shown up this morning, taken one look at this revision, and flown straight to L.A. to play a cartoon caveman, a comparatively dignified career move. Just then it occurred to me that Saludo might take not only artistic but also personal offense at the speech's embellishments: This overwritten Angelo was unwittingly announcing the sad fact of the *actual* actor's descending career trajectory, obviously a tragic misstep by the Avellinos. The once-modest cameo had been transformed into a parody of hubris, an immortal being turned desperate, all talent dissolved, greatness gone.

I flipped back to the page preceding the monologue to discover that a few added effects had already answered any question about the scene's symbolic intentions. *RAY, high and heartbroken, stares into his drink when a voice draws his attention to a blinding light. As the words wash over him, we are not sure if ANGELO, aglow and sitting beside him, is real or a figment of RAY's imagination—a hallucination, a heavenly vision.*

"Okay, Johnny," Patty said.

"Take two," Sue said.

I closed the script, feeling at ease as Patty and Sue finalized their adjustments while I amused myself with accents, doing Saludo in *Neighborhood* and *Runaway,* my tongue flailing in thick, drunk New Yorkese. I went on for several minutes, blissfully delivering highlights from those early masterpieces. My heart swelled and I stopped when I discovered Patty and Sue watching me, smiling.

We were ready to go.

12
ONE SHOT

The interns tested their trusty reflector disks, circling the monstrous island-bar set, whose hardwood base rolled on wheels. I kept my balance as Handsome Bill and Mitch nudged the set into position, the two of them, along with the interns, fielding silent signals from the gaffer, a dark, featureless figure on a tall ladder, aiming a lamp poised on a tripod. Mike and Joe were back in their chairs, thigh-to-thigh, hissing like nervous surgeons, their pencils poised like scalpels.

Beyond the frantic activity, a beam of late-morning sunlight on the concrete floor divided us all from a shadowy figure, checkered sleeves hanging from slouched shoulders and unbuttoned at the wrists, crisscrossing and murmuring to himself in the dark corner. He could have been an intern or a janitor conducting some menial business. It took me a moment to realize it was him. His face never turned toward the light, but that body, though smaller than I'd expected, was unmistakably his, firm of frame yet agile, as he seemed to be calibrating every minuscule movement he was planning for his part.

Patty said, "Entertain us, Johnny."

Sue said, "Do more Saludo."

But I was done with that for now. He must have entered the main room through the nearby gray door, left ajar. And just like that, he once again disappeared, through the gray door, exiting into the hidden room where I assumed he'd been rehearsing this whole time. After a moment the Avellinos followed and shut the door behind them.

"Not what you expected," Mitch whispered into my ear, jolting me from my strange reverie and nearly out of my seat.

"What happened to the script? Angelo's speech, they changed it."

"We'll talk about it later."

"It's *terrible*."

"I'll fix it. Don't worry. You ready?"

A charge shot up my spine. "You talked to them?"

He set his hand on my shoulder. "Patience."

"Okay." I didn't press him for details, for fear of jinxing whatever plan he was cooking up. He kept his hand on my shoulder. Suddenly I felt relaxed, as if Mitch and I were finally united in our secret artistic purpose, as I'd always hoped we'd be.

"Joe and Mike are about to have two heart attacks apiece."

"Why?"

"Because Saludo didn't come here today to play Angelo. He came here to tell them to get Kauffman to play Angelo."

"What? Why?"

"Because his face looks like fucking raw hamburger, bro."

I cringed.

Mitch said, "I also think he'd like to keep it a secret from the tabloids that he did a faceplant into a docked yacht off the coast of Malta."

"Doing his own stunt?"

"No, they were finished shooting—fortunately for *them*. Or else *their* movie would have been fucked like *ours* is."

"Ours isn't fucked," I said. "You could make the injury fit Angelo's character."

Mitch nodded, possibly intrigued. "Like he stuck his face in a meat grinder."

"Well, that's—"

"Method acting and all that."

We stared at the dark gray door in the distance.

"Stanislavski," I said.

"Huh?"

"Nothing." After a moment I asked, "Is Ray here?"

"Ray who?"

"The actor who's playing Ray."

"He's back in L.A., shooting *Hansel*."

"Don't you need him for the scene?"

"His work is done."

"He's *in this scene*," I said.

"It's called editing, bro. We shot the scene with Kent, up to the point where Angelo enters. And then again when Kent exits. Now we just fill in the blank. Ray blacks out at the bar. We cut to the Brooklyn Bridge, sunrise to sunset, which we shot yesterday. A bright flash of light, Ray wakes up—*voila*, there's Angelo, who delivers the perfect monologue to end all monologues."

"It *used* to be perfect," I said.

"Mike told me he tinkered with it last night."

I shook my head. "He destroyed it—and it's really long now."

Mitch didn't flinch at this news. "Welcome to my nightmare, Johnny boy."

"You need to change it back."

He closed his eyes and smiled, demonstrating the kind of unfathomable patience he kept imploring me to have—and trust in something I couldn't comprehend.

Then I remembered, "Who's Kent?"

"The guy who plays Hansel on the TV show."

"Never heard of him—or the show. What show?"

"You're kidding. *Hansel*. It's in its second season."

Then I realized, "*Kent Clarkson?*" I laughed.

"So, you *do* know him—"

"That's his name? As in Clark Kent?"

"Who's Clark Kent?"

"The guy that turns into Superman? His parents actually named him that?"

Mitch shrugged. "Kent and Mike went to Syracuse together. Mike wrote *Shadow King* for Kent."

"What do you mean, for Kent?"

"I mean, they needed a lead with recognizability. Figured they weren't going to get an A-lister for their first feature, so Mike came up with a concept for the movie that kind of plays off the TV show, figuring Kent would play the part well and the show's fans would fall over themselves to get to the theater. They pitched Kent. He loved it. On the show Hansel has amnesia, after a car accident. His sister supposedly died in the accident, but he doesn't believe it, so he's looking for her."

I said, "Don't tell me her name is Gretel."

"Greta. Good guess."

The distance between Mitch and me seemed to expand, despite his hand gripping my shoulder.

Mitch said, "In *our* movie, Ray *can't* forget anything—the opposite of amnesia."

"I get it."

"Cool, right?"

A rumbling under the legs of my stool drew my attention to the other end of the bar, where Dante Saludo was now taking a seat, a shocking beak of white bandages protruding from between inhumanly large eyes, black circles either bulging or cavernous, I wasn't sure. Mitch helped me off the stool and led me out of the spotlight, while my eyes stayed locked on Saludo, his left arm in a sling under his unbuttoned shirt. The thin fingertips of his right hand emerged from the loose cuff and rested gently on the bar top.

"He looks so small," I said.

Mitch said, "They always look smaller in person."

His masked face flashed hideously. But then, tenderly, as if he had already incorporated the unfortunate costume into his character, he leaned with detectable affection toward an invisible figure to his right—toward Ray, that mysterious protagonist, who was already gone but whom I imagined entering through the side door and taking his place next to Saludo.

"I can't believe he's really here," I said.

"He's in no condition to do this," Mitch said.

"I'm in the same room with Dante Saludo."

"I tried to tell Joe, but he doesn't listen."

We stood frozen together, Mitch's hand still clutching my shoulder.

"Is he okay?" I asked.

"Grade-three concussion, bro. He's half-zonked on painkillers. I couldn't understand half of what he was saying earlier, back there guzzling coffee—or who knows what—from a thermos. Mr. Method Actor, right?"

I was watching Dante Saludo rehearse—this transformed, seemingly shrunken man muttering to himself at an empty bar. He raised his face into the spotlight, eyelids closed as if being warmed in the sun. His fingers seemed to be reaching for something, and I wondered what past experience he might be channeling. My instinct was to jump behind the bar and pour him a drink. And then pour myself one.

"Why's he doing this," I said, "if he's in such pain?"

"Loyalty," Mitch said. "Integrity. Do you know this term, integrity? It's sort of like character. You don't hear about it much anymore. It was fashionable when our grandfathers were young."

I mirrored Mitch's grin. "My grandfather may have mentioned it, actually."

"It means: He said he would do it, so he's doing it."

"What if he *can't* do it? Because of his injury," I said.

"Mike told me he's trying to write *in* the injuries—like you said."

"He took my advice?"

"Apparently he thought of it all on his own. Now and then, Mike gets lucky. Only now he's making it like he fell out of the sky."

"As in, literally fallen angel?" I winced. "It's worse than I thought."

"I tried to tell him."

"Why aren't you more upset?"

"It's a team sport, Johnny. There's always a chance he adds something worth keeping—and I'll fix the rest of it later."

"When?"

Mitch gaped at Saludo, whose fingers twitched and crawled aimlessly as if in search of crumbs. "I don't know if this is the best thing for the movie anymore. It feels forced—or *cruel*."

"Did you call Jay Kauffman?" I asked.

Mitch shook his head and sighed. "We're gonna save this sinking ship, bro."

Saludo sat up and wagged a finger at Joe, who in an instant signaled to the crew to take their places. Saludo sank back into character, if that's what he was doing, shoulders slouched, fingers splayed on the bar. Mike went for the door that opened to the sidewalk. A moment later, in came Buddy in his familiar Hawaiian shirt and cutoff jean shorts, white stubble aglitter beneath the shadow of his fishing cap. He might have been snoozing in the van all morning—or all night. He situated himself behind the jib arm, shaking his hands to get the blood flowing, itching to get to work, or itching to wrap this job and get back to wherever he came from. The warehouse lights, a dim gray haze hovering in the rafters, dissolved overhead; the light crew's ensemble thumped and clicked, a white glow showering the lone man at the bar. Sue handed me the cord extending from the boom above her head and said, "Follow me."

Buddy obeyed Joe's silent direction, maneuvering around the side of the bar, which itself inched slightly on its wheels, a pair of interns nudging it at each end. Reflector disks in position, Joe cued the sound team, all of us transfixed by Saludo, who might have gone on grumbling his rehearsal into the night, seemingly oblivious to the universe orbiting into position around him.

Buddy flicked his hat brim. "Yo, Dan! Don't get any funny ideas just because it's me behind the camera."

Saludo squinted into the lights, his eyes like dark marbles. "I'm too old for that, Buddy."

Buddy laughed. "Makes two of us."

I stepped behind Sue, the boom raised overhead like a harpoon.

Joe approached the bar. He stepped into the light. "I just want to say, with everyone listening …" He clasped his hands together. "Dan, thank you so much for this. This is such an honor to work with you, and just to be witness to your talent, to your genius—"

"All *right*," Buddy hissed, spinning his cap backwards. "Are we done suckin' each other's dicks, or can I go finish my nap in the van?"

Joe crossed his arms and backed away from the set. "Charming, Buddy."

Saludo uttered vaguely in Joe's direction, "We have a bartender?"

At once Joe locked eyes—not with Saludo, but with Mitch, who seemed to shuffle nervously in place. As Joe inched toward the bar, I stared at Mitch, wide-eyed, until he turned and gave me an extended, solemn wink. I nodded in solidarity.

Joe said, "No, there's no bartender in the shot, Dan."

Blood rushed into my shoulders. Mitch didn't budge.

"And Ray?" Saludo said. "The guy I'm talking to here?"

"Also, not in the shot. It's just you, Dan." Joe pictured it all in the square frame he made with his extended fingers. "The focus is all on you. It's going to be the best long one-shot take in movie history."

"On my zombie face?" Saludo said.

"We're going to work around the injuries," Joe said. "Or *with* them. We'll shoot it a couple different ways."

Saludo pondered the shelves full of bottles and his empty hands.

"Let's fuck!" Buddy cheered.

Saludo toasted with an invisible glass and faked a sip.

Joe called action, and Saludo stared vaguely into the empty space around him. I mouthed the words, as he started, "You know why I drink bourbon, son?" He hung his head. "I'll tell you—sorry— How can I get a real drink without a real bartender?"

I laughed. Sue shushed me.

After several seconds of beaming dumbly into the silence, I realized no one else had heard Saludo's grumbled quip—a convincing bit of improv?—or maybe no one else knew the script well enough to know he'd strayed from it. Saludo kept staring in my direction, into the shadowy stretch between us. Finally, he announced, in a deeply apologetic tone, "I don't think this is going to work for me, Joe."

Joe called, "Cut!" and approached the bar. "Is that Johnny Demos on the boom?"

Only then did I realize.

"Oops," Sue let out.

Joe said, "The boom is in the goddamn shot!"

My heart sank, along with the giant microphone overhead. "Sorry," I said.

All eyes in the room had turned to me, or so it seemed in the dark. At that moment, it was no consolation that Joe Avellino had had my name on the tip of his tongue.

Saludo followed the boom pole and the cord clenched in my fingers. Our eyes met.

He sat up on his stool and looked at Joe. "You understand my concerns. It's not going to look good on screen."

"Trust me," Joe said. "We're going to be *very* close up on your face."

"That's my concern," Saludo said.

"There's nothing to be concerned about. We'll avoid the injuries entirely."

"I don't see how that's possible." He took a deep breath. "I need a bourbon. In a glass. With or without a bartender."

Mitch said, "You got it," and hopped onto the elevated floor behind the bar.

Joe said, "Hold on, Mitch," and then, "Dan—to be clear—we won't see the glass, let alone the bartender."

"Can we take five?" Mitch said.

"No, we cannot take five!" Joe snapped. "It's Ray's P-O-V. So we see the eyes. The lips moving. We're *extremely* close up, Dan. Literally, the eyes, the lips."

Saludo said, "What about the ears?"

Buddy said, "I'm in so close I'm getting nothing but tongue!"

"Verisimilitude," Dante Saludo said. "Consider it my limitation as an actor. You shoot it how you want it, Joe, but I have my needs. It's gotta feel real." He waved for Mitch to bring him a real drink.

"Whatever you say, Dan," Joe said. "Mitch, you getting that bourbon?"

The seal on the bottle was already crackling in Mitch's hands. He set a tumbler on the bar and poured. He took his time. For a moment I imagined Mitch lingering there and playing the bartender himself. Saludo seemed to be playing along, sipping, nodding, as Mitch's lips began to move.

Joe said, "We set?"

Buddy said, "Can't get it up, Dan?"

Saludo emptied his glass in a single slug. "Just chatting with the bartender." He gestured to his glass. Mitch poured him another.

"Quiet on the set, everybody," Joe said. "Mitch, back off, please."

Saludo straightened up on his stool and turned once again to Joe. "Let's not rush this, Joe. The more I think about it— You're gonna be zoomed in so close, the audience won't know who they're looking at. It could be anybody. I think you should call the other fella."

"It cannot be *anybody*," Joe said. "The audience knows your eyes, your voice …"

Saludo was leaning toward Mitch, evidently asking for his name. "*Mitch*—Mitch here says he's got an idea."

"Yes." Joe blew out a breath, uncrossed his arms, and marched toward the bar. "I'm familiar with the idea, which—I already told Mitch—does not interest me."

My stomach sank. I inched toward the developing scene.

When he saw me approaching, Joe hissed, "This is some first-rate unprofessional bullshit, Mitchell."

Mitch stood his ground. "Dan said he doesn't feel comfortable—"

"What the hell are you trying to do? Sabotage my goddamn film?"

Mitch said, "I am trying to *save our* film."

"I'm the director," Joe said.

"I'm invested in this, too," Mitch said.

Saludo raised his hand to flag Joe. "Hold on. I'm the one—"

"Your measly thirty grand?" Joe kept his aim on Mitch. "Inheritance money you coughed up at the last minute to buy a producer credit?"

"Where'd you get *your* money?"

"God damn it." Joe made a fist and held it lamely near his shoulder. "Do not say another word, or God help me …"

Mitch stepped toward him. "What are you going to do?"

"That's enough for me," Saludo announced. A cold silence filled the warehouse as he carefully maneuvered himself from the stool and landed on his feet.

Joe said, "Dan, please."

"You boys work out your differences." Saludo shuffled toward me at the end of the bar.

I stepped aside for him to pass, but he stood before me. I held the boom like a staff.

He aimed his black-circle eyes at me. "You believe this?"

I shook my head in reply. "No, sir."

A grin grew under his absurd bandage. "My Vicodin's wearing off, and unfortunately I do not have anything stronger back home. I'm not sure how much longer I can take the pain." His eyes smiled. "You understand, young man?"

"I do."

"Dan?" Joe said.

Saludo leaned toward me in mock privacy. "He calls me Dan. I don't know where he picked that up. The name's Dante." He held his hand out for me to shake.

"Johnny," I said. His hand was small, his fingers soft and dry in my grasp.

Saludo called out, "You two make up yet?"

Mitch returned my bemused gaze, while Joe turned restless under the spotlight.

Again, Saludo leaned toward me, as if to impart another secret, and this time I leaned toward him, the two of us shoulder to shoulder, in confidence. "For weeks I had to watch stunt doubles have all the fun. Day after the shoot I finally get on a jet-ski myself. This is the price I pay." He took a deep breath and let it out. "If this were *Night of the Living Dead,* we'd be in business."

I laughed and breathed in the welcome smell of bourbon.

He turned and faced the set.

Joe pressed his palms together in a display of peace. "We'll make this work, Dan. If the close-up doesn't work—"

Saludo cleared his throat. "Joe—"

"We can work the injuries into the monologue—"

"I want to help you," Saludo said, "but—"

"Mike's been working on something all morning." Joe turned around and shouted, "Mike!"

"We all get a little crazy when we get desperate," Saludo said.

The words fell on the room with finality. In the long, silent moment that followed, Joe—and all of us—seemed to be considering what fate would be born out of this evident truth.

"We *need* you," Joe said.

"You *want* me," Saludo said. "That's different. I understand your interests. But you don't *need* me. You've got to trust the work. The screenplay is good. This *scene* is good. Or it *used* to be good. And then I don't know what happened. You overdid it in the rewrite. You let your fear take over. I can feel it. You want it too much. You want it to be great. You want it to be perfect. But you fear it won't be. And so now you're panicking. And guess what? I want to run in the opposite direction. And so will your audience. Art is the opposite of fear."

Mitch stepped into the spotlight. "Mr. Saludo, it's *got* to be you."

"How's that, Mitch?"

"We shoot you from behind. We don't see your face at all—"

Saludo laughed. "In that case, you *definitely* do not need me."

"The audience will know it's you," Mitch continued. "They'll know you're in the movie, and they'll be waiting for you the whole time. And then they'll hear you."

"And wonder why they're looking at the back of my head and not my face."

"That's exactly right. And the answer is—" Mitch pointed at me. "Because we're looking at *his* face—*you* at eighteen—while you deliver the monologue. The audience will make the connection. They'll be mesmerized by the resemblance. They'll understand that Angelo is looking back at himself on the brink of manhood, wondering at the choices that led him to become who he is now. It's got to be you because the audience will never shake the thought that it's Dante Saludo talking and they'll understand that everyone, even you, the *greatest*, must wish his life had gone in some other direction, or at least wonder at the different paths he might have taken, and the different outcomes, if only he'd made other choices. They'll believe you're talking to them, and they'll picture their own young selves staring back from behind that bar. You have to play this part, and Johnny has to play the bartender. It only works with the two of you together."

Mitch set his hands on the bar. His look was one of calm confidence, resting patiently on Dante Saludo, who returned his long stare.

Joe's eyes lingered on Mitch before lifting off, almost reluctantly, as if to preserve the hope that had been momentarily resurrected, and landing on Saludo, who seemed still to be taking in this new angle and maybe even basking in the beauty of Mitch's words, as I was.

Saludo nudged my arm. "What do you think?"

"I love it," I said.

"Me too," he said.

I smiled. Joe let out an audible breath.

"Mitch, you been holding out on us," Saludo said. "Are you a writer or director?"

Mitch smiled.

"He's an actor," I said.

Saludo looked right at me. "The question is, are *you* an actor?"

The warehouse was silent.

"I am an actor," I said.

Saludo said, "Acting is ninety percent listening. It's *re*-acting. Understand? If you really listen to people, your actions will come to you naturally and empathetically. Your expressions will be *true*—not just in your face, but in your whole body, right down to your fingertips." He held his hands up between us and looked at them, as I did, as if they had just appeared miraculously. "The whole story is right there in your hands." He paused. "Got it?"

I stayed motionless.

"Good." He looked at Joe, who was nodding approvingly from behind the bar. "The kid's going to need to practice."

"Absolutely," Joe said.

"Another thing," Saludo said, "the monologue has got to be restored to the original length—as short and sweet as it was—especially now that it's just one long shot on Johnny. No offense, son."

"None taken," I said.

"No ten-minute showstoppers, or whatever it was you guys were trying to pull with those two pages of on-the-nose drivel.

We have to go back to the earlier version. It was very good—brilliant, actually. But I do think even the original could be tightened a bit. *And* …" He tapped a finger to his head. "It's already in *here*."

"Mike!" Joe called out again, but Mike was already hurtling toward Joe, huffing anxiously, a worn screenplay curled in hand, a yellow pencil wedged above his ear.

Saludo said, "I'm going home for lunch and a nap."

Joe checked his watch. "Break for lunch! Reconvene at two o'clock."

"No, no," Saludo said. "We're done for the day. Everybody goes home. Rehearse with the kid now. If we're gonna do this, it's gotta be right. The scene isn't about the words I say anymore. It's about how Johnny hears the words. How he *reacts* to every syllable."

Murmurs from the crew accompanied sounds of uncertain shuffling.

Joe glared anxiously into the large room. "So, what are we saying here? See you in the morning?"

"That's what we're saying." Saludo put his uninjured hand on Joe's shoulder. "Call me in a few hours and we'll talk. I have a few minor suggestions. And then I'm going to need some time with Johnny, obviously." He glanced back at me and grinned. "One long shot, kid. I'm getting nervous already."

The bar lights blinked out, and for a brief moment, we were in the dark. Then someone turned on the warehouse lights.

Joe squinted and raised an arm to his eyes. Mike said something into Joe's ear. Joe clapped his hands and shouted, "Reconvene eight a.m.!"

I was beaming, delirious with excitement, half-glad that the shoot had been delayed since my facial muscles would need the time to relax, or just to lose the smile. I gave a silent cheer for Mitch as he ducked offstage into the shadows, where I imagined him staking his claim once and for all. For a long moment, I stayed at the end of the bar, staff at my side, just watching everyone move toward the daylight pouring in through the door cracked open in the corner.

Interns and crew members formed quick huddles, shook hands, and patted backs, before exiting. Saludo joined Mike and Joe in a private pow-wow. Mike held the script scrolled open and made a few quick gestures with his pencil. After a long minute, Joe put his arm around Saludo and shook his hand. Joe escorted Saludo toward the door, where in an instant the small, dark figure seemed to merge with the blazing daylight, the silhouette swallowed up in a flash. Joe took a deep breath and arched his back, confidence seemingly restored.

Just then I spotted Mitch across the room. I let the boom cord fall from my fingers and darted toward him.

"Hey, bartender!" Buddy cheered somewhere in the distance. I stopped in the center of the warehouse floor and located him with Sue and Patty near the other exit. He saluted me with a wagging finger, and I returned the gesture. "See you in the morning," Sue said. "Little Dante Saludo," Patty said.

When I caught up to Mitch, he was talking with Joe, who saw me approaching and raised a finger that told me to wait one minute. I began to inch backward, just as Mitch swiped at Joe's hand and said, "For two years now, when you needed something done in the office and you weren't about to drive an hour from Jersey, who was here to do the job?"

"Get out of my face, Mitch." Joe's hand once again curled into a fist, which hovered at his side. "If you think we can't make this movie without you, think again. You've got an inflated sense of your importance. With Dan committed, we could triple your investment in a day. Don't tempt me."

"You can't *fire* me. That's what contracts are for." Mitch turned his fierce look at me. "You can stop smiling now, Johnny."

At once my cheeks were in free fall, along with my stomach.

Mitch bore down on Joe. "Unfortunately for you, Dan's commitment now hinges on my cousin's involvement, and, without me, there's no Johnny."

Joe looked at me, grinning maliciously. "Did you hear that? There's no Johnny without Mitch. That's pretty much how it works with your cousin—"

Mitch said, "I saved you today, Joe. Admit it. And it's not the first time. The script would not be what it is without me—"

"Oh, please! Not again with the script!"

"You turned a perfect monologue into—"

"It's *our* project, Mitch. Mike's and mine. Not yours. You're an '*executive*' producer." He stabbed quotes in the air with his fingers. "We're the *actual* producers, with one hundred percent creative control. *That's* why we have contracts. To say who's who and what's what. And now *we* are going to rewrite the scene again. The way *we* want to."

"Are you crazy? He said he wants it restored to the original version—which *I wrote*."

Joe laughed. "You helped. Someday when you own your own company, you can take all the credit."

"I think I'll do that. And I'll deserve it, unlike you."

Joe looked at me again, still grinning. "Did you know this about your cousin? This is how he sees people. Only in relation to him. Without him, you wouldn't even exist."

"You've got it all figured out, Joe," Mitch said.

Joe said, "None of us would be here without you, Mitch. You keep on believing that."

Mitch nodded and drifted toward the exit. "The slightest thanks is all I ask. And the actual credits I deserve. You can go fuck your contract." He turned for the door. "You know my number if you need anything."

"Where are you going?" I said.

"Listen to the director, Johnny." And with that, Mitch made his exit. "Have a nice day!"

"You look like you just saw a ghost," Joe said to me. "Jump behind the bar."

"Right now?" I asked.

"Yeah, right now."

I stared at the sealed exit door, picturing Mitch in the street, hunched over and shuffling back to his apartment.

"Don't worry about him," Joe said. "You just witnessed his monthly meltdown. If I had a nickel for every time we repeated some version of what just transpired right there …"

I nodded, as if I were all too familiar with Mitch's mood swings.

"I should go talk to him," I said.

"He'll be fine. Believe me. I'll join you in a minute. Get familiar with the set. Go ahead." Joe walked toward the door to the back room. "I gotta pop in here and make a quick phone call."

I did as I was told and headed for the bar. Incredibly, the warehouse had been vacated, and I was alone in a gray haze, still stunned by the latest disruption and fearful of its ramifications, for both Mitch and me. Entering the spotlight, I squinted at my own fuzzy image of Mitch, distracted once again by memories of him on stage, and puzzling over why he hadn't chosen the life of the actor, which I still believed he could have if only he'd set his mind to it.

In a few minutes, Joe returned from the back room, stepping into the spotlight and wearing my fedora, as if this were all just business as usual.

"I believe this is yours," he said, and set my hat on the bar, just out of reach.

I nodded.

"You won't say a thing, Johnny." Everything was invisible beyond him. He studied me intently and took Saludo's seat. "Grab the bottle and fill it halfway."

I found the bottle and flinched at the light.

"Your cue is Dan tapping the glass."

I stared at Joe's hand resting on wrist and fingertips.

A vague nausea spread through me.

"Are you sure about this?" Joe asked.

"Are *you*?"

Joe went right on examining my face as I nodded absentmindedly. He tapped the glass. "Whenever he does this, you fill up."

I gripped the bottle's neck. "What's my motivation?"

"Hah!" He shot me an amused look. "Once we're into the scene, you wait for the tap, but we start the scene with a full glass." He tapped the glass again. "Fill it up."

"Sorry." I poured slowly.

Joe peered at me through a tiny frame he made with a finger and thumb. "Your job is just to stand still and listen carefully, like a good bartender. Okay?"

I nodded.

"You listening?"

"Yeah," I choked out. I let my eyes float toward the exit.

"Hey, in case you're wondering, I'm not exactly happy, either, about what just happened. But if I want Dante Saludo to be in my movie, I don't seem to have a choice, thanks to your cousin, who doesn't know when to keep his mouth shut." Joe let out a long breath. "I need a drink, so let's do this, okay? Pretend I'm Dante Saludo. Ready? Lights, camera, action."

I turned my attention to Joe's hand wrapped around the full glass.

He tossed the drink back in one gulp, set the glass down, and tapped the rim again. He cleared his throat. Unable to stop my shifty eyes, I continued to ignore my cue, my vision resting, finally, on Papou's fedora. For some reason I didn't fully understand, I wanted to remain in this moment forever. I had the sinking, growing feeling that my one shot had already passed me by.

13
CALL BACK

The door was hanging open when I got to the apartment. Mitch stood in the corner, staring at the blinking red light of the answering machine.

"What is it?" I asked.

He hit the play button, methodically, as if for the tenth time.

The machine beeped. Joe Avellino started in: "Pick *up*, Mitch. You there yet?" Long pause. "It only takes a minute to walk to your apartment, so I know you're there. Pick up." Another long pause. "All right, just listen. I did not appreciate you upstaging me there, Mitch. Unlike you, I was trying to exercise some discretion in front of your cousin, who does not need the added pressure of understanding just how high the stakes are here. Next you're going to be asking for a directing credit. I don't care how much money you've invested in this thing—which by the way is pennies compared to what my brother and I have invested. Executive producer does not mean you have creative input, much less creative control. And right there on the set? You chat up Saludo in the middle of the shoot? And then you're giving me ultimatums, trying to blackmail me with your cousin—right in front of the kid? This is a new low even for you, Mitch. You got your way, but guess what? This better work. The kid better be great. He better be *fucking perfect*. He better be the next Dante Saludo! Or else we are completely and totally fucked. Thanks to you." The tape hissed before it clicked off.

Mitch remained expressionless.

I put my hand on his shoulder. "Don't worry. It'll work out. Joe said—"

"There's more." Mitch's finger made a long arcing dive toward the play button. There was an anxious stretch before the next depression.

My mother's consecutive messages progressed from warmhearted—"Johnny, please call"—to impatient—"Your uncle had a heart attack. You need to come home."

"What?" I let out, my thoughts scrambled, feeling more awakened than surprised.

Mitch and I stood together as though in mournful prayer. The red light blinked out, and we went on staring at nothing, contemplating our uncertain, or all-too-certain, fates.

Just then the phone rang. Mitch answered. "Yes, Mrs. Demos. He's right here." He handed me the phone and slipped into the kitchen.

"Hello?" I said, playing oblivious.

"I've been calling you all day."

"We just got back from the set. I have to tell you what happened."

"Did you get my messages? Your uncle's in the hospital. You need to come home."

"Now?"

"Did you hear what I said? Uncle Paul is flying in. Big drove home this morning."

I was in a daze, pacing. "Mom, you don't understand—"

"*You* don't understand, young man. Your uncle needs surgery to save his life." She was bubbling up. "We're all here—or we're *going* to be."

"But he'll be okay, right?"

She fell silent.

I believed I had her attention, finally. "Mom, I can't leave. The movie depends on me. We're shooting the last scene tomorrow morning—"

"He might not *make* it till tomorrow morning, Johnny."

"He's had a heart attack before, Mom. He'll be fine."

Mitch cleared his throat. I looked up to see him in the kitchen, shaking his head at me and mouthing the word, "No." I mirrored his frown. *No what?* He closed his eyes with a sadness or shame I didn't feel.

"Hello?" I walked toward the gray daylight in the window. "Are you still there? Mom?"

"Yes."

"I'm not coming home," I announced.

"Is that so? You're independent now?"

"Yes," I said.

She said, "Take a cab from the train station to the hospital. Or walk the six blocks—if it's not too much trouble. I hope it's not too late when you get here."

"Mom."

Then she hung up.

When I turned around, Mitch was standing there, sipping a Bronx Brew and extending a fresh can to me. "I never gave you this beer. Understand? You are not permitted to drink alcohol under my roof or in my company." He swiped the hat off my head and flicked it like a frisbee toward the door.

I gestured a silent thanks with a tip of the can, cracked open the tab, and took a long slug. "Sorry," I said, as if Mitch were the one I owed the apology to. "I can't believe this," I groaned—vague, uncharitable strategies forming in my mind.

"It's terrible," Mitch said. "About your uncle, I mean."

I nodded. "I know, I know."

"So, what are you going to do?" Mitch asked.

"I'm not leaving, if that's what you're asking."

Mitch took a sip of beer.

"I don't have a choice," I said. "Do I?"

He took another sip.

I dragged myself to the window. It was already late afternoon. Time seemed to be racing by—or slowing down. Too much was happening too fast, or not fast enough. I put the cold can to my lips and took a long swallow, my eyes tearing up from carbonation.

"I mean, what would happen—if I didn't stay?" I wanted to hear how the movie would fall apart without me.

The silence suggested otherwise.

Eventually Mitch said, "We'd figure something out."

I turned to face him. "I can't believe you're saying that."

"If you're asking me for the truth, I'm telling you. We'd come up with something, because we'd have to. Something better or worse. But we'd finish—"

"I'm staying," I said.

"We'd finish the movie. The movie's existence does not depend on you. I'm just being honest."

I sipped my beer and stared out the window, beyond Ferrara's across the street and past the bank building on the corner where Saludo lived, searching in vain for the horizon in gaps between far-off skyscrapers.

"At least you're being honest," I said.

"I promised your mother I'd take care of you, Johnny."

"I don't need you to take care of me!"

"I can't be the reason you stay—"

"I'm not doing it for you! I'm doing it for me!" I bowed my head. "Joe would kill you if I left." I looked up.

Mitch smiled. "I can *not* be the reason you stay—*or go. You* need to decide." I turned away from his devouring eyes. "I'll survive," he said, and I felt the knife in my side. "The *movie* will survive."

I kept my eyes on the sky. "So it doesn't make a difference what I do."

"It makes all the difference," Mitch said. "But it has to be your choice."

I finished my beer and set the can on the windowsill. I imagined Dante Saludo sitting alone at the bar, no one there to hear him, his words of wisdom rising into the bright empty space all around, into the darkness above the hot lights beaming down, into the gray sky over the warehouse, into the clouds and into black space, outward and forever, into nothing.

"He's like a father to you," Mitch said.

For a strange moment I thought he meant Saludo. Then, in the haze, I saw Uncle Nick, white-faced and thumbless, staring up from white sheets clutched at his chest.

"How would I know?" I said, resisting the powerful pull of home.

—

We started down the sidewalk toward the subway, passing the bright diner windows. The booths were full, and waitresses in black slacks and vests crisscrossed the aisles with steaming plates. At the stove, two mustachioed Greeks slid spatulas under sizzling meat, while dark-skinned boys by the serving counter scooped vegetables with big dripping spoons. I picked up my pace, hunched over, my duffel bag filled with freshly washed and folded clothes weighing me down.

Mitch trailed me. "You're doing the right thing."

"I don't have a choice," I said. "Isn't that what you're telling me?"

"Stop," Mitch said, "right there."

I stopped at the entrance to the subway tunnel, at the precipice of a long stairwell.

Mitch met me face to face on the sidewalk. "I can be a selfish prick when I need to be," he said. "In fact, it's not hard for me to be one—in case you haven't noticed. And a selfish prick is what you need to be sometimes if you want to make it in this business. So, if I were being a selfish prick right now, I'd be telling you to stay and be in this movie tomorrow because I think the scene is going to be brilliant. Not to mention, I have no fucking idea what we're going to do without you. Okay? There, I said it. But I'm trying really hard not to be a selfish prick in this particular case. Under the circumstances. Do you understand?"

"So you think I should stay?"

He squinted at me. "What's the matter with you? I'm not telling you what to do! That's the point!"

I shook my head and turned for the stairs. Down in the tunnel, I laid my piece of luggage at my feet and drifted back against the tiled wall, gazing at the iron, tree-trunk girders separating me from the opposite platform and the letters in mosaic, spelling out "Franklin Street." Next to me Mitch leaned back and let out a mournful hiss, as we took in the scene and all of its players.

Beneath the maroon-tile border, a man with a red Afro sat on a plastic crate, playing a harmonica he clutched with big round hands. Nearby, a teenage girl with a gym bag strapped over a shoulder floated toward the music buzzing over the tracks. I glanced at Mitch to see that he was watching the girl, too. She circled the beam with ballerina grace, one arm stretching out of a sleeveless yellow top, a knee shyly rising in some practiced move. When the uptown train roared in, lights blazing, she planted her sneakered feet behind the yellow safety stripe and hiked up her gym bag.

All of this happened in a flash, but in my mind the girl went on dancing for an eternity, as her silhouette disappeared into the train and the train disappeared into the roaring tunnel toward Penn Station.

"You just missed your train," Mitch said.

The image of the girl was replaced by the thought of my socks in their tightly rolled bunches, snug in the rounded end of my duffel bag.

"I'll get the next one," I choked out, aching for courage.

"This is one role," Mitch said. "There will be countless opportunities for you. Movies, plays, whatever you set your mind to. You've got your whole life ahead of you."

"You can stop trying to convince me now," I said, sniffling. "Or trying to convince *yourself*."

"Why are you crying?" Mitch dipped his head to see the tears sliding.

I tugged at the brim of my hat.

Mitch said, "He's going to be okay."

"It's not that," I admitted shamefully.

Shoulder to shoulder, we stood idle. The buzz of harmonica returned in the wake of the barreling train. Another train arrived and vanished into its own mysterious future.

I swiped at my eyes. I was into some serious bawling now.

"I don't know what to tell you," Mitch said.

I caught my breath. "How can I miss my one shot?"

"It's not your one shot."

"Those were *your* words—my one shot."

Mitch sighed. "So what are you saying? You want to call her back?"

My eyes met his.

He shrugged. "Does she know you're going to be in a scene with Dante Saludo?"

"I've told her a million times. She did *read-throughs* with me."

"So much for our confidentiality agreement."

"She's my *mom*," I said. "She figures everything out anyway."

"So, she appreciates what's at stake here?"

I nodded.

"Then maybe you just need to tell her—that it's actually happening. Tell her you'll be on a train by noon tomorrow."

I let out a long breath, wanting to believe in this revised plan.

He asked, "Did she tell you what the situation is, exactly—with your uncle?"

I hesitated. "She said he might not make it through the night." I wiped my nose.

"Oh."

"My uncle's flying in from California right now."

The next train's lights burned in the distance.

Mitch said, "I can't put you on that train, bro."

"Maybe he would *want* this for me," I said.

Mitch furrowed his brow. "Who would want what for you?"

I shouted over the train thundering in, "Wouldn't a father want this for his son?"

Mitch's frown deepened.

The train doors opened, and I darted for the stairs and the sunlight.

"Wait a minute!" Mitch raced to catch up. "Have you lost your mind?"

—

Back in the apartment, I dropped my duffel bag by the door and began searching halfheartedly for the phone. I grabbed a pair of Bronx Brews from the fridge and returned to the living room. Mitch found an intact cigarette on the coffee table and put it between his lips. When he looked up at me, he froze.

"What's this?" he asked.

I handed him a beer and opened mine. We stood on opposite sides of the coffee table.

"You *have* lost your mind." He opened his can.

Before sipping, I raised my beer. We clicked cans. We took long swallows.

He said, "You've got it all backwards."

"What backwards?"

"The question." He took a long drag and exhaled. His eyes rose with the invisible smoke.

I followed his gaze at the cracks in the ceiling, long dribbling shadows caked with paint.

"The question isn't what a father would do for his son."

My vision blurred behind thin watery domes building once again on the surface of my eyes.

He sat in his big chair and kicked his boots onto the table. "I'm not trying to upset you."

"You're not." Tears ran down my cheeks. I took a deep breath and sat on the couch. I draped my arms across the back.

"The question …" He picked up the phone from the coffee table and tossed it onto my lap.

I flinched and trapped the phone as it landed. "I get it, Mitch." I set the phone back on the table. "You don't have to say it."

"… is what would a son do for his father?"

"Thanks a lot."

"Well …" He took a long sip, giving me ample time to think. In my silence, he smacked his lips, exaggerating satisfying refreshment, and set down his can. "That's the question you need to answer."

"It's a stupid question," I said, "because I'll never know the answer."

"You're an *actor*." He sat back. "Use your imagination."

"Why bother? I don't have a father!"

I slugged my beer, got up, and walked to the window.

"But you have a mother," Mitch said.

The slow orange glow on the horizon seemed permanent, infinite as the sky itself, the darkness of night still a lifetime away.

"—and an uncle who's probably a better father to you than most fathers are to their sons."

His words took me by surprise. I clenched my throat, trying not to picture my mother alone at a pay phone in a hospital hallway, Uncle Nick's small, gray room somewhere far off in the distance.

"You gonna call her or not?" Mitch set his boots on the floor and sat up. "You're procrastinating."

"I'm thinking."

"About what?"

I turned to face him. "Why you gave up acting."

"Hey, bro." Mitch looked at his watch. "Worry about your own life right now."

"You're the reason I decided—"

"Here we go again. I am not responsible for you. For *this*—"

"Tell me the truth!" I stood up.

He looked at me calmly. "You need to call your mother and tell her you're doing this movie—or else we need to get out of here right now …" He sipped his beer. "Because I've got some unfortunate news to tell the director."

I stared down at him in his big chair. "I want an answer." I sipped my beer, matching his calmness.

"What's the question?" He took a long swig.

I tipped my beer back and finished it. "The question is—" I let out a long breath. "Why should I even bother trying when I'm not half as good as you were—and you quit?!"

"I didn't *quit*."

I took in gulps of air.

Mitch tapped his pack of cigarettes, pulled out another, and held it out to me. "Sit down." He aimed the cigarette at me, waiting for me to take it, but I didn't budge. I slurped at my empty can. He stood up, drained his beer, and gestured for me to hand him mine. He took the empties to the kitchen and returned with two more cold Bronx Brews. We cracked them open. When Mitch sat, I sat.

He said, "You have to promise me you're going to remember what I'm about to tell you."

"How can I promise I'm going to remember?"

"Because you remember everything, so if you listen carefully, in ten years you're going to remember what I'm about to tell you."

"Why ten years?"

He took a deep breath. He sat at the edge of his big chair. He took a long drink. I leaned forward to take the cigarette he once again offered. He surprised me with an actual lighter. I let the flame flicker inches away, puffing. Then he sat all the way back and laid his arms out along the armrests.

"I've been at this for ten years," he said. "*Ten years.* You know how long that is? For an actor? It's a lifetime. Since you were *eight*. I'm thirty, bro. It didn't take me long to realize I was never going to be that young hotshot actor. That dream's done. It was done a long time ago."

Invisible smoke rose between us.

"You're *thirty?*" I sat back and drank my beer.

"I spent two years in L.A." He scooched forward again and propped his elbows on his knees. "For a year I did nothing but audition. TV shows, commercials, movies. Three-hundred-twenty auditions." He paused. He had my attention. "Not one callback. But I met people. I started writing, doing other things—directing, producing. Three short films. Who's seen them? Nobody. But they became my resume. Met Joe and Mike. Showed them my work. Moved to New York." He took a deep drag, squinting, and tapped a finger to dislodge ash that didn't fall. "I've spent ten times more money than I've made. And I don't just mean my *own* money." He licked his lips and stared at me gravely. "My father bought this place when I couldn't pay the rent. You understand what I'm telling you? I'm not proud of this."

"*Three hundred twenty* auditions? You *counted?*" I took another fake puff and set my empty on the coffee table. "How could you not get *one* callback?"

"Listen to me. My grandfather left me fifty grand. Decent chunk of change, right? Joe and Mike were scraping the bottom of the barrel. They needed thirty, so that's how much I invested. The other twenty I need for rent and food, and money is dwindling by the day. My grandfather knew how I'd spend the money. Maybe not that I'd dump it into a long-shot indie flick, exactly. But I wanted in on this movie. I need the credits—on a *feature film*. This is my *career*. I don't care if they shoot Saludo's *hands* for three minutes. This thing is going to have his name attached if it kills me, and I'm going to be executive producer—of a Dante Saludo movie."

"That may not be a bad idea, actually—his hands." I took a thoughtful drag. "Think about it. Just his hands—remember—?"

"Johnny, please focus."

"Not for *three minutes*, but you could start close-up and then—"

"I'm trying to tell you something important here." He teetered at the edge of the chair. He finished his beer and set the can on the coffee table. "Just hear me out, okay?"

"Sorry." I tapped fake ash into the blue ceramic dish between us.

He took a gentle puff and blew out a long cool breath. "Can you imagine what it must be like for my parents, watching me and wondering what the hell it is I'm doing all these years? You can't explain it to people. The industry is changing so fast." He gave me an earnest, hopeful look. "I have big plans, bro—for movies, TV shows ... I want to produce, *direct* ... *everything*. This is just the beginning for me."

"I just want to *act*," I said.

He stood up slowly and shook his head. "Am I getting through to you *at all?* Acting, writing, directing—it doesn't matter, it's all the same, we're *artists*—"

"You're getting through to me. You're saying this is just the beginning."

"Not for *you*, but for *me*—after *ten years. That's* the point. You need to want it *that bad.* You need to be ready to give ten years, minimum, before you can expect any kind of success—before you can expect to be *any good.* Are you ready to give ten years—just to get to that point? Ten years to get in the door—or even *up* to the door, to get close enough to knock? Starting right now?"

The inevitable, foolish question bloomed in my mind, and I couldn't help asking it: "Do you mean if I *leave* tonight or if I *stay* and do the scene tomorrow?"

Mitch let out an exasperated breath, then mocked my puzzled expression. "Call back." He grabbed the phone and shoved it at me.

"I can't," I said.

"Okay, then you've made your decision." He set the phone down and walked to the door. "Let's go home."

I looked away—out the window at the gas-blue sky. Night was coming on. I imagined Dante Saludo tapping his glass, giving me the cue. I filled it to the rim, the two of us awash in light. I took another fake puff and held my breath. I imagined a thin orange ring burning before my eyes. The light vanished, and I felt alone and hopeless, as if I were already back in Kornfield.

I stabbed my cigarette into the blue dish and looked at Mitch. "Can I ask you another stupid question?"

"Why stop now?" He crossed his arms.

"Is this really helping you—this whole cigarette routine? I mean, isn't it torture, tasting the very thing you're trying to quit?"

He took a deep, tired breath, then a long drag of a cigarette I didn't know he was holding. "You're right. I'm a masochist."

"Why not at least reuse them?"

He walked over to the coffee table, crushed the cigarette in the dish, and extended an open hand for me to take, prepared to escort me out once and for all. "Exit, Demos."

"Why spend all that money on fresh packs?"

He grinned at the blue dish filled with tobacco dust, white scraps of paper, and untarnished filters. "Verisimilitude."

I smiled, though the word was no more familiar to me now than it had been when Dante Saludo used it earlier in the day. Still, I was convinced of its truthfulness.

"Without paying the price," Mitch said, "I'll never commit." He leaned forward, squinting and grinning at me with a face that was suddenly not his own. The spotlight was back, and so was Saludo. "Consider it my limitation as an actor." His voice dropped an octave. "You shoot the scene how you want, Joe, but I have my needs. It's gotta feel real."

I laughed. "If I were the director, you'd play the lead."

"You better stick to being an actor—not a casting director. Come on."

I stood up. "Or—I know—you could play Saludo *playing* Angelo. How about that?"

Mitch didn't ponder this nonsense for long. "Get your bag. Don your fedora."

I followed him to the door.

"I have to talk to him," I said.

"I'll tell Joe there was an urgent family matter."

"Not *Joe*." I hoisted my duffel bag onto my shoulders. "Saludo."

Mitch laughed and opened the door. "A couple beers and you're delirious." He stepped into the hallway, digging a ring of keys from his pocket. "You still have to get to Penn Station and buy a ticket."

I donned my fedora as instructed and toed the line inside the doorway. "Can you call Joe, please? They're probably all together."

"Are you nuts? At this rate you'll be lucky to catch the last train."

I backed up another step. "Shouldn't you be with them, anyway? Helping with the script?"

"Didn't you hear Joe's message?"

"Yes, but you're still a producer."

"*Executive* producer. It's a euphemism. Look—" Mitch grinned, a hand on the doorframe. "I'm sure Dante Saludo will forgive you for bailing on the film. Actually, he'll probably want to thank you because now he can bail, too—seeing that *his* role now depends on *your* role and not vice versa." The keys jangled. "Exit, Demos—*now*." He let the door swing nearly shut, as if to lock me inside the apartment—a threat he immediately realized was counterintuitive. Then he slowly reopened the door, dramatizing his exhaustion with a completely expressionless face.

"I can't just *leave*," I said.

"I can see that." Mitch stepped back inside. The door shut behind him.

"Can you please call the office?"

He walked to the coffee table and picked up the phone. "You just want to say goodbye?"

I shrugged.

He stared at me gravely and dialed a number. He put the phone to his ear and said, "Not picking up."

"Let's walk over and see."

"They're not there, Johnny." He tossed the phone onto the couch and went to the door. "It's time to go home."

"Maybe they're at Saludo's."

He shook his head. "Saludo's in bed, tanked up on bourbon and Vicodin."

I stood by the couch. "He told Joe and Mike to call him later so they could talk. He said he had *minor suggestions*. He said, if we're gonna do this, it's gotta be right."

Mitch blew out a long, slow breath. "That's true, isn't it?"

"Call Saludo." I reached for the phone.

"You see that? You remember everything."

"Do you have his phone number?"

"Not yet."

He checked his watch, and I chased him out the door.

14
LAST CALL

We rushed out onto Franklin Street, into the hazy lamplight. Scuttling down to the Ferrara Center, I imagined us walking in on them, Saludo in a high-backed chair, pencil in hand, delighted to see me, bemused by the duffel bag and fedora, rehearsing his soliloquy while paring it down to its essence. The Avellinos would be too consumed with the precious scripts in their laps to notice the intruders at the door, trembling at the great actor's next edit, their failed revamp scrapped in favor of Mitch's original, which itself was now diminishing by the minute, along with the bottle of bourbon at the center of the table—and Saludo's invaluable screen time.

In the lobby of the Ferrara Center, the doorman, a hatless short-sleeved man, sat behind a counter, sipping from a paper cup and watching a small, gray-screened television, a still shot of a furnished room someplace inside the building.

"Hey, Len," Mitch said, leaning coolly on an elbow. "Anyone around tonight?"

"Nawp." The man's eyes glared at Mitch's elbow on the countertop, then shifted back to the motionless room, in which sofas and plants surrounded a coffee table.

"We got to, uh—" Mitch aimed a thumb at the elevator. "—grab something from the office real quick."

Len pursed his lips. "Joe or Mike send you for it?"

Mitch smirked. "Yes, Len. As always, Joe and Mike sent me for it."

Len reached for a button under the counter, glaring at me and the duffel bag—or maybe at the fedora. I followed Mitch onto the elevator.

Mitch held the door. "Dan here?" he called to Len.

Len looked up before the doors sealed shut. "Ain't nobody here, I just said."

Mitch waved to reassure him, and I tipped my hat, as the door closed.

"What are we doing?" I said. We were going up.

"You said you wanted to talk to Saludo."

"Nobody's here, he just said."

"Well, we can't just waltz into his penthouse, so we're going to have to call first—which means we're going to need a phone number." Mitch watched the numbers light up above the door. "Now that we're here, I might as well show you where the big shots work. Our office is on the fourth floor—Avellinos, I mean. Saludo's on seven, but you can't take the elevator up that high. *We* can't. There's a special key." He pointed to the special keyhole on the panel. "Maxema's on five. Gabriel, too."

"Paul Gabriel?"

"Yup. He comes down to the fourth floor now and then to check on his nieces—a few lousy actresses trying to be producers. I see him in the kitchen getting coffee now and then."

"Amazing," I said.

The elevator doors opened. I trailed Mitch down the dim hallway.

"Took a piss right next to Saludo once," Mitch said. "Four urinals in the bathroom, he comes in, stands right next to me."

"No way."

"True story—"

"You talked to him?"

"Yes, I talked to him. I said, 'How ya doin'?' but that's not the point." Mitch plucked a bunch of keys from his pocket. "

"What did he say?"

"The *point*—"

"Did he ask how *you* were doing?"

"No. He said he was good, and then I stood there pretending to pee, while he zipped up and washed up and left. Then I kicked myself for not being ready with a pitch. Like I'd blown my one shot with Dante Saludo."

"Damn!"

"Yeah." Mitch nodded. "That's what I thought, too. *Damn*—"

"And you never saw him again?"

He grinned. "The *point* is … after I saw him another *hundred* times, I realized he's just a busy guy like you and me who's trying to take a leak or grab a coffee, and he doesn't want to read your fucking screenplay—or hear your stupid pitch. See what I'm saying?"

"You wrote a screenplay?"

"I wrote *seven* screenplays."

Mitch rounded the corner and stopped at a closed door with a nameplate that announced *Avellino Brothers*. A gold key sprang up from the bunch clenched in his fingers.

"You *do* have a key?" I said.

"How else do you think I could do all the work that needs to get done around here?" He unlocked the door, which fell open with ease. "And how else do you think we're going to get Dante Saludo's phone number?"

I followed him through one sparsely furnished office into another, where he circled the desk. I said, "Len made it sound like you need the Avellinos' permission to be in here."

"Well, they *do* pay the rent ..." His fingers fluttered through the wheel of index cards on the desk. "*Voila*. The ol' Rolodex. Look at this." His grin was heating up. "Take your pick. Office, car, home—*Italy*."

He plucked the phone from its cradle on the desk and leaned back in the leather chair, cord stretching to his ear, at once inhabiting an inflated version of himself. He leaned forward and held his finger down on the button as he rehearsed the call: "Dan! Mitch here! Oh, you're all together? Wonderful. Dinner at your house? No, I understand. I'm sure you guys were looking for me. I'm a tough guy to track down. Don't apologize. What? No, thanks, I just ate—"

"This cannot be a good idea," I said.

"Would you put that bag down, please?" Mitch said to me. "You're making me nervous—with your Dick Tracy hat."

"*I'm* making *you* nervous?" I glanced back at the door, halfway open.

Mitch rested the phone on his shoulder. "You know why I have these keys?"

I let my bag drift to the floor. "How else would you do all the work that needs to get done around here?"

His jaw dropped in exaggerated shock. "That is *exactly* what I just said. Do you have, like, perfect recall or something? I think you were born to be an actor. That's what I think. And *I* was born to be a *producer*, and one of my talents is identifying talent—and recognizing opportunity." He leaned forward. "The reason I have these keys is that for the last two years, when something needs to get done and they're not about to drive from New Jersey to do it, who's here to do the job?" In a flash, he snapped the card clean from the rings that held it in the circular deck.

"*Now* what are you doing?!" I blurted.

Mitch put the phone on speaker mode and dialed. The shrill beeps filled the room. "I have done as much as they've done for this movie, but because my name is not Avellino, they won't let me in *all the way*. Because I'm not *family*. You see? Human beings are tribal creatures. I've learned from my experience. It's important you learn from your experience, Johnny," he added wryly. "Are you learning?" He hesitated. "I'm trying to teach you the value of *family*."

Dante Saludo's phone rang. The volume swelled, and I felt swallowed up by the noise.

I took a deep breath, hoping no one would answer. The room went silent.

"Machine," he said.

"Please hang up," I said.

Mitch held up a finger to shush me. "Uh, hey, Dan, it's Mitch. Thought I'd try and catch you at home. I'm here at the office with my cousin Johnny, talking about the shoot tomorrow. Turns out I've got a new idea I'd like to bounce off you. It might end up Plan A, but it's at least Plan B. Hoping you can give me a call back here as soon as possible." He hung up the phone, a sour grin taking shape.

"Now what?"

"We wait."

"What's this *new idea?*"

"All I know is you're not in it." He pressed his palms flat on the desk. "We should be hearing from Joe any second."

"You think the Avellinos are with him?"

"Of course they're with him. You said yourself—"

"Joe's gonna be pissed," I said. "Don't you want to be a producer anymore, either? He could kick you off the project for breaking into his office."

Mitch held up the keys. "I did not break in, Sherlock."

I pointed to the Rolodex. "You stole Dante Saludo's phone number."

"You cannot *steal* a phone number." He let out a long breath, filling the air with his fatigue. "God, I need a cigarette."

"I just wanted to talk to *Saludo*," I whined, exaggerating my exasperation.

Mitch sat up straight. "Here—" He flashed the torn-out Rolodex card and thrust it toward me. "*You* call."

I shook my head. "You already left a message."

"There's no message."

"You just—"

"I was acting." He shook his head. "Had my finger on the button. Call Saludo."

"Maybe you're acting *now*."

He hesitated. "This isn't just about *you* anymore, Johnny. I bet all my chips on you today, and now you're leaving. This movie is all I've got."

"Sorry."

"I'm not blaming you. It's just a fact."

There was a knock at the door. My heart sank as I swung around. *They're here*, I thought.

The door opened, and Len appeared. "You boys get what you came for?"

The phone rang.

Len said, "Mr. Joe called and told me to come up here and tell you boys to leave."

I looked at Mitch. "How'd he know we were here if you didn't leave a message?"

"Maybe my good friend Len called and told him we were here."

The ringing didn't stop. I said, "Are you going to answer that?"

Mitch picked up the phone and sang out, "Avellino Brothers, the future of American cinema!"

I shrank back.

Joe's voice rang clear: "What the fuck are you doing in my office, Mitch?"

"*Shee-it*," Len said, sidling up to me.

Mitch silenced the receiver against his chest, his expression one of mock distress. "Len, I'm hurt. I thought we had an understanding. All these months I've been coming here—"

Joe exploded, "Are you insane? Did you not get my message?"

Mitch grinned crazily, extending the phone toward Len and me, as Joe railed on, his voice filling the room: "… There's *one* director! Why can't you understand that? After tomorrow, we are finished, you and me. We're done. *You're* done. If you want to have anything to do with the film business, you should pack your bags and go back to L.A., and I wouldn't get my hopes up *there*, either …"

Mitch kept the phone extended and shouted at the mouthpiece: "Johnny's going home, by the way!"

The line went silent. Mitch winked at me, as if we were in on a prank together.

"Family emergency," Mitch said.

Finally, Joe said, "He *can't* leave," and then, "Please tell me you're fucking with me."

Mitch said, "I am not fucking with you. He doesn't have a choice."

I scowled at Mitch and hissed, "*I do have a choice!*"

"I stand corrected," Mitch said. "He *does* have a choice. And he's choosing to go home."

Joe sighed. "What do we tell Dan?"

"You're the director, Joe. You're going to have to get creative. I know that will be difficult for you."

"This cannot be happening," Joe said.

I approached Mitch, my thoughts scrambled.

"Dan won't do the scene without him," Joe said. "He loves the kid—loves the *whole idea*."

"*My* idea," Mitch said.

"We've gotta make this happen, Mitch."

"I gotta go," Mitch said.

I grabbed his shoulder. "Wait!"

Joe's voice cracked desperately. "Is that him?"

I held my hand out for the phone.

"He's in a hurry, Joe. He got terrible news today."

"Give it to me," I said.

Joe cried out, "What's Plan B, Mitch? You said in your message you've got a new idea …"

My jaw dropped. I shoved Mitch. "You said you were acting! You said you didn't leave a message!"

Mitch backpedaled, cupping the mouthpiece with a hand. "You were right the second time. I was acting when I said I was acting." The phone cord stretched tight. He lifted the receiver to his mouth. "Kid's gotta catch the last train."

"It's my choice!" I steamed toward him.

He held a hand up to stop me. "I'll call you back later, Joe."

Len said, "What the hell is going on in here?"

Mitch sidestepped me and hung up the phone.

"Call him back!" I shouted.

Mitch rounded the desk. "I told you, Johnny, this isn't about you anymore. Some of us have a movie to finish tomorrow. We've gotta get this show on the road." He moved toward the door, where Len stood, speechless.

"Is this you being a selfish prick?" I let out.

Mitch crossed his arms on his chest. "Yes, it is. Between now and tomorrow morning, I need to come up with a solution to a problem that no one else is going to fix. And the problem is that you're leaving and you're the only reason Dante Saludo is still here. So, forgive me. I'm in a bit of a pinch!" He slapped the torn Rolodex card into my unsuspecting hand. "I got his number for you. Call him if you want. I'll wait for you downstairs."

Len stepped aside, and Mitch was out the door.

I was staring at the phone number when Len swiped the card from my grasp. For a long moment, we swapped hard glances. Then I hiked my duffel bag onto my shoulders, tipped my hat, and raced out.

I caught Mitch in the elevator just before the door closed.

"Change your mind?" Mitch said.

An expression I didn't recognize—a grin, pleased or cruel, I couldn't tell—started on Mitch's face. But I didn't care what he thought anymore.

Outside, I hustled across the street toward a pay phone beside the glowing window of Three Brothers Pizza.

Mitch followed. "*Now* you're calling your mother? From *here?*"

I dropped my bag on the sidewalk, withdrew a handful of change from my pocket, and fished out a quarter.

"You'll need more than a quarter for Kornfield."

"I'm not calling *Kornfield*." I inserted the quarter and turned my back.

"You're calling Saludo? Where's the phone number I gave you?"

I tapped a finger to my head and dialed.

"You're insane," he said. I shook his hand off my shoulder as the phone rang. "Johnny, listen to me—"

"Answering machine." I twisted to see the dark building at the other end of the block where Saludo lived. "Mr. Saludo, this is Johnny Demos, the kid from today, calling from the pay phone down the street. I'm sorry to bother you, but I need to talk to you." I choked up. "My dad died, and now my uncle—"

"Take it easy," Mitch said.

The inevitable crying started. "Joe said you won't do the scene without me. He also said …" I wiped my tears. "He said you …"

"Jesus Christ with the drama," Mitch muttered.

"I want you to know," I blubbered, "I want to be in this movie with you more than anything. I want to be an actor and come to New York, but—"

Mitch planted a hand on the pizza shop window.

"—my uncle had a heart attack, and now I have to go home, to Pennsylvania, but this is my one shot, and tomorrow … and tomorrow …"

I could see Uncle Nick and me in Papou's living room, bracing each other with firm grips.

There was a click at the other end of the line. My heart swelled, and I thought I'd float off the ground: "Hello?" But the line was dead.

Mitch placed his hand on my shoulder. "Kid."

I looked at him through a thickening haze.

He took the phone from my hand and put it back in its place. He hoisted my bag over his shoulder and took my arm. "Come on." We stepped out onto the street, Mitch's eyes shimmering under the streetlights.

15
EXIT DEMOS

Mitch dropped my duffel bag inside the open doorway, where I stood waiting—for what, I didn't know. In the dark kitchen he made a phone call—a gravelly whisper, "Corner of Hudson and Franklin"—and set the phone on the counter. The flame from a lighter appeared, followed by the glowing tip of a cigar. He entered the living room in a cloud of sweet-smelling smoke.

"You're smoking?" I said.

"Follow me," he said.

I once again hoisted my duffel bag over my shoulder. "Did you call me a *cab?*"

"Called a guy I know drives a car." He pointed to the floor. "Lose the bag, kid. Don't have much time." He lifted the hat from my head and tossed it onto the couch. He puffed and squinted behind the bright orange tip of the cigar.

"What are you, a gangster all of a sudden?" I said.

"The name is *Dante*." Smoke streamed from his gleaming grin.

I managed a weak smile.

"I want to show you something, kid."

I set my bag down and followed him into the hallway. We wound our way up flight after flight of stairs until we arrived at a dimly lit landing. A white door opened onto a fragment of the roof, surrounded by the brick walls of other buildings, as well as by a section of the building that rose up farther. He puffed his cigar and gripped the railing of a wrought-iron spiral staircase that led to the sky—deep blue despite the night. He wound his way upward, and I followed, my eyes at the thick heels of his black boots.

His voice sounded in the night: "You were telling me in your message, you want to be in this movie more than anything else? Is that true?"

My mind groped for a response to the question, which felt like a trick. I was a little dizzy from the thick smoke, and I didn't trust my own thoughts.

He went on, "You were saying you want to come to New York and be an actor …"

At the top of the stairs, he looked down at me, nodding.

"Afraid of heights, kid?" He smiled and stepped out of view. "Top of the world up here!"

I decided I was willing to play along.

Another step and my eyes met the roof facing west and followed the brief flat blacktop plane to where it blurred with infinity. He stepped toward the edge of the roof, and I quickly followed. I let out a gasp, in general wonder, as the air of the world drew my gaze to those Twin Towers—those gloriously mammoth columns appearing in a miraculous flash as something heaven-sent. So near were these giants of mass and light that it was impossible to comprehend how I had been blind to them, how my vision must have been downcast, or inward—or just blocked, during my embarrassingly brief stay in Manhattan, by the buildings standing between here and wherever these monoliths were rooted however many blocks away.

Turning around, I couldn't tell which way was home. New York seemed to go on forever, mountains and ridges and valleys of buildings and flickering car lights emerging from and vanishing into caverns of darkness, everything around us moving like a slow ocean, this island a magnificent world of its own, anchored and buoyed by bridges with sparkling arcs like chains over the water, glittering like the stars, reaching onward and outward and connecting us with the universe.

"Cigar?"

He pulled a cigar from his breast pocket and held it out to me.

"No thanks."

He planted the cigar in my hand. "Never turn down a cigar, kid."

I held the cigar at my side. "Come on, Mitch—"

With a flick, a flame appeared before me.

"Cut the act now, please," I said.

He thrust the light toward my face and narrowed his eyes. "Acting is listening, remember? *Re*-acting."

I puffed, and smoke rose from my cigar.

"You must be crazy sneaking into my building like that, stealing my phone number." He turned toward the infinite lights. "Look at this place. It's past midnight on a Tuesday, and it's buzzing like a hornet's nest. Look at that, like bugs and bees swarming all over." He fluttered his fingers. "A Tuesday night it's like this here."

I could feel the earth moving beneath us and around us.

"Where you from? Jersey you said—?"

"Pennsylvania."

"—New York is nothing like Jersey. You gotta be nuts to come here."

He turned toward the Twin Towers, and I shouldered up.

"You're born here, you got an excuse. Most people born here stay here." Cigar in hand, Mitch tapped his big middle finger to his skull, encasing a brain that was nuts or not nuts, I wasn't sure anymore. "These Avellino boys—you think they're smart guys?"

I shrugged, playing my part again. "Sure."

"Maybe you're right. I don't know, to be honest, but they're definitely nuts. They got Buddy Klein shooting the thing. They got college kids doing lights and a sound team with a tape deck and a milk crate. And they're broke! You know why? Because for three years they been renting a very expensive office they don't need in my building down the street. That sound smart to you?"

I shook my head no—the right answer, I figured.

"See, you're too smart for this business—or for this *town*, anyway—because *of course* it's crazy. These guys actually *think* they're movie producers. Have they made a movie? Not yet. No. But they're trying, so we'll see." He cackled. "What matters is, they *believe* they're *filmmakers*. Understand? *Before* they've made anything. What do they know? Their dad died when they were kids—"

I felt my face turn white.

"—well, not kids, exactly. They were in their twenties—old enough to know better. And what do they do? They go and sink their whole inheritance into this one thing. But don't you dare bring that up to them. They want you to think they worked their way to the top. Rags-to-riches story. Sons of immigrants, the whole thing—"

"Come on, Mitch," I choked out. "We're not so different—"

"That's right, Johnny. But I'm trying to make a point here, if you listen. These guys are not trying to *become* producers. They just decided that's what they *are*. You know what you have to do to be a movie producer?"

"Produce a movie?"

"You're listening. Good." He smiled. "But that's not the correct answer—not exactly. *Produce a movie* comes later, when it's complete. In the meantime, the answer is, *whatever it takes to get it done, until it's done.* They wake up one day and say we're gonna make a movie. What's stopping them? They write a screenplay. It's good enough, it's not a masterpiece, *not yet*, but now they've got something. They work their butts off. They call people up and say, *We're producing a film, Shadow Whatever-the-Fuck, You can reach me in my Tribeca office, in the Ferrara Building*, they're being honest, it's all true, and, bang, people are buying the whole act, they want to know who these young hotshots are with the screenplay and the office in *my* building. Impressive, right?"

I nodded.

He went on, "The Avellino Brothers. It's got a nice ring to it. Italian kids. Family working together. Who doesn't want to be a part of that? They're optimistic, they're passionate, they *believe*. They come to me—*they pay me rent*—they ask me for a favor. I say maybe. Now people are investing money in the *possibility* of a Dante Saludo picture—*before* it's officially a Dante Saludo picture. People take the risk, they're willing to lose their money, because they want to be *in the movies*. It's like magic. It's delusional. They think, *If I can't be* in the movies, *well, then, here, take my money, let me help you* make *a movie. Take the money my grandfather earned by building bridges, breaking his back. Take it all, take everything I've got.* It's crazy. This is America. We're in love with the big screen. Don't ask me."

I shuffled and sighed. The bridges blinked and waved.

"But being an actor is different. Being in the movies isn't being an actor. There are a lot of people in the movies who are not actors. You wanna be in the movies or you wanna be an actor?"

I'd lost my way in his meandering speech. "I want to be in movies, and now the one chance I get—"

"Give me the cigar. How you ever gonna be a real actor when you don't listen?"

I put the cigar in my mouth and took a long puff.

He walked into the middle of the roof toward the shallow brick ledge. The breeze was mild and warm, but he shouted as if into the wind. "You know why I'm doing this movie? This miserably long scene where I blather about nothing?"

"I thought you liked it?"

He put his hands on his hips. The wind picked up. With his front teeth, he bit down on his cigar and took brief, measured puffs. His untucked shirt whipped like a flag at his sides. "C'mon. Why would I do this godforsaken movie?"

I feigned a thoughtful puff and licked my lips, spiced and tingling. "Because you admire these guys, the Avellino brothers? Their guts, I mean?"

"I don't know about their guts. Maybe they have guts." His grin gleamed as he took the cigar from his mouth. "It's because they're family. Their mom is a Saludo. My father is cousins with their grandfather. They were in business together here in New York for decades. Fabrics. Textiles. Importing, exporting. They did very well for themselves—"

"Are you making this up?" I asked, entirely myself.

"It's the truth. Joe and Mike are my cousins. Like you and Mitch are cousins. And they're my *friends*. Not long ago they were just family—my cousin's kids. Now it's more than that. Understand? *That's* what it's all about. Nothing else matters, kid. Your family and your friends. If you're lucky, they're the same people."

For a moment, Mitch seemed to break character as he turned to face the Brooklyn Bridge, its red lights blinking like dragon's eyes, the burning orange nub of his cigar pulsing as he puffed and blew. "I love this city," he let out, and then added, his voice gangster-tough again, "A man's lucky to live a single day here."

I breathed in the smoke of his exhalation, which mixed with the pungent taste of tobacco already on my tongue. I had crossed over, lost in the scene, along with Mitch, who was Dante Saludo, while I was a kid from Kornfield who had made it all the way ... I inched forward, pretending his breath were my own, my tainted saliva heightening my already distorted sense of the largeness of everything around me.

"I want to live here," I said, anticipating his approval.

When he said nothing, I dared to step up to the edge, beside him.

"How's that cigar?" he said.

I'd been holding it at my side, when, suddenly, tears welled up. I hammed a puff, then held my breath—I should leap to my death before I started crying again.

"There's no one shot, kid. Some things you get one shot. Not acting. And if it was true, it wouldn't be some movie you just showed your face in, pouring drinks behind a bar, even if I'm the one doing the drinking. You're not an actor because you hang around with actors—or even appear in films with them." Squinting, he took a long drag, the sizzling tip penetrating me like a third eye. He awaited my reply.

I nodded.

He said, "You acting? I mean, taking classes, that sort of thing?"

Okay, I thought. Enough, Mitch. End of scene. Cut to: et cetera.

"I'm not trying to insult you. Have you done some acting, is all I'm asking?"

"Come on, Mitch." I shifted my cigar from one side of my mouth to the other. "We've been through this."

"Answer me."

"Biff," I said.

"What else?"

I sighed. "Geppetto."

"What's 'at?" He cupped a hand to his ear.

"I was Geppetto, in *Pinocchio*."

He nodded. "Uh-huh. That's what I thought you said." His cigar was a stub, black-tipped with bits of light. "Now listen. You could be in this movie tomorrow, or you could take the car I sent for you and be home in two hours. It's *your* life." He twisted and pointed his cigar toward the fainter lights in the distance. "Where you live? Parsippany? New Jersey?"

"*Pennsylvania!*"

"Good. The farther from here the better."

I chuckled, ready to go.

He puffed and looked at his dark cigar. When he stepped up to the ledge, I stepped back, unsteady and out of breath. He pressed the dark ash into the pale concrete and left the stump jutting like a finger from the black residue, a lifeless smudge.

"You can't quit because of me," I said.

"No one's quitting anything."

"What about our scene? What are you going to do without me?"

"It's going to be beautiful."

"What's your new idea? Plan A or Plan B?"

"It's Plan A now, Johnny boy." He bit his cigar with a giant smile. He took a series of puffs. "Voiceover. Close-up on my hands. Just like you said. At first, clenched and anxious. Ray blacks out at the bar, and *boom*, we cut to the Brooklyn Bridge and that first ray of sunshine. Nice and easy. With my voice. We hear the words of that magnificent monologue penned by Mitch Mitchell. We see the sunrise over the river. We slow it all down. All those colors in the sky. Sunset. A complete life story in a single day. We come back to my hands, calm and peaceful. Ray wakes up and walks outside into sunshine. Heaven on earth. That's it. What do you think?"

The whole story is right there in your hands.

"I like it," I said. "It'll still be a Dante Saludo movie."

"That's right."

"You're gonna save the day," I said.

He winked. "So, what do you want to do?"

I looked away and then up at the stars. "I'm going to miss this so much."

"I'm going to miss it too."

I faced Mitch, who was also Dante Saludo. "Now we're family *and* friends."

"That's right," he said.

"I want to go home," I said.

"That's good, son." He walked over to me and set his hands on my shoulders. "Someday maybe you come back here, but not for a long time. People live here because they *have* to. Anywhere else, they feel like they're dead. You'll know. You'll feel it, *here*—" He thumped a finger on the hollow center of my chest and turned for the staircase. "Your ride …"

My tongue scoured my mouth for disintegrating leaves. "You really called for a car?"

"Remember what I said." Mitch turned, gripping the handrail. "You gotta be nuts to come to this city. Just be glad you weren't born here—like me. I've been nuts since I could think." His face was in the shadows. As I approached, I could see that he was grinning.

Alas: End scene. *Exit Demos.*

16
WILD WEST

In the wake of Uncle Nick's death, I couldn't bear to acknowledge the embarrassing insignificance of the details of my life—and of all of our lives. Or maybe I just couldn't bear to recognize the devastating *significance* of them. I could hardly bear to face the implications of the choices we had to make in life. And so, for days, as we revisited the family plot in the cemetery, and then weeks into the summer, as we returned to the restaurant, we seemed to float in and out of each other's lives, politely acquiescing, making no bold moves, avoiding disruptions.

On a Saturday night in July, during Wheatcroft College's Class Reunion Weekend, I was working the bar, chit-chatting with Bates about the hopeful state of the Phillies, when my mother, seasoned hostess and recently self-appointed acting general manager, signaled to me with a wink from the corner table by the door.

Two familiar old couples sat opposite each other, bedecked in summer suits and floral dresses. The nearer pair twisted and beamed in my direction—at the grandson of the founder of this place, to which they'd been coming since Johnny and then his son Nick, God rest their souls, transformed the old truck stop into the area's finest restaurant. I smiled back and delivered another four drinks on the house. Bates worked on a mouthful of prime rib while I added cherries to a dozen Manhattans, another in a series of such rounds, for a table in the Wild West Room, where I imagined a reunion celebration crescendoing into a real geriatric barnburner. Papou had always reveled in Wheatcroft's Class Reunion Weekend, when these rooms became aglow in nostalgia and the past was made present. The old revelers would cheer his name when "Johnny!" walked into the room, and Papou would reward them with desserts and sweet wines, prolonging their stay and deepening their devotion.

"They don't look like much," Bates offered, eyes on the TV, "but in three years, these guys are going all the way." I nodded agreeably, though I couldn't see how he could be right about a bunch of banged-up, no-name hacks. "They've got grit," Bates added, and I wondered if he was somehow trying to encourage *me*, since my own future seemed no less uncertain than the Phillies'.

Just then, my mother arrived at the cash register, which was embedded in the rear wall between rows of liquor bottles.

"You know who that is, don't you?"

I returned the bottle of gin, and our eyes met in the mirror behind the whiskeys.

"That's Dean Wilson from Wheatcroft. As in, Dean of Admissions."

My stomach sank, along with my eyes.

"He said your late application won't be a problem. Your grades and test scores are way above average."

"We knew that already," I said. "Getting into Wheatcroft was never the issue."

"Not until you didn't send in your application—and then lied to me about it."

"I didn't lie"—another lie.

I had nearly managed to convince myself that the unsent college applications buried in my bedroom desk drawer had actually been sent, rather than designedly tucked, sealed, stamped and all, to appear accidentally forgotten, as evidenced by the fact that they had not been trashed or burned—an airtight strategy that my conscience had failed to allow.

"I suggest you make a good impression," my mother said. "He didn't guarantee anything."

"I'm not going to Wheatcroft. I told you, I have to get out of here."

"So where are you going to go? Your father went to Wheatcroft—"

"Mom!" I took a deep breath. "Maybe I'll go to Penn State with Big." With this unplanned announcement I'd taken myself by surprise, and for a moment I believed that this was a viable prospect I might actually consider, despite my unsent application.

In a flash her face softened—a prolonged expression of sympathy that indicated I was missing something crucial and obvious. I shrank back, embarrassed by this sudden kindness—not the shocked reaction I was expecting.

"Oh, honey," she said.

I hesitated. "What?"

She gently reached for my arm. "Do you really think he's going back there?"

I frowned and bowed my head, ducked past her, and rushed through the lobby, skirting the impatient mob and Aunt Helen looking up curiously from her clipboard, toward the stainless-steel doors at the far end of the Wild West Room, a blur of good cheer I couldn't pass through quickly enough. I blasted into the kitchen, into the routine crisscrossing of waitresses in their timeless short-black-dress getups, gravity-defying salads and desserts on corkboard trays attached to their palms; the cooks and dishwashers, in their thick white aprons, dutifully manning their stations, grumbling and mumbling to each other or to themselves—these were the clicks and groans of an old machine that showed not one sign of faltering, despite the absence of a few key parts.

I circled back to the butchering room, but it was empty. Then I pulled open the door to the walk-in fridge, and there he was, right in front, by the bin full of sliced lemons, eyes slowly opening as I entered, his hands invisible under the lifted black skirt of the recently hired Guadalupe, who, moving only slightly more quickly than Big, and not exactly urgently, untied her tongue from his. I pulled the door shut behind me and held firm to the handle, as if I were here to play protector and they'd been expecting my welcome arrival.

Big grinned, not at me but at Guadalupe, who put her innocent hands up as she backed into shelves lined with plastic bins filled with frozen fish.

"You're bad," Guadalupe breathed, lowering her arms and pressing her palms to her thighs, silver rings flashing along with her glowing smile, her gorgeous nest of black hair spreading out before a backdrop of Tupperware covered in cellophane.

They hadn't exactly acknowledged my presence, aside from having suspended their tryst—that is, assuming I'd had anything to do with their stopping in the first place, an assumption I was beginning to doubt, until Big said, "You and I will finish this later."

For a moment, I believed he was addressing *me*, about a feud I didn't know had already started, until Guadalupe said, "If you're lucky," in a strange voice I both despised and envied.

"How much luckier could I get?" Big said.

"That's for you to find out," Guadalupe said.

Steam poured from their ridiculous smiles. All of this was playing out before me as if designed for me to witness, to both inform and taunt me. And yet, I was just about to offer to stand guard outside when Big asked, "Were you looking for me?"

Guadalupe gathered her hair in a fist, patted my cheek, and informed me on the way out, "Your cousin is very bad."

Once she left, Big said, "Oh, man, I am so in love with that girl."

I frowned at the stranger before me.

"I can't even tell you," he said. "She is like nothing I have ever even dreamed of."

"When did this start?" I asked.

"I don't know. Few weeks ago."

"Wasn't she just *hired* a few weeks ago?"

"Exactly," he said.

"Doesn't she have a kid?"

"So what?" Big's smile managed to grow. "Her ex is out of the picture."

"Are you crazy?" I leaned back against the door, my hands on the latch.

"What are you talking about?"

I shook my head. "You're an idiot."

"What's your problem?"

When I thrust the door open and spun into the kitchen, I upended poor old Dotty, hammered her like a pinball, sent her flying into Guadalupe, who then tripped into Hank—or, rather, into the edge of the stainless-steel serving tray being carried by Hank—the veteran bus-man, who, despite a balletic attempt to save the dozen entrees stacked in three piles of four, couldn't keep the silver plate covers, nor the plates they protected, from sliding and catapulting over the tray's raised ridge, nor could he keep the crab cakes and steaks and flounder specials and all the assorted side dishes—the mashed potatoes, the carrots, the buttered string beans with shaved almonds—from sailing into the wide-open space of the kitchen, into the air, where for an endless moment it seemed my actions could be reversed and all could be saved, my fears assuaged, our respective fates averted, until everything reached its peak and then came falling onto the floor.

This tremendous, seemingly endless sound of crashing trays and their spilling contents preceded the sight: first of my mother, who'd entered through the double doors just in time to witness the catastrophe I'd caused, before leaping to the aid of the fallen Dotty; then of Guadalupe, who sat on the hardwood floor, Big already kneeling at her side with his hand on her forehead, alongside strewn iceberg lettuce and a dark-orange smear of French dressing shot from a stainless-steel cup; Hank quietly stacking plate covers—all of them sparing me their scolding stares.

As I inched away in shame, I let myself believe I was turning my back on them for good. The springless screen door smacked shut behind me, and in minutes I arrived at Sierra McCloud's house, where I leaped from the old Honda onto the front yard, never more certain about anything in my life. I was sure I understood at last what love really was, felt strangely free, ready to sacrifice everything, so I rang the bell and waited, cupping my hands to the glass and looking for a sign, of any kind, and then circled the house, once, twice, peered into the small square windows of the garage door, at a single parked car, and then waited some more, ten minutes, twenty, just sitting there on the driveway, until I returned to my senses.

But I didn't leave, because I didn't know where to go. Instead, I just lay down on the quiet, empty driveway and stared at the infinite, white sky. I thought about crying but didn't. I wanted to cry but couldn't. I breathed in and out and wondered at the invisible universe beyond the pale blur that I could see. Everything and everyone drifting out and away on their own paths. A jangling sound roused me, and I sat up. A man and his dog turned the nearby corner and continued their walk, sneakers and paws scratching and padding on the pavement, leash and collar and tags all clanging their light tune. Then it was silent again. I waited for Sierra or anyone to arrive, to bear witness to my agony.

A car appeared seemingly out of nowhere, turned into the driveway, and took aim on me. I shot up to my feet. This was not how I wanted to be found: paralyzed, holding my breath, exchanging troubled glances with a stranger, desperate to formulate some explanation for my being here, for my very existence, to identify myself. *Who are you and what are you doing?*

When the car backed out and returned in the direction it came—someone who'd gotten lost or traveled too far down the road and was simply making a U-turn—my lungs collapsed in relief. It was time for me to go. Time for me to leap, headlong, into the path of my own design.

17
OFF BROADWAY

Attending Wheatcroft College would prove to be, if nothing else, time for all my grieving and yearning to transform from an anxious pit in my stomach to a polished, burning jewel in my gut. And so, four years after that tantalizing, agonizing summer—after the acting classes and the monologues and the play performances; after the improv and the playwriting and the short-film productions; after deconstructing Shakespeare and Ibsen and Chekhov—there I was again, at last, alone in New York City, gone and not gone, certain only of my uncertainty, and yet mesmerized anew by the concrete, the surrounding waters, and the city's incessant hum, poised for my true education. In my pocket I dug for that cardboard coaster with the address of a certain renovated church, indeed a small Byzantine structure after all, just around the corner from that familiar street, from that summer of promise. Inside, the rear wall domed out behind the altar, the original artwork fading to orange shades, twelve cloaked and sandaled men, six per side, reaching up toward the white star that spread out in splintered streaks across the ceiling and faded into water stains. A chandelier lit the stage, a worn, red-rugged platform above two steps.

In the side aisle, Jay Kauffman stood contemplating, beyond the pews, the three men and three women leaning into one another, shoulder against shoulder, and bowing at the waist as if surrounding, unhurried, a lost diamond in the rug. He glanced half-interestedly in my direction and tapped his own shoulder, gesturing for me to leave my bag and join the group.

"Okay," he said to them, "breathe deep, close your eyes."

The students stayed huddled as Jay looked at me hovering at the outskirts.

"Forget the circle," he said. "Just feel the connection."

I was paralyzed, still outside. He waved me in.

"One more minute."

I felt the carpet moving beneath me, the others gliding blindly through each other.

"Forget who you are. That's the only way to get there. Close your eyes!"

His hands gripped my shoulders.

"You must lose yourself before you can become somebody else."

In the dark I made fists as he directed me toward the center of the circle and let go.

Eventually, drifting among these strangers, these relative veterans, I was joyful in the sense that I had taken my place among them. Soon they became my friends, like family. As years passed, they kept me close when I wanted to give up, when all hope seemed dashed and I felt drawn back home for good; they held on to me when I longed for the security I believed I might rediscover by retreating to familiar ground or, in the darkest times, into uncharted wilderness, when all of us wanted to be anywhere else.

It was during a stretch of those loneliest days that I happened to cross paths with, of all people, Sierra McCloud, as I rounded a corner where she exited a Krispy Kreme. For as long as I was in Kornfield, and then for more than a little while after that, I had imagined winning her back through a series of unpredictable and increasingly impressive accomplishments that would fortuitously reunite us and that I had yet to achieve. By now, I had loved exactly three women in my life—Sierra, whom I remembered as most elegant; and much later, and for much longer durations, a banker and a medical student, who each admired my grim determination and so adored me as one might adore an exotic pet.

The moment I saw Sierra, her smile erased all the years that had passed between us and rekindled in a flash those long-buried and persistent longings. She appeared to me exactly as she had over a decade ago, despite the cropped hair, skirt suit, and running sneakers women wear to avoid heels, trekking to and from the office. We'd known each other only three weeks the night we first proclaimed our love, giddy in the recognition of this glorious newfound truth, and only three months before she foresaw our demise and wisely cut her losses. She'd managed to fend me off then, despite my formulations and our relentless proximity to each other. At last, pure chance had brought us face to face.

I'd somehow missed the stroller she was pushing, along with the shining pale faces whose narrow eyes matched their mother's.

"Twins," she said, directing my attention with a forgiving grin to her treasures, fair-haired toddlers nibbling politely at their donuts.

The expanding emptiness in my chest was replaced by a momentary swelling of my heart, which no doubt she detected. "You're married," I said, re-establishing in an instant my dull preoccupations.

Sierra answered with a fluttering of fingers, flashing the unmissable evidence. "And you?" Before I could improvise a thought, she drew a buzzing phone from a pocket and expertly thumbed a reply to the sender. "My husband," she said, without looking up. "One sec." She then gestured to the phone in her hand and smiled. "It's constant, right? Can you imagine if we'd had these when we were in high school?"

"I'm glad we didn't."

"I know. I think I wouldn't have been able to avoid you."

"Oh. Well. Then I wish we'd had them."

I was amazed to feel as unembarrassed by these easily made confessions as she appeared to be. When she returned my smile, my imagination exploded with possibilities.

"So," she remembered, "are you married?"

"No," I blurted, and bumbled on about how busy I was and how hard everything was in this city, what with my countless auditions and exhausting nights bartending …

Her eyes narrowed further. "You were always a natural on stage, Johnny. You need to try harder, and don't give up so easily."

These words flowed off her tongue—as did the diminutive nickname, which she so confidently (and rightly) assumed I'd kept. She smirked, it seemed to me, seeing that I was stunned, and evidently gauging my expression as the moments passed.

I managed, "What are you up to?" and went on brooding on the possible implications of her advice, as she went on about the joys of motherhood and urban planning. Her tone went unchanged when she recalled a life-altering turn of events, her water breaking six weeks before the due date, in the pre-dawn hours of that dreadful September morning, when her husband raced with her to the hospital instead of heading downtown to his office in the World Trade Center, from which he would not have returned. She beamed, talking of renewal and growth, when, suddenly, an irrational, aching hopefulness bloomed in me, in the presence of this optimistic salvager of strewn debris. Here was a woman who had engineered her life with daunting shrewdness, even in the face of calamity. I allowed myself a moment of pure fantasy (the life that could have been, *if only* …) and then resigned myself for the millionth time to the unknown future and the unsettled past.

She'd taken out her phone again and said something I mistook as intended for her toddlers, who were licking at their empty hands. When I failed to respond, she gave me a look that seemed distantly wounded or even alarmed. "*No?*" she asked, with a grin that belied the question.

"I'm sorry?" I said. "I didn't hear you."

She beamed. "Can I call you?"

"Call me? Seriously?"

She laughed. "I mean, right now. So you'll have my number. To keep in touch."

"Right," I said. "Of course."

I gave her my number, which she promptly called, and, as my phone buzzed in my hand, she said, "If you're in a show, I want you to call me. I mean, *when* you're in a show. I want to come see you."

"I will," I said. "I'm in a play now, actually. But maybe wait for the next one."

She smiled. "What's wrong with the one you're in now?"

"Nothing's wrong with it. It's just—*Off*-Off-Broadway. The next one will be better, I hope. I just found out yesterday, I got the lead—my first big lead."

"That's great, Johnny! You must be so excited! I'm so proud of you."

"Thanks."

"What's the play? When is it and where?"

"It's Off-Broadway—"

"Not *Off*-Off?" She beamed, waiting for me to elaborate, to show my excitement, or to acknowledge my apparent lack of it.

"I *am* excited," I said. "And nervous. You know how it is here. One bad review …"

"Or one *good* review! And then you're an overnight success."

I returned her grin. "True."

"You haven't changed," she happily said, and in the seconds that followed, I tried, as I would for the rest of the afternoon and well into the next week, to read hopeful messages into this and every other delightfully ambiguous comment she made.

"Neither have you," I said, and to be sure she understood what I meant, I added, "You're still beautiful and amazing," which seemed to have the surprising effect I intended. She didn't say another word. Not even goodbye. Perhaps understanding that I wanted nothing in return for the compliment. To this day I'm grateful I said those unambiguous words, wholly aware, both then and now, that my kindness was the direct result of hers, a fact I believe she understood at least as well as I did.

My one mistake with Sierra—until that moment on the sidewalk—was that I'd failed to realize that she'd always meant exactly what she said, and she did so in a way that presumed the best possible outcome under the circumstances. She believed in her hopeful vision, and I, and no doubt others who came into her path, could hardly trust that she was as confident as she seemed to be or that the universe could live up to her optimistic expectations. But even the greatest skeptic could be swayed by her outlook. And why the hell not? She would maintain that hopeful vision, I imagined, until her dying day.

Standing there on the sidewalk with her, I chose, right then, to try to live like that. When I typed in "Sierra McCloud"—adding, as she pleasantly informed me, her married name, "Chamberlain"—to match the recently received phone number, life felt a little fuller. I felt somehow more like myself, a happier version that seemed distantly familiar, and more connected than ever with this person I still loved, only differently now, a sentiment she seemed to share as we tucked our phones back into our pockets and stared intently into each other's eyes.

Hope, like love, should not be measured out cautiously. The revelation made me smile, and she returned the smile, along with a firm, unhurried hug, before departing.

—

Two months after running into Sierra—and after three nights of decreasingly dreadful previews, at the Randolph Theater, in Tribeca—I climbed the gallows as John Proctor in the debut performance of *The Crucible*—a modernization in which the accusers are high-school girls; the hero, their

English teacher—and, in the moments before my execution, erupted into nearly uncontrollable sobs, maintaining just enough composure to make this unrehearsed expression of sorrow appear to be the character's and not my own. I stared both gratefully and mournfully through blinding lights at my beloved Salem, which seemed, now, idealized through my sentimental tears, a kind of heaven that no fool, or even righteous hero, would willingly leave, but such had been my choice and there was no turning back now.

Returning my gaze were the ghostly faces of my adoring mother, hand in hand with her devoted, and now clean-shaven, Bates, who sat beside her, clad in a brown leather sport coat and bespectacled in dark-rimmed glasses that made him appear almost cool in his retirement, almost worthy of the great beauty by his side; my dear cousin Big and his wife, Guadalupe, still, after all these years, gorgeous in their lustiness—it was a wonder they didn't have five of their own children by now—arms intertwined, fingers interlaced, all possible body parts interlocked despite the arm rest between them; and queenly Aunt Helen, adorned with large gold earrings dangling with ornaments and matching necklace that lay flat on her chest and plunged toward a low-cut sea-green sweater, a vision that would launch a thousand ships, or at least inspire battles among Kornfield's more senior local suitors. How was it, I wondered, that their losses had made them so much stronger, larger, somehow more fully themselves? And then, for a long moment, before the house went black and I hung there lifeless, I felt myself expanding in size and stature, soaking in the glow of their ardent smiles, up there on the upraised stage, welcoming my own annihilation.

When the lights returned, my eyes fell on a hundred nameless faces, all of them dead silent—all ruthless critics, I was sure. Say what you will of me, I thought. I will die here a million times before I'm finished. All at once I found, beyond my family, Sierra McCloud and her husband, their hands poised to clap, and rows behind them, rising to his feet, in from L.A. just for the night, as he'd promised, Mitch Mitchell, extravagant instigator of standing ovations. By then I was beaming back at them, completely out of character, and loosening the noose.

When I arrived at the after-party—at nearby Ferrara's, of course, in the barroom, filled with family and friends, cast and crew—Big wrapped his arms around me, crying and laughing.

"What the hell's the matter with you?" I cracked, and, before he could get a word out, my eyes widened at the sight of Guadalupe's marvelously round belly.

She said, "We wanted to tell you in person …"

I shouted, "You're going to be a father!"

"You're going to be a godfather," Big said.

Just then Mitch approached and cheered, "Let's get this party started! I've got a plane to catch in three hours!" With beer raised, he turned to the room and announced, "To Johnny Demos! Our very own Dante Saludo!"

Big pressed his head to mine and choked out, "I wish he could have seen you up there."

"Me, too."

Still standing inside the doorway, I smiled privately at the thought of several men in addition to Uncle Nick, all of them with us tonight, among the living, out there with me at the edge of that ecstatic whirl of celebration, overcome with joy and gratitude, as I was.

The crowd moved toward the bar, but I walked outside and stood at the curb, feeling transported back to that night when all had seemed lost—I could see myself at eighteen, right across the street from Ferrara's—as I trailed Mitch, after our sojourn on the roof, down the steps of his apartment building and out onto the sidewalk.

And I could see Mitch, setting down my duffel bag and asking me, "What the hell are you crying for again?"

"I'm *not*," I said, swiping at my cheeks. "It was windy up there."

"Yeah." He leaned back against the brick wall. I leaned back next to him. For a few minutes we stood there, shoulder to shoulder, taking in the faint sounds of the city. We'd said all there was to say to each other, at least for now. When a long, six-door Cadillac turned onto the street, Mitch said, "Your ride."

"A stretch limo?"

Mitch shrugged, pretending not to be impressed.

At the curb a hatted man emerged from the dark car. "You Mr. Saludo's boy?"

"This is him." Mitch wrapped an arm around me and smiled. "You've always got a place to stay. As long as I'm here."

I nodded. "Thanks."

Mitch would be gone by the fall—gone west, to fare well in that other city, to become—inevitably, it would seem a decade later—the creator and producer of the multi-season smash-hit and eventually syndicated TV reality series *Strangers!*, which featured, in each new episode, orchestrated by Mitch, "chance" meetings between unwitting strangers, who, through their distinctive talents and Mitch's flair for matching personalities, transformed each other's lives.

"I forgot my hat," I realized.

"Your papou's fedora. I'll get it—"

"It's okay." I believed I would return for it one day soon.

And then, for what felt like a very long time, I thought I'd never return.

That endless night and morning became one. One minute I was gazing into the sky above New York City; the next, I was home, gazing down at Uncle Nick, in the hospital, his hands folded over his broken heart. Sometime after midnight, a violent shudder woke us from our sleepy optimism, hours before the scheduled operation. We awaited the inevitable reports in the room across the hallway. I said nothing of my delayed homecoming, and no one asked me to explain why it had taken me all day and half the night to return.

I waited beside Big, who sobbed in choked inhalations, gripping the armrests of his chair, as though the chair itself were speeding toward his fate and it was all he could do to slow down progress. Even Uncle Paul might have felt the pull toward home—*back* home, for good, to Kornfield—twisted up in the corner, hand trembling at his forehead, the head man of the family now, his wife and son, unaware of this twist of misfortune, anticipating his happy return, three thousand miles west, where a generation ago he'd gone to be forgotten, or just missed. We were three sons without fathers, I realized, and I began to cry—for my cousin and uncle, whom I wished I could console. For the first time, it occurred to me that I had never actually grieved for my own father. I had never experienced the jolt of loss, only the mysterious increasing awareness of his absence.

My mother stroked Yiayia, who would not last long—she had witnessed the impossible, and her mind must have been doing tricks. Aunt Helen wailed in the hallway. How many times had she convinced herself, with good reason, that her husband was invincible, that there was nothing in the universe fierce enough to take him down, that he would outlast us all? We had all shared that delusion. I could not have been the only one in that room, in that terrible silence, to be formulating his selfish escape from the wreckage, even as we all clutched one another desperately—or, I must have been the only one.

Gripping Big's shoulder, I studied the covers of tattered magazines and the patterns of drying fern leaves and indulged my reverie of return to New York. I tried to imagine being Papou at eighteen, rising up from the ocean and banks of the island, alone in the endless maze of streets, with only his instinct and a dream, wondering which doorway would be his first and how, without knowing the language, he would ask for a shot. He had done something beyond my ability to imagine. When he arrived, he'd had nothing, and then somehow—

There were my mother, Aunt Helen, and Uncle Paul, hugging in the center of the room, their three heads pressed together—they were the fractured center of my universe. We're the only ones left, I thought, as I drifted toward them, for a moment defying the laws of entropy.

"Here you are, Johnny," my mother called to me, now, from the doorway of Ferrara's.

I turned to her, in strange rapture; not for the first time, nor for the last, she took my hand and guided me back in from outside.

18
JOHNEES AMERICAN

A year after *The Crucible* debut, on the Sunday morning before the baptism of Big and Guadalupe's baby, I hovered at my mother's bedroom dresser, inspecting pictures and jewelry, opening drawers and tiny boxes, being a general snoop, while she sat on the bed, twisting her hair into a clip and stepping into heels.

"You look very handsome," she said. "Are you ready?"

I was holding the old, framed shot of my dad alighting from his car, in skinny black tie, briefcase in hand. I shook my head. "I never understood what you went through. I'm sure I still don't."

She straightened my collar. "You were a child. Why should you have understood?"

"I'm older now than you were then."

"That's true."

She opened a slim drawer located just under the overhanging lip of the dresser's surface, a shallow, red-velvet-lined vault that for decades had achieved its apparent purpose of hiding her most cherished valuables, at least from me. From it she retrieved a small photograph from beneath an ornate wooden box, its pressed flatness failing to disguise ancient cracks and creases.

"Remember this?" She handed me the photograph. It was an old shot of my dad hunched over me at a red plastic batting tee set up on some sprawling lawn I didn't recognize, his hands gripping mine, bat poised at the shoulder, ball ready to be struck—all potential. "You loved that picture."

"I do love it. I just don't remember it exactly. How old am I? Where is this?"

"That's Papou's back yard. You're two. It's that summer—"

"There're no trees. But I thought … So this is—?"

"I wish we had more shots of you two like this. Parents nowadays, with cameras in their phones, can you imagine?"

"I think I *do* remember this. The picture, I mean."

"You used to take it to bed and stare at it before you fell asleep."

"I remember that. Or maybe I just remember you telling me I used to do that." My grown fingers sank into the folds of the picture. "I wish I could actually remember. *Him*, I mean."

"Keep it. Put it in your wallet."

I took my wallet from inside my sport coat, then changed my mind. "I don't want to ruin it."

She chuckled as I tucked the wrinkled picture back beneath the box, beyond which I spotted the shadowy edge of a short stack of paper.

"Dad's book," I let out.

I opened the drawer, quickly then slowly, as the words on the top sheet, stamped out in evenly shaped letters, announced themselves as if from a life I vaguely remembered living myself: "Cypress Street: Stories." I could hear the clap of the metal arms leaving their mark, one inky imprint after another. In the top lefthand corner the author's name, Steve Lemondakis, was that of a man distinct from my father; it was the name of a peer, a friend, a kindred spirit whose forgotten work, and name, I felt suddenly driven to save from obscurity. I took the pages, soft and bowing in the middle, into my hands.

"I forget—did he ever try to publish these?"

"He tried, with a few of them. But not the book."

"Have you ever thought about it? Publishing it—posthumously, I mean? I could take it to New York. I'd make a copy—"

"He was never finished." She reached for the book, but I turned away. "I think he would want you to live your life. You were the only thing he loved more than writing."

"Don't say that, Mom!"

She laughed. "I don't mean *me*. You were a welcome distraction."

"From what? The writing?"

"The rejection."

I shrank from the word, toward this sole, typed copy I wanted to free from its long dormancy.

She said, "He would have been very proud of you. Jealous, probably."

"Jealous of what?"

"Your courage. To keep trying."

"It's not courage. There's nothing else for me to do at this point."

"There's always a choice."

I stiffened at the thought.

"So he just gave up?" I asked.

"No. He took a break. He loved being your father. He spent every moment he could with you. He would have gotten back to it."

"I'm why he stopped writing."

"Believe me. He had no regrets. We were a happy family. He loved his life."

Bates called from the kitchen, "You two hungry?"

"Yes!" my mother called back, then said to me, "Things have turned out okay, right?"

I took a deep breath and nodded. "You and me till the end of the world."

She held her tender stare, despite welling tears.

Bates had taken nothing about my mother for granted, and I respected him for that. I remembered her telling me how for years she delighted in watching him from the upstairs windows, through the trees, by his car down the street, as he checked his watch and timed his arrival. Bates had never lost hope, even with the cruel knowledge that my mother had settled for camaraderie—that is, until she fell in love with him and married him.

"You're a good man."

I heard Papou's voice in hers.

She took the pile of paper from my hands and returned the book to the hidden drawer.

I said, "You did everything right."

"I guarantee you that's not true."

"You were alone. You were so young."

We hugged.

Bates called again from the kitchen.

"I was never alone." My mother took my hand.

Time to eat.

—

Hours before the last train back to New York, I sat with Big, eating gyros and fries, on a sprawling, upraised patio filled with iron picnic tables the color of daisies and a dozen red umbrellas, under a glowing sign that read "JOHNEES AMERICAN GYRO." From inside the small, newly constructed building, set in the corner of the Old Kornfield Inn's huge parking lot, came the chatter of teenagers working cash registers and flipping burgers at sizzling grills, carving and stuffing meat into pockets of bread, the smell of singed pork fat drifting by. A tall boy with a pad and pen fielded phone calls for pick-up orders, already answering with routine, comfortable efficiency: "Johnees American."

"You ever think of coming home?" Big asked.

"You mean here?"

He grinned.

"Every day," I said.

"I could use the help."

"I'll bet."

I stared at the old restaurant, still closed on Sundays, remembering Uncle Nick in the kitchen, forever busy with shrimp, before a thick wooden counter, the surface wounded but smooth, a white plastic bucket at his side, dipping a hand into crunching ice and pulling out, one after another, at rhythmic intervals, the orange fleshy wedges; jiggling the wrist, palm up, cold water drizzling from his fingers; slipping a thumb under the flaky shell, in one quick arcing scoop, until it covered the knuckle like a helmet; and snipping it off at the tail, his hands reaching and fingers pinching and snapping all at once, like finely tuned machines.

I remembered Big at eighteen, on a certain spring afternoon not long before that long, lonely summer. He was making mashed potatoes in a giant mixer, pouring cartons of milk and sour cream and testing the whipping batch with a finger.

When it was perfect, he anchored the bowl's base at his belt, reached his arms around, squatted, and twisted toward the steamer table, where with a spoon he guided the thick flow into shoebox-sized bins. He caught my eye and turned for the butcher room. I heard the screen door slap shut, and I followed him outside, where he sat on the stoop, the green dumpster to our right smelling of everything on the menu—steak, soup, fish. I remained standing as he went on staring at the hill across the street, his apron spotted with yellows and pinks.

Finally, I sat down next to him. "You must be dying to get to Penn State," I said.

He glanced back through the screen door.

"He'll be okay without you," I said.

Inside, Uncle Nick dropped metal baskets into sizzling vats.

"You don't belong here," Big said.

"Neither do you," I said.

He grinned and wrapped an arm tightly around my shoulders. In that gaze he must have seen how all of this would be erased, and replaced—there was a veritable city of asphalt and concrete before us, of shopping malls and traffic and bright lights, and a place called JOHNEES AMERICAN GYRO—a burger and gyro joint, *the first of many,* Big, wise heir and investor, would one day announce to me, still grinning after all these years, that weird spelling, with the double "e," he would explain, necessary for the purposes of franchising. And when I asked about the missing apostrophe in "Johnees," he would say, "There's more than one Johnny," and smile, but offer no explanation for the paradoxical "American Gyro"—nor for the bizarre and somehow perfect incongruity of the plural followed by the mysteriously singular.

Now here we were slugging Cokes, a softball game going on under brightening lights in the park across the street. The hill was gone, leveled, along with the stockyards, which had been replaced by a maze of concrete and macadam. Cars came and went all summer long.

Big lit up when Guadalupe stepped onto the porch, carrying their baby girl. "Mia!" Big announced, as Guadalupe handed me the baby. Mia let out a brief cry, and I patted her back. "Godfather," Big said, intoning the respect one would give Brando on his daughter's wedding day.

I let my cheeks and voice sink. "One day, and let's hope that day never comes, I will come to you, Johnny, and I will ask you for a favor."

Guadalupe laughed. "Anything you ask, Godfather."

Just then, Guadalupe's grown daughter, Sofia, hopped onto the porch, beaming in a sundress like her mother's and displaying a giant black key in her hand.

"I drove!" she announced, her black hair tumbling past her shoulders.

"God help us," Big said. "Miss Independent hits the road."

Sofia handed Big the car key and kissed his cheek. "Thank you, Daddy."

Guadalupe said, "We were in the mood for chocolate shakes. You guys want anything?"

Big gestured to the saucy remnants on our trays. He palmed his belly.

Mia settled into my arms.

Sofia took her mother's hand, and they went inside.

"You are positively fatherly," I said and kissed Mia's warm head.

Big sighed. "So, how's life in New York?"

The air was still. Sounds of the game rose from the green field across the street. I listened for Papou's voice in the twilight. *New York is a good place for a young man.* I still believed it, only I wasn't so young anymore.

"It's good, it's good," I said.

Big smiled as we set our eyes on the irrelevant game. Above giant poles, clouds of light suffused the blue evening sky.

ACKNOWLEDGEMENTS

Thank you to Jack Wheatcroft, Robert Love Taylor, Dennis Baumwoll, Dan Loose, Charles Baxter, Wilton Barnhardt, Alex Lyras, Chris Matonti, Dan Jahns, Libby Mosier, Giacomo Fizzano, John Fried, Robin Black, Julie Odell, Tony Knighton, Kath Hubbard, Nathan Long, Kevin Maness, Ashley Hile, and Elise Juska. And to the amazing and wonderful people at Vine Leaves Press, Jessica Bell, Amie McCracken and Melanie Faith. Thanks also to Thom Didato and *failbetter.com* for the publication of "Behind Curtains," and to *The Hawaii Review* for the publication of "Snapper Soup." My deepest thanks to my family, especially to Vana, for your love and support throughout the years it took to write this book.

VINE LEAVES PRESS

Enjoyed this book?
Go to *vineleavespress.com* to find more.
Subscribe to our newsletter: